The Dashing Miss Fairchild

Aristocratic Society looked upon Miss Clare Fairchild as a lady of mystery – but now she was caught in a maze of mysteries of her own.

Who had placed a beautiful infant boy in her hands, and why?

Who was trying to foil her attempts to discover the baby's identity and threatening her life if she came too close to the startling truth?

Why had the rakish Richard Talbot taken such an intimate interest in her, and how could she stop this devilishly handsome, wickedly charming womanizer from making her his latest conquest?

And most disturbing, in the depths of her heart and core of her being, *did she really want to?*

By the same author

Hidden Inheritance
Lady Sara's Scheme
The Gallant Lord Ives
Queen of the May
Double Deceit
The Wicked Proposal

The Dashing
Miss Fairchild

Emily Hendrickson

ROBERT HALE · LONDON

© Doris Emily Hendrickson 1992, 2009
First published in Great Britain 2009

ISBN 978 0 7090 8283 5

Robert Hale Limited
Clerkenwell House
Clerkenwell Green
London EC1R 0HT

www.halebooks.com

2 4 6 8 10 9 7 5 3

Typeset by Derek Doyle and Associates, Shaw Heath
Printed by the MPG Books Group, Bodmin and King's Lynn

CHAPTER ONE

The Honorable Miss Clare Fairchild gazed from the window of her jouncing carriage with great patience. At her side the delicate and well-bred voice of Venetia Godwin droned on and on about the folly of a near spinster rattling off to Bath in such a harebrained fashion. Or was it called droning when the voice was high and clear . . . and most penetrating?

Clare glanced across the carriage to meet the gaze of Priddy, her abigail. Not a word was exchanged, but Clare sensed she was in for a gentle reprimand later, the most Priddy ever allowed herself to vent, for inviting the delightful Miss Godwin along for company and to lend countenance to Clare's advanced age of twenty-three. It was not done for a young woman to set up an establishment on her own, and Clare was too prudent and proper to overlook the conventions of Society.

London had grown dreary in the heat of summer, and suddenly she had felt as though she couldn't bear another round of visits to her happy brothers and sister, all married. It was the children, actually. Although Clare loved them dearly, it pained her to see them and feel as though she would never have one of her own. It was her reward for being too choosy, she knew. Everyone scolded her ever and anon about it, Venetia being no exception.

Clare turned again to face the view, attempting to ignore the verbal ramblings of her chosen companion. The day was drawing to a close with still many miles to travel before they should reach their final destination. Venetia had set the pace, declaring they must proceed at an aggravatingly slow speed due to her sensibilities and a stomach that tended to queasiness when jolted about in rushing vehicles. Patience being one of Clare's more admirable traits, she consented. If one sought company, one did not quibble at the tender susceptibilities of that person.

'I shan't wonder if we are set upon by highwaymen, dear Clare,' Venetia stated in summation of her opinions on travel in the English countryside by young women without a gentleman to protect them, even if men in general were most annoying creatures. Although she had to admit they had their uses. Male servants did not figure in Venetia's estimation of possible saviors.

'Too early in the day,' murmured Clare. 'Besides, this road is far too well traveled for such. We have been passed by any number of carriages and coaches since departing London.' A snail might have whizzed past them, but she refrained from that comment, lest Venetia become upset.

'Nevertheless, I daresay we shall all rest more easily once we are inside the Castle Inn at Marlborough.' Venetia gave an emphatic shake of her head, and for once Priddy nodded her agreement. The abigail, usually given to a sentence now and again, had remained silent since their departure from London. Clare guessed her long-suffering maid would welcome the peace of the inn, for Clare had bespoke separate rooms for herself and her friend, a decision she was coming to view as wise indeed. It was to be hoped that her invitation to Venetia Godwin, prompted partly by pity, was not destined to be regretted.

Bath had appealed to Clare, its choice being no whim of the moment, although Venetia seemed to believe otherwise. Clare had recalled her mother's fond recollections of the town in its prime, and decided it was time she paid the place a prolonged visit. It was still a pleasant city, or so she had been assured by Mr Popham, her agent, who was to arrange suitable housing for the Honorable Clare Fairchild, the daughter of the late and exceedingly wealthy Viscount Seton. They were to be met by him at the Castle Inn with the results of his search.

'Oh, dear Clare, do look. I believe we approach the town of Marlborough. Can it be?' Venetia clutched at Clare's arm in her excitement.

'Unless we have crawled off the London to Bath road, I suspect it is undoubtedly what you see.' In preparation for their arrival, Clare gathered up her reticule and other impedimenta that had scattered about the coach.

Venetia sat with her gaze fixed on the approaching town, hoping for the first glimpse of the inn where they were to spend the night. When she saw the imposing structure, once the home of the Earl of Hartford, she ventured a broad and satisfied smile.

Clare's agent assisted her from the coach with obsequious attention, walking with her to the inn while Venetia was left to do with the attentions of the innkeeper and a groom. Priddy coped with the bandboxes and portmanteaus deemed necessary for an overnight stay, directing one of the servants with the faintly superior mien of an abigail to Quality.

'I believe you will be most pleased with your direction while in Bath,' Mr Popham declared. 'I have managed to procure for you a highly respectable address. The gentleman who had engaged the house failed to appear at the specified time. Thus I am able to offer you a residence in the Royal Crescent,' he ended with an expectant note.

Clare did not have the slightest notion as to whether this was good or not, but the man had the air of one who has performed the impossible, and now looked like a little boy who desired a pat on the head. She nodded graciously, saying, 'How good of you to go to such great trouble for us. I am sure we shall be most comfortable. I recall my mother saying something about that place. It is convenient, I trust?'

'Most convenient, Miss Fairchild.'

Clare suspected he was disappointed in her reaction. 'I see. I gather this is more than a mere house, but a residence that will give me proper countenance.'

Her gentle irony was lost on the agent. He nodded eagerly, then handed Clare the keys and documents necessary to her settling in for two months.

When she at last closed the door to her room in the Castle Inn, she found she longed for nothing more than a light repast and her bed.

'How odd that such dreadfully slow travel should fatigue one so much, Priddy. I daresay I am showing my age, but I feel to be at least eighty.' Clare tossed her bonnet onto a small table, then stared longingly at the bed. It was a massive affair, large enough for three, if need be. She cared not in the least about the rest of the world, if she could slip beneath the sheets and close her eyes in peace.

' 'Tis that Miss Godwin,' Priddy muttered in a barely aubible voice.

'Now, Priddy,' remonstrated Clare in an amused tone. She undid her pelisse and handed it to the waiting maid, then fluffed out her blond curls, her serene blue eyes only slightly troubled as they glanced in the looking glass to discover the effects of the journey on her appearance. Anyone might have assured her that her years sat lightly upon her attractive person.

A gentle knock at her door preceded the entrance of Miss Godwin, who promptly regaled Clare with everything that had occurred from the moment she entered the inn.

'And do you know,' Venetia concluded, 'I am told the Marquis of Aylesbury has a place not far from here. Savernake Lodge it is called. Does that not sound delightful?' Her hopeful gaze settled upon Clare, who wondered what she was supposed to do about the matter.

The question was set aside by a knock on the door. A young maid entered the room bearing a tray with appetizing dishes for their evening repast. Clare thought the maid's searching looks a bit forward, but said nothing. Surely two ladies traveling with an abigail was not so unusual a thing?

Venetia chattered all through the light meal while Clare concentrated on keeping her eyes open and tongue between her teeth. It was to be hoped that once Venetia discovered the delights of the Bath shops and tea parties, not to mention the charms of the Pump Room, the circulating library, and other social festivities, she would prove to be less taxing to the nerves.

'Do you know I feel it in my bones that something momentous is going to happen, dear Clare? I have this feeling at times, you see. 'Tis most exciting. I wonder should the marquis chance to visit this inn? Not that I am in the least interested in men myself, you understand. Mind you, they have their uses, but I chose my independence. From every observance of mine, they are tedious, tiresome, and most annoying with their lightskirts and gaming and hunting. Bothersome creatures, would that they all drop into the sea!' she declared in a high, plaintive tone.

Considering what might happen to the population in such event, Clare prudently kept her gaze fastened on her plate, lest she chuckle and provoke her friend. She quietly replied, 'Now, Venetia, do not set your face against them all. One gentleman may just capture your heart, and you will change your opinion.'

Venetia darted a quick glance at her benefactress and snapped her mouth closed. After a moment of silence, she ventured to say, 'And what about you, dear Clare? Were the marquis or any other proper gentleman to appear, what would you do?'

'I have been introduced to every *proper* gentleman in the realm. They are all a lot of dead bores. If I must marry, and I daresay it is not mandatory, it shall be to someone who is different from the norm.'

'Clare!' Venetia cried in horror. 'Men are disagreeable enough without resorting to one who is beyond the pale.'

'I never said I would do the *im*proper. But,' Clare replied in a patient voice, 'I should like to think that somewhere in the world exists a man, a gentleman, who has a lively curiosity about life. A man resolute and steadfast in his affections, yet good-natured and possessed of a sound intelligence, one I could admire.'

This shocking declaration proved too much for Venetia to tolerate. Her hand fluttered to her brow as though to ward off an evil blow. 'Well!' She sniffed loudly, then continued, 'Men are grief and trouble. I detest the lot of them. Mark my words, one will bring you tribulation, and then you shall understand what I mean.' Venetia gracefully rose from her chair. Looking down at Clare, she added, 'I only hope you never know that pain.' Then she whirled about and left the room, taking the last of the sweets with her.

'Rubbish,' pronounced Priddy with a wry twist of her face.

'I have never heard of an affair of the heart that deeply affected Venetia, but one never knows,' Clare said with a thoughtful look in her eyes. She erased the frown from her forehead and pushed away from the small table where they had eaten their light meal. 'Why do you not leave me now and seek your own dinner? I shall fare well enough, for I want nothing more than sleep.'

Priddy silently nodded, then assisted Clare out of her traveling gown and into her night rail before going down to her own hearty meal.

In the quiet of her room, which was a relative matter given the noisy nature of public inns, Clare slipped beneath the covers and stared up at the ceiling while she contemplated the conversation. Was there such a man, she longed to know? She had found the pretensions of the fops and dandies of Society too, too dreadful for words. Venetia was right in her estimation that most of them seemed to care more for their sports and entertainment than a wife and family. Perhaps. . . .

A crash of china and cutlery in the hallway woke Clare from a sound sleep. Peering out the window to the rear of the inn, she noted it was quite early in the morning.

Priddy softly entered the room shortly following the domestic disaster, nodding with annoyance when she saw her mistress awake. 'I knew that silly girl would wake everyone on this floor.'

'I might as well get up and be gone from here, although this is an excellent bed and I slept like a baby. I wonder, did Miss Godwin hear the racket?'

'She would have to have cotton wool in her ears, and even then I suspect it would wake her,' Priddy grumbled as she went to assist her mistress to dress for the trip.

Clare swung her feet over the edge of the bed and began to prepare for the day ahead. She prayed nothing would delay their arrival in Bath. She had a longing for the quiet of her own home, even if it was a temporary lodging.

Thus it was that within two hours the ladies were able to enter the carriage, Clare having personally complimented the innkeeper on their excellent accommodations. She climbed into the traveling coach, then paused before sitting down. A strange basket reposed on the seat Priddy usually occupied. Clare knew it did not belong to any of her party.

Hesitantly she stretched out a hand, leaning forward to see the basket's contents. Inside, she discovered a soft woolen blanket over white linen sheeting. Probing further, she saw what appeared to be a tiny hand. Alarmed, she hastily pulled apart the coverings to see a sleepy baby nestled deep within. A fringe of pale red curls peeped from beneath a starched white cap trimmed with delicate lace. The infant now quite awakened, Clare found she was being studied by a somber child with enormous eyes as blue as her own.

'Gracious!'

'What is it?' Venetia cried. 'I knew something was going to happen. What is wrong?'

Clare poked her head back out through the coach door to give Venetia a wide-eyed stare. 'There is a baby in here! How do you suppose it got in our coach?'

Before Venetia could begin to vocally contemplate the various possibilities, Clare disappeared again. The infant had decided to exercise its lungs with terrifying intensity. With her experience as an aunt to draw upon, Clare expertly picked up the baby, cradling it gently in her arms, patting and stroking its back with soothing results.

'We must find the mother, Priddy. There has to be some mistake here. Surely no one would simply place their child in a traveling coach and go off?'

Priddy's eyes had softened at the sight of her mistress holding the infant in such a maternal and skillful manner. What a pity she did not have a clutch of her own to nurture. She

11

merely nodded, holding out her arms to accept the child so Clare might get out of the coach.

'Come into the inn. We must make inquiries.' Clare led the way inside followed by a curious Venetia and a wary Priddy. Priddy was not accustomed to being around infants, not that she minded them. She had hoped long before this that her mistress might present her with such a one to admire . . . from afar.

The infant took exception to Priddy's less than tender hold and began to howl once again. With a rueful smile, Clare paused in her steps, took the baby in her arms, then charged into the common room in search of the innkeeper.

That gentleman looked askance when Clare approached him, obviously recalling that the ladies had come *sans* infant yesterday.

'Sir, we need your help. It seems there was a confusion in the inn yard. Someone placed their infant in our coach by mistake. Could you direct us to the family, please?' She jiggled the baby in her arms to quiet it, hoping that soon she would be rid of her increasingly odiferous and damp bundle.

The innkeeper looked even more distressed. 'No one came with a baby yesterday, Miss Fairchild. Leastways, none I recollect.'

Venetia inserted herself into the conversation. 'Someone obviously came here with an infant, sirrah. I cannot believe you could scarce fail to take note. Think, sir, think.'

At this point the infant began to cry again, more loudly than ever. 'It has an admirable set of lungs,' Clare murmured to Priddy. 'See if you can find out anything for me in the servants' area. I shall cope the best I can until we decide what must be done.' Turning to the innkeeper, she added, 'I believe the best thing for me to do is return to the room I occupied last night to see if the baby can be made more comfortable.' As her abigail headed toward the kitchen door, Clare prompted, 'And inquire about a wetnurse, Priddy, do.'

The parade up the stairs would have been amusing had someone been around to appreciate it. Clare sailed forth with the squalling infant in her capable arms, followed by a

12

distraught Venetia complaining that she was about to have vapors at the very least due to the delay in their plans. Clare heroically refrained from any comment about the slowness of the journey to this point.

Once in the privacy of her room, after firmly closing the door behind the ranting Venetia, Clare efficiently stripped off the outer garments from the baby, noting as she did the exquisite quality of each item. All were handmade of finest cambric and flannel with lace trim and embroidery worked with skillful fingers.

A gentle rap on the door brought a young maid with the basket from the coach. 'Your coachman says as how you might wish this, miss.'

Leaving the maid to keep an eye on the squirming infant, Clare dove into the basket to discover a packet of clothing in the bottom. Upon opening it she found shirts, caps, bed gowns, blankets, bindings, petticoats and stays, and last, but scarcely least, at least two dozen napkins.

'Thank heavens. This does simplify things considerably.' Armed with the necessary item in hand and the maid holding a basin of water, Clare performed the needed change while Venetia, after one peek, took herself off to the windows.

When the baby was again neat and sweetly clean, though inclined to whimper unless Clare cosseted it against her shoulder, Venetia declared roundly, 'You might know it would be a boy. It is always the male of the species who causes trouble!'

'I doubt the baby had a thing to say about it, my dear,' Clare answered serenely.

The maid gathered up the soiled napkin and bathwater, promising to return with the washed and dried item as soon as possible.

'What do you plan to do?' Venetia asked, a frown creasing her forehead as she stared at the unwanted guest in Clare's arms. 'Really, it is too bad of you to fuss so over him.'

'I could not be so heartless as to dump him on the inn. It seems to me there was a reason this baby was placed in my coach.' Clare dug about in the basket to see if there was anything to pacify the increasingly hungry babe, if his nuzzling against her was any evidence. She found nothing, so permitted him to gnaw on her finger.

'Nonsense!' Venetia cried in alarm.

'Explain, if you please, how an infant in a large basket could be tucked into any coach by mistake and not noticed immediately. I saw him at once.'

'Well,' drawled Venetia while eyeing the delicate embroidery on the petticoat and gown now worn by the boy. 'That looks like remarkably fine work. It is probably stolen,' she concluded smugly. 'The baby might belong to anyone.'

Clare gave her friend a narrow look. 'I doubt it. It is precisely the proper size and is all of a kind. I mean to say, the fabric is of the best, the embroidery the same quality. No, all of these items,' she gestured to the contents of the packet now spilled across her bed, 'were made just for him.'

At that moment Priddy entered the room, a young woman cautiously edging into the room behind her. 'No word at all belowstairs, miss. Seems like the babe just dropped from the sky.' Behind her, the young woman peeped at the baby, her eyes round and questioning. Her hands twisted her starched white apron with quiet anxiety.

'That is errant nonsense,' Venetia declared.

'He is far too real to be a figment of our imagination. What else did you find out?' Clare glanced at the stranger, hoping that she proved useful.

'This is Jenny. She recently lost her babe to a fever, but still has her milk. She's agreed to be wet nurse, for I know we have need of one and promptly.'

'How wonderfully convenient, Priddy,' murmured Clare while Venetia flounced from the room at the mere thought of feeding an infant. Disgusting. Too, too shocking.

Once the shy Jenny was settled in a chair by the window, Clare drew Priddy to the far side of the room, keeping an eye on the gentle young maid all the while. 'Does it not strike you as odd that she would be so handy?'

'Aye, that it does. But the cook swears to the truth of the matter. Not a soul would admit to knowing a thing about a stranger with a babe.'

'Did Tom Coachman learn anything of interest?'

'No. 'Tis like I said. The babe seems to have dropped out of the sky.'

Clare glanced at the baby nursing heartily away, a small fist waving about in the air, and shook her head. 'He does not look to be an angel.'

'You sound like Miss Godwin,' Priddy muttered.

'I do not intend to rail against the male sex. I mean, he is too real, too substantial to be other than what he appears. But to whom does he belong is the question. And why in my coach? There were others before the inn this morning. We were not the first about to depart, thanks to the crash in the hallway.'

'True,' agreed the abigail.

'We have a mystery on our hands, I believe,' Clare murmured, then walked to the maid. Seating herself on a nearby chair, she softly inquired, 'Could you travel with us to Bath? I fear I must get there tomorrow at the latest. Your husband?' Clare hated to probe. The death of a new baby was difficult to accept, and it must be painful for this young woman, scarcely more than a slip of a girl actually, to handle another's child in her arms.

'I don't have a husband,' the shy creature replied, dropping her gaze to the baby in her arms. 'I was got with child by one of them swells that was stuck here last October when we had that terrible rain. 'Twas lucky for me that the cook let me stay on. I didn't need no baby, though she was that sweet, she was.' While Jenny's face remained impassive, she exhaled a gentle sigh.

'I see,' Clare replied, seeing a great deal. Venetia would find this a prime example of the thoughtlessness of the male species. Take their fun regardless of the consequences. The idea that servants were somehow less than human had always been repugnant to Clare, and she found herself very angry with the man who had treated this shy girl so badly.

The baby sated, he let out a resounding burp when placed against Jenny's shoulder. The sound brought smiles to all faces. Priddy surveyed the scene from behind Clare's shoulder.

'Will you come with us, then? I cannot leave the baby here, untended and unwanted. I have this feeling, you see. I believe there is a reason that a baby so obviously belonging to someone of refined background would be placed in my coach, my care as it were.'

'Yes, miss. I think it be mighty fine of you to take him on,' the maid declared boldly, then subsided in blushing confusion at her audacity.

'You will remain in here with me, I believe,' Clare announced decisively. 'I trust no one will harm the lad, but one cannot be too careful.' She glanced about the room, then turned to Priddy. 'Order up a cot for Jenny, and anything else you and she deem necessary. I believe I shall wander about the area to do my own bit of searching.'

In the hall Clare found Venetia about to go downstairs. She joined her, encouraging her to take a stroll in the inn's charming garden.

'I am told there were fish ponds here at one time and a bowling green as well. That appears to have been kept at any rate,' she observed as they strolled along a path. 'No doubt something to while away the hours should one be delayed.' She thought of young Jenny, and her mouth firmed.

' 'Tis a rather rambling place, is it not? Charming, however.' Venetia paused, then went on. 'Do you actually intend to take that child with us in the morning?'

'What else can I do?'

'Leave it here,' Venetia declared with a disdainful air.

'That I will not. Perhaps my destiny is bound up with this baby?' Clare gave a musical little laugh at this preposterous idea. 'I am being fanciful, I fear. But truly, I must see this matter through. Surely you can see my point of view?'

Venetia sniffed, a very telling sound revealing her total opinion of the scheme. 'If you must. I can see that nothing *I* may say will sway you from your tenacity. You realize that creature must travel with us in the coach . . . unless,' she said with hope in her voice, 'you hire a conveyance to take them to Bath?'

'Rubbish,' Clare said, her even temper frayed just a bit. 'If we speed up our pace a trifle, we can be in Bath in a trice.

16

Hiring a carriage is an expense I will not stand. However, should you care to. . . ?' Clare allowed her voice to trail off suggestively. Tom Coachman would be overjoyed to increase their speed. It must have galled him yesterday to have every vehicle on the Bath road rattle past him.

'Mercy, no,' Venetia stated fervently. The condition of her finances was such that only the needful was acquired. 'I daresay we shall manage.'

Clare appreciated the die-away air Venetia affected for what it was, a grateful, if grudging, yielding.

Thus it was that come the following morning, after Clare had made repeated efforts to locate the true parents of the baby, the little troop entered the coach. Within a very short time, the vehicle rumbled off toward Bath watched by the ostler, a couple of grooms, and an elderly nursemaid who happened to be passing by at the moment of departure.

'Fine leddy,' commented the ostler to a groom as he headed toward the stables to prepare for the next customer.

'One of a kind, oi'd say,' came the reply.

The journey was strained to say the least. Venetia remained in wounded sensibilities the entire trip. Jenny did her best to keep the baby quiet, but infants being what they are, it was not always possible.

Priddy was torn between her loyalty to her mistress and her growing affection for that scrap of humanity that, whenever she picked him up, tugged at the ribbons on the gown that covered Priddy's flat bosom.

'We shall have to think of a name for him. I mean, we simply cannot go on calling him the baby or whatever comes to mind.' Clare gave the infant a fond look, then turned to Venetia. 'Do you have any suggestions?'

'No!' Venetia snapped. Then, seeing the annoyed expression on her friend's face, she shrugged. 'John?'

'Was there nothing in the basket? No other clue I might have missed?'

Jenny frowned, then shook her head. 'Only a scrap of paper in the bottom.'

Guessing the girl could not read, Clare gently asked, 'Is it

17

there still? I cannot think how I missed seeing it.'

'Yes, miss. I never threw it out.' Jenny fished around, then came up with a small piece of fine hot-pressed paper from which Clare read to the others, ' "My name is William. Please care for me." '

'William? Common enough,' Venetia said.

'Our beloved king thought it good enough to bestow on one of his boys. William it is,' Clare said thoughtfully. 'Although, I believe I shall call him Willy, for he is such a small fellow.'

With the increased speed, and no apparent ill effect on Miss Godwin, the coach rumbled down the hill into Bath in far better time than Clare had expected. They coped with the jolting ride over the cobbled streets with a degree of composure, then, when they stopped before a handsome edifice, got out to look about them.

The door opened, and a dignified man came out to greet them. 'I am Bennison, Miss Fairchild. We welcome you to the Royal Crescent.'

Clare had taken William from Jenny and stood before the house, appraising it with shrewd eyes. It looked to be just the sort of place her family would approve. A lady passed them by, bowing slightly with an inquiring look in her gaze.

'I believe we shall quite like this house, Bennison. Please show us in, for we are all quite fatigued.' Turning to Jenny, she added, 'See to Willy's things, and tell me if you think anything is needed.'

'Yes, Miss Fairchild,' replied the wet nurse with a happy glow about her. She had landed on her feet, she had. The lady was kind and gentle, not the least condemning. There was nothing Jenny would not do for the patient and plucky lady who had hired her from the kitchen.

Along the street, the woman who had lingered to overhear the identity of the newcomer to the crescent raised her delicate eyebrows. A single lady with an infant? Here? Disgraceful. Mrs Robottom huffed off to spread the latest tittle-tattle to her neighbors. Why, she might dine off this news for a week, at least.

CHAPTER TWO

Clare and Venetia wandered up Milsom Street, pausing frequently to gaze in the shop windows. Venetia possessed the intent mien of the dedicated shopper. Mind you, she was not one who purchased much, but she adored looking, trying on bonnets, and examining trimmings as though she intended to spend prodigious amounts of money. Amazingly enough, she was one that shopkeepers fawned over, apparently deciding that while she might not buy, she could have influence over others.

Clare stared at the contents of the windows with an abstracted air. She was not a vain miss, nor given to pretensions, but she had rather expected to meet with more politeness than so far experienced. Their foray to the Pump Room had been dismal. Not one person had sought to make their acquaintance. Had Clare not known it to be impossible, she would have said everyone present already knew her identity and did not care to become better known.

In a way it was fortunate that she had the matter of Baby William to worry about. Why had no one come forward to claim him? She felt in her bones that there was a hidden significance to the appearance of the baby in her coach. But she had cudgeled her brain time and again for the solution, and come up with nothing tangible. She needed another head, one wiser than her own, and certainly more concerned than Venetia, who felt it an affront to have the baby in the household.

Of course, the baby was housed in the room two doors down from Venetia on the top floor, right next to Priddy. There were three bedrooms there, with only one on the floor below across from the drawing room. After the much larger home in London, it was a change to fit into the more modest abode in Bath. It bothered Clare not one whit, but then, she had taken the slightly larger bedroom. She knew that the servants would expect it of her and that, while she might complain in her genteel way, Venetia did as well.

'Just look, Clare, dear. Is that not the dearest bonnet in the world? I rather fancy those primrose ribands would match my favorite gown. Do you not agree?'

Venetia turned to bestow an impatient glance on the quiet young woman at her side. 'I declare, you are most annoying today. You wished to come to Bath. Now that you are here, you act most peculiarly. The house is quite satisfactory. We have settled in with no problems at all – in spite of that infant.' She spared Clare another darting look, then returned her attention to the bonnet which, with the clusters of fine primrose silk ribands, she was certain would match the gown she hoped to improve by purchasing something new and becoming to go with it. 'I shall try it on.'

Clare and Venetia entered the shop where several ladies sought the attention of the owner. When that imposing woman observed Clare's quiet elegance, most assuredly gained from London and the best modiste, she deserted the others to attend her.

'I wish to see the bonnet with the primrose ribands that is in the window,' declared Venetia in a sweet but commanding way.

Possibly disappointed to serve the other, less chic young lady, but never revealing it, the shop owner reached for the bonnet and assisted Venetia in trying it on.

Standing behind and off to one side, her thoughts now dwelling on her imagined slights, Clare was soon aware that the other ladies in the shop were raking her with haughty glances, then whispering in a most ill-bred manner. Shortly they murmured vague excuses to the owner, and filed from the shop. Clare firmed her lips and tried to concentrate on Venetia's demands for attention.

'I believe it is just the thing, dear Clare.' Venetia turned from the looking glass to face Clare. 'You do think it looks well on me, do you not?'

Rebuking herself for being distracted from her friend's dilemma, for choosing a bonnet was no small matter to Venetia, Clare smiled. 'Indeed, I cannot think of one we have seen that becomes you half so well.'

Sighing with satisfaction, Venetia turned back to the shop-keeper to conclude a sharp bit of bargaining.

Clare and Venetia left the shop and strolled along in the direction of the Royal Crescent, intending to cross through the Circus on their way. At the corner of Milsom and George Street, they encountered one of the ladies who had been in the millinery shop. The woman gave them a pointed look, her nose in the air, then sharply turned her back, rather than politely nod as might be expected.

'Well, I never,' exclaimed Venetia at the slight she managed to observe.

'I do not suppose you have,' Clare replied with her usual self-possession still intact, though somewhat frayed about the edges.

They turned away, heading up George Street toward the Circus. Venetia chattered about the cut direct that had been given them until Clare was ready to scream.

'I do wish,' murmured Clare, 'that I knew what was going on here. It is a mystery to me.' She had her suspicions, but could scarcely credit she might be right.

'What are you doing about the identity of Baby William? Have any of your inquiries proved of help?' The mention of a mystery had brought the baby to mind, a subject Venetia usually tried to avoid if possible.

'None,' Clare replied with chagrin. She could not imagine how a baby might be 'lost' without someone being greatly concerned. 'I suppose we ought to have remained at the Castle Inn at Marlborough a bit longer so that whoever it was could come to their senses, and we might restore Willy to them. However, I left my direction so that any inquiries would come here.'

'I say it was deliberate,' Venetia stated with more firmness than was her wont.

Clare sighed yet again and nodded her head in agreement. 'I fear you have the right of it. But why? becomes the question. I have racked my brain ever and anon, and cannot supply the answer. He is such a fetching little fellow. I should think it would break a mother's heart to part with him.'

At this point Clare caught sight of a young woman coming toward them that she had met in London, one she felt she had known fairly well. She approached Miss Oliver with some trepidation. She need not have feared, for her casual friend did not fail her.

'How lovely to see you, Miss Fairchild and Miss Godwin. You come to Bath to escape the summer doldrums of London? I am surprised you are not with your handsome family, Miss Fairchild. Did you not say that you usually visit one or the other of them during July and August?'

'I sought to do something different.' They chatted on about the weather and visiting a new town. Then Clare dared to ask, 'Pray, would you join us for tea this afternoon?' Clare found herself awaiting the reply with more than customary suspense.

'That would be delightful.' Miss Oliver beamed a pleased look on them both. 'I am visiting my aunt. She is in the habit of frequent naps, and it gets rather dull just sitting by the window without making a sound. One can embroider only so long.' She gave Clare a winsome smile.

'Goodness,' Venetia ventured to say. 'How glad I am that Clare is not given to naps as yet. Although William is,' she added in an annoyed afterthought.

Clare studied Miss Oliver to see if there would be a change of expression on her face at these heedless words from Venetia. There was, but not the freezing sort.

'I shall be there, you may rely on that,' Miss Oliver stated, avoiding comment on Venetia's remark. Her eyes sought Clare's with a glimpse of warm understanding in them.

Susan Oliver knew about whatever was going on in Bath with regard to the 'cuts' given Clare. She knew, and she did not let it prevent her from coming to tea. Clare extended her hand in a warm clasp, for this young woman she suddenly appreciated far more than before.

'I shall be looking forward to a comfortable coze with you,' Clare said with a wealth of meaning in her voice after imparting their direction to Miss Oliver.

'How nice to find an acquaintance in Bath,' Venetia commented as they turned to walk up Gay Street. 'She is the sort one always welcomes at parties, for she knows how to make herself agreeable without being encroaching.'

'I hope she will be able to tell us what is causing this uncomfortable business going on.' Clare studied the attractive houses along the street, thinking Bath would be a charming city if only the occupants were more accepting.

'You refer to that cut direct from a stranger? How foolish. I should not allow it to bother me in the least.' Venetia ignored the fact that she had droned on and on about that very cut not so long before. She shifted the bandbox that held the new bonnet from one hand to the other. She had taken it with her, not wishing to part with it for even a moment.

'That is easy for you to say,' Clare retorted in an even tone. 'We have not endeavored to attend to any of the assemblies or other entertainments found here as yet. There is a concert at the Octagon soon. Should you like to hazard a try for tickets?'

'It sounds rather interesting, although I would like to know what is to be played. I will not go if there is to be a soprano.'

For once, Clare was in agreement with Venetia. She had no love for the often distressing sounds of a soloist ill chosen. Why they usually seemed to be sopranos, she didn't know.

'Fine, I shall make inquiries and purchases – provided that this silly business does not interfere with such.'

Clare hurried Venetia across the Circus and into Brock Street. There were ladies abroad, but evidently it made no difference to them as to Clare's identity. Or perhaps Clare was indulging in a fit of self-importance. They were most likely intent on their own business, and not paying Clare and

Venetia the least heed.

As they marched up the steps of their Bath house, Clare commented, 'I am undoubtedly filled with windmills in my head, and there is nothing amiss but my own sense of worth. I am most likely missing the attention of Londoners and must earn my way in the local Society.'

Venetia gave her friend a puzzled look, nodding absently at Bennison as he held open the door for his temporary ladies.

'The post, Miss Fairchild,' he said, offering Clare a neat pile of letters. She flipped through them, finding them to be from her sister and sisters-in-law. They were good to write, and she felt she might be comforted from reading their news. There was nothing for Venetia, and that young lady strolled to the window with a miffed expression on her face.

'Would you excuse me that I might read the news?'

'Never say I kept you from learning all about your family,' replied Venetia with a pettish sigh. 'I shall go upstairs to try on my new bonnet again. And,' she added softly, with a worried frown, 'I had best see that it matches.' She scurried from the room with an intent look in her eyes.

Later on that afternoon, Clare was pleased to welcome Miss Oliver to the neat little drawing room. This room, as well as her bedroom, had a lovely view of the green beyond the crescent. She had been standing by one of the windows when she saw Miss Oliver approach the house. Since Bennison had been apprised of the expected guest, she was brought up to Clare immediately. Venetia still remained up in her second-floor bedroom.

Eager to explore the confusing circumstances before Venetia might insert her opinions, Clare drew Miss Oliver to the comfortable chairs. 'Tea shall be brought up shortly. May I perhaps call you Susan? I feel our both being in Bath brings us closer, somehow.'

'It would be nice, I own,' Susan replied, studying her hostess with a kindly gaze.

'I shan't bother with any roundaboutation but come straight to the point while we are yet alone. Since my arrival here a few days ago, I find the climate distinctly frigid. Would you by any chance know anything about this?'

Susan shifted as though suddenly uncomfortable. After studying her nicely gloved hands for a moment, she gave Clare a direct look. 'You have always been most amiable to me, Miss Fairchild, that is, Clare. I hesitate to reveal the source of the chill in Bath, for it seems so preposterous. They say that you, a single lady, have arrived to reside here with your infant.'

From the doorway Venetia exclaimed, 'I knew that male would bring trouble!'

Susan gasped, then turned troubled eyes to Clare, seeking an explanation without being censorious.

'I must explain, I see. There truly is a baby here in the house.' Clare was pleased to note that her new friend did not blink an eye at this horrendous bit of news. 'Actually he found us, for when we went to depart the Castle Inn in Marlborough, I discovered him inside a basket in my coach. Poor little babe abandoned to a stranger! I have been trying to locate his family, but with no success in the least.'

'How romantic!' Susan declared, thus earning a warm smile from Clare.

'You would not have been so charitable had you been required to remain over an additional day when you were longing to see Bath,' Venetia stated somewhat bitterly. 'But Clare would see if she could find a relative. Without success, I might add.'

'So I gathered,' murmured Susan, sharing a look of sympathy with Clare. 'What shall you do about him? And how might we counteract the gossip floating about Bath? For I must tell you that every quidnunc in town is flapping her tongue nineteen to the dozen.'

'I have thought and thought, and come to no sensible conclusion. I fear it may be to your detriment should our acquaintance be known, Susan,' Clare cautioned.

'Oh, pooh!' Susan said with a nice contempt in her voice. 'I am not dependent upon those tabbies for my wellbeing. They do nothing for me, I assure you.'

'But how uncomfortable,' Clare murmured. 'But your aunt?'

'My aunt, Lady Kingsmill, is immune to any darts sent in her direction, for she has quite the grandest consequence of any of the elderly ladies in town.' Susan laughed, a pretty, silvery sound, and Clare was very glad they had found each other this afternoon. 'I very much doubt I shall be in line for any malicious talk. But what to do?'

'I had thought to obtain tickets for the concert at the Octagon a few days hence. Do you think I shall encounter any trouble over this?' Clare frowned in her concern.

'Not in buying tickets. Your very name insures your welcome.'

Clare raised a brow in question. 'Welcome? Hardly. I should think they would more likely bar the door than let me in. Why did not one of them come to me to find out the truth rather than jump to conclusions?' Her voice clearly reflected her exasperation with the gossiping ladies of Bath.

Susan shook her pretty head, hazel eyes crinkling with amusement. 'What! And miss the chance to share the latest *on-dit*? London is not so very different. There are always those who adore being the first to pass along bad news.'

The three women put their heads together over the teacups to see the best way they might reveal the truth of the matter. At the conclusion of tea, nothing had been decided. 'You must come again tomorrow, Susan, for we have yet much to discuss.'

'Why do you not join my aunt and me for tea instead? I suspect we could use another head in this scheme, and hers is a wise one. You need never worry about her guarding her tongue. She is as close as wax. I rather believe she enjoys baiting the tabbies if she can.'

Clare darted a glance at Venetia, wondering if she would tolerate a visit to an elderly lady. She underestimated Venetia, it seemed, for that young lady brightened and smiled. 'I think it is a fine idea.'

'I agree,' Clare quickly hastened to add. 'We shall see you tomorrow, then.'

The remainder of the day was spent in speculating about Lady Kingsmill and her influence, or lack of it. If, as Susan

26

had indicated, the lady preferred to nap frequently, she might prove of little help. Still, she might know someone useful. And at this point, Clare was ready to turn to nearly anyone.

The following afternoon saw Clare and Venetia approach the front door of the Kingsmill dwelling in Laura Place with a faint air of trepidation.

It was just as Clare had feared. While Countess Kingsmill still possessed a twinkle in her eyes and uttered murmurs of sympathy to Clare, it was clearly beyond her to exert herself on Clare's behalf, or William's, as the case might be. While the girls sat chatting, trying to find an agreeable subject to discuss so that Clare might not be downcast, the housekeeper entered. This being an entirely female establishment, no butler or footmen were to be found.

'Lord Welby, my lady.'

Behind her a portly gentleman attired in the height of fashion some years past entered the room. His neatly powdered bagwig was tied with a flair, and the multitude of brass buttons on his coat shone brightly with polish.

'Welby! Good day, sir.' The countess snapped out her fan to languidly waft it to and fro while she preened slightly at the visitor.

He executed a remarkable bow, considering his girth, then acknowledged the young guests.

Another tray of tea appeared as if by magic. A pile of macaroons soon disappeared from the plate, and Clare suspected they were in part responsible for the weight Lord Welby carried about him.

'Are you enjoying your visit to Bath, young ladies?' His remark was general, but he studied Clare as he spoke.

'Not as much as I hoped,' Clare admitted.

'You do not mean to say there is a word of truth in the tittle-tattle going about town? I refuse to believe a syllable of it, especially now I have met you.' He brushed the final crumb of macaroon from his lap, then again peered at Clare intently.

'You are very kind, sir.' She looked first to Susan, then her aunt. The countess gave a regal nod of her head to indicate that Clare might speak freely.

27

She revealed the scant details of the story as swiftly as she might, then concluded with her admission about the motive. 'What that might be eludes me completely.' She ceased pleating her napkin and set it aside, feeling a bit foolish for airing her views regarding the baby.

'Hm. A bit of mystery to enliven our days. Havey-cavey sort of stuff always did appeal to me. Alas, my dear, would that I might champion your cause. I fear you need a younger knight-errant than I.' He sighed, then exchanged a sad look with the countess, who nodded in reply.

'Pity the fellow who was supposed to lease the house where you are now failed to arrive on time. Dashing sort of man, just the type you need. Blame me if I can think of his name.' He bestowed an apologetic look on Clare, ignoring the pouting countenance of Venetia completely.

Lord Welby might be old, but the perverse Venetia enjoyed the attentions of every male in sight, even as she declared how miserable males were in general and how much she detested them. Clare had ceased trying to untangle Venetia's reasonings in that regard.

'Do you believe my countenance might be restored if I reveal the identity of the babe, or lack of one, to the quidnuncs?' At the nods of agreement from both the elders, Clare countered, 'I fear that such a move might endanger his life. Surely it must be something drastic to force a mother to part with her son? No, as much as I would desire to be free of the stain on my name, I cannot jeopardize that little boy. He is a very dear child, you know.'

'Most worthy,' murmured Lord Welby, taking an enormous white handkerchief from his coat pocket and blowing his nose. He wiped his eyes, then said, 'Blame me, if you ain't a good girl. We shall have to think of some way to help you.'

Come the time to depart, they were no closer to a solution. Lord Welby suggested he linger in the coffeehouses and about the post to see if there might be any news floating about. That seemed the best idea anyone possessed.

The following morning, Clare decided she had had quite

enough of the entire matter. Jenny was looking a trifle down pin, and Clare boldly announced she would take the baby for an airing in the Sidney Park.

'Do you really think you ought?' Venetia timidly inquired, hesitantly taking a step in the direction of the stairs down to the ground floor. 'I daresay I might go with you.' This was said with such a distinctly reluctant air that Clare immediately shook her head.

'I believe 'tis bad enough you live with me. I will not have you feeling put upon.' Besides, it seemed Baby William had taken an unreasonable dislike to Miss Godwin. Whenever she came into view, he was wont to cry until she disappeared. It seemed Venetia's feelings regarding him were reciprocated.

Clare wrapped Willy up well, though the day was fine enough. One never knew about the weather. Just when one was set to enjoy sunshine, a cloud would come up to spoil it all. There seemed to be a great many clouds around Bath these days.

Rather than take the carriage, Clare ordered a chair to take her to the gardens, feeling she was not quite ready to brave the crowds going to and from the baths just yet. It was pleasant enough, and the baby seemed to enjoy the chair very much indeed.

Once there, Clare paid the men, then strolled into the gardens, intent upon finding a bit of pleasure in the day.

The baby was extremely well behaved. He gurgled and cooed with great good nature when she showed him the pretty flowers and the lanterns that were lit at night.

She was about to sit down for a bit of rest when she espied a gentleman she had not seen in ages. He caught sight of her at the same time, and Clare wished for a moment that she had left little Willy back at the house with Jenny and Priddy. There was nothing to do but brave it out.

She nodded graciously at his elegant bow. 'Lord Talbot, how nice to see you after all this time.'

'Miss Fairchild, I am flattered beyond words that you remember me.' His green eyes danced with humor until the significance of the babe in her arms sank in. The warmth of his smile faded, and Clare decided she must explain the circumstances to him. She had been quite fond of Richard Talbot, and was sorry when financial problems that often faced a younger son forced him to seek his fortune overseas.

'Please join me on the bench over there. I fear I am unaccustomed to carrying this young lad, and he is heavier than I anticipated.' She nodded to her left, hoping her chic bonnet would not suffer in the move.

'He is not your own?' came the cautious words.

Clare shook his head, relieved the matter was going to be so easy to approach. She had an instinctive trust of this man. In spite of those dancing green eyes and the sun highlighting his chestnut hair in a dashing manner when he swept off his hat in greeting, he had the look of solid dependability about him.

She then related the tale of the stopover at the Castle Inn in Marlborough, ending with Lord Welby's offer to watch the post and listen at the coffee houses.

Lord Talbot chuckled at the tale, shaking his head at the predicament she described. His admiring look did much to restore Clare's feeling of worth.

'I daresay it is a horrid mix-up, with a nursemaid running off or some such thing. I can only hope that someone steps forth to claim him soon.'

'Surely a lad his size doesn't require much?' Lord Talbot studied the infant with an indulgent eye.

'Besides the wet nurse we found for him, there is an astonishing amount of laundry to be done each day. For one so small, he has the house topsy-turvey.' She gave William a fond look, making it clear she was teasing and truly enjoyed the baby.

Richard Talbot studied Clare for a few minutes as she fussed over William. She seemed as lovely as he remembered from their encounters at various London balls and soirées. There was a fresh charm about her, from her pert blond curls and aristocratic little nose right down to the dainty foot that peeped from beneath the hem of her fashionable pelisse.

He wondered why she had never married, for surely it

could not have been for the lack of suitors. A fellow could scarce get near the lady a few years back, and he doubted if things had changed overmuch.

'You surprise me,' he said, giving voice to his thoughts. 'I expected you to be married, and that lad your own.'

Clare blushed as she hadn't in years. Flustered as a green girl, she said, 'I am scolded by my family ever and anon for placing myself on the shelf, sir.' She made a pretense of checking William, tucking the flannel blanket about his chin.

'Well, I, for one, am quite pleased to see you in a blessedly single state.' He chuckled at her surprised glance, so revealing.

Her long lashes fanned over warm cheeks at his laugh and what he implied by his words. Goodness, she was as bad as a Bath miss, to feel so upside down, so allover queer. Just because a devastatingly handsome man tells one he is glad she is unmarried does not mean anything serious.

'I might say the same for you,' she began, then realized immediately how that must sound. 'That is, I am surprised you are yet unmarried. You were much sought after, as I recall.'

'Until the mamas determined I had not a feather to fly with. Leastways, only a very small feather.'

'You sound remarkably tranquil about the matter. I gather you must have landed on your feet wherever you went.' She patted the baby where he snuggled against her shoulder, smiling at Lord Talbot as she rubbed her cheek against the fine wool.

His reply was lost a moment as he observed the sensual movement of her face against the soft fabric. Her eyes had a dreamy quality to their gentle blue, and he wondered why some man had not claimed this lovely creature for his own long before this. Did she have any notion how appealing she looked with the babe in her arms? A man might get ideas, very permanent ideas, just looking at her.

Clearing his throat, he continued his explanation. 'I went to the family plantation in Jamaica. With a spot of good fortune, I was able to expand our holdings there and increase the prof-

31

its. When my father died, I discovered he had willed the entire place to me. I have managed to do well enough.'

Clare liked his modesty, for another could have bragged about his wealth. Richard Talbot revealed as much by what he didn't say as by what was uttered.

'I had hoped to do well enough in Bath, myself,' she teased. 'I fear this young man has put paid to my ambitions. The quidnuncs have had a glory day with the *on-dit* of an unmarried lady and an infant.'

'No!' he replied, shocked that any taint of gossip should be placed against the lovely woman who had always been above suspicion of impropriety in years past. He shook his head, unwilling to believe the ladies of Bath could be so silly and blind. 'Did no one inquire as to the truth of the matter?'

'There's the rub. I suspect there may be a secret motive for placing the baby with me. How can I broadcast my innocence without putting him in danger, be that the case?'

Richard found it utterly absurd to even think she might be right about the whole matter. Surely one of the women would decry the gossip as being ridiculous?

At that moment, Clare decided she had best get home before one of the tabbies saw her with Lord Talbot and added to the gossip. Rising, she bowed her head, unable to shake his hand or curtsy. 'Thank you for the lovely visit, sir. I trust we shall meet again while you visit in Bath.'

'I lost my lodging because of a delay and have been put to finding another place to live. But I am settled in the Edgar buildings now and surely will seek you out at your address.'

Pleased he was to pursue their friendship, Clare informed him of their direction. She was surprised at his reaction.

'Oh, ho, so you are the ones who took my house! Well, I must say, I'd rather you than anyone else.'

'Most handsome of you, sir. We are in your debt.'

Just then Clare saw two of the women she had seen at the millinery shop. Raising her chin, she gave them a cool, defiant look. She was cut quite dead.

At her side, Richard Talbot stiffened, incensed that anyone could be so rude to one he knew to be of the finest quality. He bestowed a searching look on her lovely face as she tried to conceal her hurt. He was not one to jump into a controversy without due consideration, but he had known Miss Fairchild sufficiently well to also know her to be a remarkably fine person. She deserved better.

He took her elbow to usher her along from the park. 'I believe you need some help, my dear. May I offer my services?'

All at once Clare knew that she wanted nothing more than to depend on this man. He had something none of the other men she had met possessed. The quality was elusive, attractive, yet there. 'Yes,' she replied. 'I believe I should welcome that very much indeed. Where shall we begin?'

CHAPTER THREE

'I believe the first thing necessary is to return this infant to the care of his nurse. Then,' and his voice dropped to an attractive, rich vibrancy, 'we ought to make a list.'

'A list?' Clare wondered if the time spent in the heat of the Indies had affected his brain. 'What sort of list, pray tell?'

'You must recall the young angelics who frequented the halls of Almack's the past few years, the ones who married and are off breeding the future of England?' Was there a faint hint of amusement in his voice?

Incensed to be reminded of her spinsterish state, even if it was of her own choosing, Clare stiffened slightly. She glanced down at the Kennet and Avon canal that flowed through the heart of the Sidney Gardens where a painted narrow boat leisurely floated along, then back at him. Her voice chilling a few degrees, she said, 'La, sir, if I could recollect all the young girls who realized their dearest ambition, I should have a memory of note, indeed. However, I daresay that if Miss Godwin and I put our heads together, we might form a respectable listing,' she concluded after another look at his face.

'The lad has red hair; that ought to be a clue.' He continued to guide her along toward the exit of the gardens, ignoring her momentary pique.

His very presence at her side seemed to offer a shelter from the barbs she fancied might dart her way if she braved the path alone. She quickly forgave him the mention of the young women making come outs, reminding herself she had no one to blame but herself for her position on the shelf.

'I have racked my brain to think of a redheaded girl who might be driven to part with her infant. Alas, I cannot bring to mind one person. Of course, it may be that the father is the one who sports red hair. I am most utterly bewildered.' The frustration that had plagued Clare the days following her surprising acquisition could be quite clearly heard in her tone, not to mention seen in her troubled eyes. Since these were directed at Richard Talbot when she spoke, he received the full effect of the exquisite blue orbs, desolate with worry. The bewitching face framed in the attractive, and undoubtedly expensive, bonnet of the latest mode captivated his attention for a few moments before he escorted her to where a hackney carriage awaited customers by the garden entrance.

A sudden clearing of his throat preceded his efforts to cheer her. He ushered her into the vehicle, then commenced to console the young lady. So well did he succeed that by the time they arrived at the house in the Royal Crescent, Clare had quite forgotten the snub from the ladies in the Sidney Gardens. She did not even notice the stout figure of her neighbor, Mrs Robottom, as that lady paused not far away to watch Lord Talbot assist Clare from the carriage, infant in her arms.

Lord Talbot paused before the front door where Bennison stood at the ready to escort his lady into the house. 'Perhaps I might call this afternoon? That is, if you are free?'

Clare thought of how little there was to do in Bath what with the dearth of invitations. 'The only people we know in town are Miss Oliver and her charming aunt, Lady Kingsmill. Oh, and Lord Welby. I fear we are not overrun with guests.'

It was galling to be so brutally revealing about her social life, but Clare determined that the renewed friendship with Lord Talbot should be based upon that notable trait – honesty. She wished for no subterfuge in the relationship, as was customary with young ladies bent upon flirtation. She put all thoughts of intentions and hopes from her mind. She would concentrate on the problem of the moment, then think of other, more intriguing matters later.

No mocking smile quivered on the well-formed lips belonging to Richard Talbot. Indeed, if anything, he had a trifle grim look about him. 'I shall present myself at your door later this day, Miss Fairchild. Together we shall endeavor to solve this mystery.' He tipped his hat, again revealing that glorious wealth of dark chestnut hair so modishly cut and arranged, then strode off down the hill.

Clare lingered for a moment before entering the house. What a well-set man, so broad of shoulder and tall of frame. Those unusual green eyes that had turned to hard malachite when confronted with the snobs in the gardens had looked like liquid pools of serenity when gazing down at her. It brought to mind the appeal of a sylvan glade; dreamy, a retreat from the cares of the world where one would be protected from the cruel tongues of the patronizing ladies of local society.

Once inside the hall, she handed the baby to the maid with instructions to take him up to Jenny. Then, an abstracted expression on her face, she strolled into the study, stripping off her gloves, tossing them and her exquisite bonnet on the small chair before the fine mahogany secretary along the far wall of the room.

'I see you found a gallant while on your morning walk,' Venetia chided. 'I trust nothing improper occurred when you were thus unchaperoned? Or do you feel your advanced years protect you from impropriety?'

'That was unkind, Venetia,' murmured Clare, sinking down onto a large mahogany stool covered with pretty needlework. 'There is scarce need for a chaperon at my age while carrying a babe in my arms. I should imagine most people thought it mine.' The whimsical tone of voice hid her inward hurt at the malicious nature of the Bath gossips. 'And anyway, I have known Richard Talbot for simply ages. We met the spring of my entrance to society. As a matter of fact, he was at my come-out ball. He was much admired by all of us young things, but his lack of sufficiently warm pockets kept all at a proper distance, at the mamas' insistence, of course. He went away that following summer.' Clare's eyes gleamed with her delight in the change for Lord Talbot. 'He is now possessed of a proper fortune and can stare down any of the dowagers with those wicked eyes of his and be promptly forgiven. I have observed much can be condoned if one has enough money.'

'That sort of levity will get you into trouble, mark my words,' Venetia scolded. 'That man looks to be calamity in person.' Her derisive sniff added volumes to her words.

'He has offered to help me. I agreed. We shall begin to formulate a list of prospective parents this afternoon. I daresay it could take some time. If you do not wish to join us, I will understand. But, Venetia, your memory of all the doings of the *ton* is marvelously prodigious. How shall we get on without you?'

The sop to Miss Godwin's piqued pride at being left at home while Clare sallied forth to meet such a handsome gentleman was thus soothed. Never mind that Venetia would not have deigned to be in the company of the baby for a short outing, much less a foray to the Sidney Gardens.

'I trust you are correct, dear Clare,' Venetia simpered, batting her lashes in an amusingly coy manner. 'I shall attempt to help you solve the dilemma of the unwanted baby.'

'He may be temporarily unwanted, but I daresay he is some mother's treasure. Much anguish must tear her heart while she wonders if all is well with her darling.'

'You are too fanciful. Women cannot feel such emotions over a mere scrap of humanity such as he.' Venetia thought of the often damp and smelly child, and held her vinaigrette to her nose in a practiced and assuredly graceful movement.

Clare studied the young woman she had urged to travel with her to Bath to spend two months in genteel amusements, and decided the time would pass very slowly. Not bothering to answer this last particular bit of utter nonsense, Clare bestirred herself to consult with the housekeeper regarding the gentleman expected that afternoon. There must be tea and sufficient good things to serve with it. Gentlemen, Clare knew, subsisted on more hearty fare than watercress sandwiches and ratafia biscuits.

Venetia remained by the window. After giving the retreating Clare a baleful look, she stared out the window toward Brock Street where Lord Talbot had disappeared. He was quite, quite handsome. A worried frown settled on her brow.

While Clare told herself that Lord Talbot was merely serving as a sort of knight-errant to help an old friend now in distress, she studied the contents of her wardrobe with great care before selecting a gown for his anticipated call.

Cornflower-blue jaconet trimmed with cream silk flowers and fragile lace proved just the thing. It looked most feminine. And it made her seem young without being ridiculously girlish or attempting to be overly obvious. After Priddy gave the final hook a pat, then adjusted the skirt a trifle, Clare subsided on the bench of her dressing table to stare at the face in her looking glass.

She quite liked the neat little table with its muslin skirt and pretty candle holders. Best of all, it sat between the room's two windows so that the gentle Bath light illuminated her countenance, telling her that time had not been too harsh. She examined the face before her for lines or signs of fading.

'My hair, Priddy! It is disgraceful. Look at how those curls droop and the color seems so insipid. How I wish I had something more vibrant, like Venetia's chestnut, perhaps.' The wistful words were rung from a suddenly constricted heart.

The abigail frowned at her mistress. It was quite unlike her to rail at her looks. They were far superior to most young women's. Usually Miss Fairchild calmly accepted what she saw, and instructed Priddy to freshen her hairstyle before she drifted off to do whatever amused her. Today was different. Priddy determined to nose about to discover what was afoot. Why the sudden care about an appearance that was always immaculate and polished?

'Fetching blond curls and pretty blue eyes are quite the thing, my lady,' declared Priddy with a good deal of satisfaction. 'You look not a day older than when you made your come out.'

This statement seemed to lift her mistress out of whatever doldrums she had fallen into, for she brightened at the words and allowed Priddy to complete the careful arrangement of the blond curls with a matching blue riband.

'You are a dear, Priddy. Take yourself off to have a rest while Miss Godwin and I entertain my guest this afternoon. When in the Sidney Gardens, I encountered an old friend who has offered to assist with locating the parents of little William.' Richard Talbot had been more in the line of an acquaintance, or possibly a safe flirt, since both knew their relationship had limits. Clare blithely ignored this bit of history and floated from her bedroom across the hall to the drawing-room.

Here she was shortly joined by Venetia, who loudly complained about Jenny and the baby, not to mention Priddy, being housed so close to her. Priddy, quick to smooth the path for her beloved mistress, hastily offered to move her belongings up to the attic floor. Regarding Jenny and the baby, Clare balked.

'It is the outside of enough if you insist that child and his nurse be forced to dwell in the top-most floor. I strongly suspect he is of the gentry. Possibly even higher rank. How would your tender sensibilities feel if you were responsible for that dear baby being relegated to the attic?'

'Dear Clare, that is easy for you to say. You are not the one who must listen to him cry. He is but two doors away from me. He ought to be in a nursery, or at the very least the attic.

'He is directly above me. I hear him. But he is a good lad, and Jenny tries her best.' Clare admitted to no one that she would likely banish the infant to the attic if she were not afraid for him. As absurd as that seemed, she wanted the baby close by. And Jenny had undertaken to keep him silent as best she could. His outcries were brief, though Clare had found it difficult on occasion to return to sleep when awakened at three in the morning.

Bennison saved the afternoon by announcing Lord Talbot just at that moment. Venetia smiled and fluttered her long dark lashes at him. Clare drifted across the room with outstretched hands to greet him with all the gracious warmth a gentleman could desire.

It was the first time Richard had met Venetia Godwin. Although she had graced Almack's and all the requisite balls, she had never been a part of his circle. A younger son of the wealthy Earl of Knowlton, he had lived in elevated company even if his own pockets had not been deep. Miss Godwin, while of decent enough lineage, had not quite the same connections. Nor the monied background. Clare Fairchild had both money and proper ancestry. She also possessed something else. Precisely what it was, Richard was not prepared to say at the moment. But deep within him something stirred he could not deny. He didn't even wish to explore it right now.

'I know you are here to work' – here Clare made an adorable little grimace – 'but we shall have tea and become better acquainted before we do such a dreadful thing. Providentially for us, Miss Godwin has agreed to help. You see, she has a remarkable memory. We are indeed fortunate.'

Clare drew Venetia forward only to be required to take several deep breaths as that lady proceeded to flirt outrageously with Lord Talbot. Happily, he seemed to ignore her attempt.

'La, sir, I have seen you often enough in past years. It is lovely to discover you have done so well.' Venetia fluttered about, settling on the nearest chair.

Clare smoothly guided the gentleman to a chair by a rather pretty Pembroke table laid for tea. She neatly sat herself across from him, congratulating herself on her cleverness. Then she berated herself for the same trait. She was to find Willy's parents. Nothing more. For the present, at least.

After the hearty tea, which substance quite surprised Richard, accustomed to his mother's more delicate fare, they began to discuss the problem facing them.

Removing a notebook from his pocket, Richard glanced about the room. 'May I suggest we remove ourselves to the charming study downstairs? As I recall from a hasty glance as I entered the house, it has an excellent desk, though small. I trust we shall find it just the thing for our needs.'

Clare rose to her feet in one of those elegant movements that drive other women to gnash their teeth. Smiling at Lord Talbot and Venetia, she invited, 'Let us change rooms, then, for I perceive Lord Talbot is entirely correct.' To him, she added, 'I must again beg forgiveness that we forced you from the house you had selected.'

'It is entirely my fault,' he stated with a nice show of manners as he assisted Venetia from her chair. 'I had business matters in London that took far longer than they ought. After several years of being abroad, I had forgotten how slow the wheels can move here. I looked forward to a respite in Bath, one of my favorite places, enjoying a change from the heat of Jamaica. However, I am pleased to find the house thus occupied, I assure you.'

Quite satisfied that he was reconciled to his abode in the Edgar buildings as well as renewing their acquaintance, Clare ushered him down the stairs and into the study, then urged Venetia into a charming Chippendale chair close by while settling upon another next to Lord Talbot. If they were to put their heads together over this, Clare was determined to be near enough to do so. She totally ignored the interesting reality that she had never behaved so in her entire life.

'Now,' began Lord Talbot, 'I suspect we had best start with the Season before last. Since I was absent from the country, it will be up to you ladies to think of possible names for the list.' First he located a fresh quill and a pot of ink, then he glanced at Venetia before turning to Clare.

Venetia stared into middle space while considering the brilliant, and not-so-brilliant, marriages of that year.

'There was the Musgrove wedding. Quite a splash at St George's. That was followed by the Jolliffe–Claverhouse, then the Elfinstone–Fayer. Lady Du Plat married Lord Hepburn in July, such an unfashionable date, too. The Grantham–Inglis wedding took place in September just before the Kysale–Lombe affair. Gracious, how shall one ever make a list of them all? I touch only upon the London weddings. The remaining shall require a separate list.'

'I agree. The task is difficult enough, without trying to

41

figure out just who was breeding at the appropriate time to produce little William,' Clare said thoughtfully.

Venetia looked as though she longed to expire from embarrassment at this bit of outspoken language. Her brows rose to new heights, and she fanned herself vigorously as she cried, 'Dear Clare, do have a thought for propriety, please! What you said is quite enough to bring on a case of the vapors!'

'I thought better of you, Venetia. My mama was not quite so missish about life.' Clare turned her eyes, now alight with humor, on Lord Talbot. She was not disappointed. That green gaze met hers with perfect understanding.

'Can you recall who of the *ton* has red hair? That might be more to the point.' Richard studied the two young women in turn. Miss Fairchild was relaxed, yet concentrating on her thoughts. Miss Godwin seemed of a divided mind, as though she wished to do two different things at the same time. Having been around and about for some years, it was not too difficult for Richard to figure out what she had in her head.

'The Fitzgeralds, of course,' Venetia finally offered. 'And the Innes family has a number of redheads as I recall. The grandmother's side of the family, you know. I think we might ignore most of the Scots, for it would be most unlikely they would be around this area to deposit that child in dear Clare's coach.'

'She has a point there,' Clare conceded to Lord Talbot, wishing all the while that she didn't find it quite so difficult to concentrate on the matter to hand. He would think her a peagoose without a brain in her head.

'Well, it is too bad of them all. There ought to be a convenient way to merely look up all the marriages of that year without going to London,' Venetia said with a pout.

'We could do that if necessary, you know. Or I might send my man to check for us if your memories fail.' Richard looked at Clare, who seemed to have plunged into the past.

'You know,' mused Clare, while thinking back in time, 'there was a quiet little scrap of a girl I just recalled. Her name was Jane something or other. She married the Earl of Millsham. Had pots of money. He did, that is. I seem to remember that he had dark red hair. 'Tis the sort of color that just might have been brighter when he was a child. Did you not have brighter hair as a litte girl, Venetia?'

Looking as annoyed as a hornet that has been brushed away from a chosen flower, Venetia hastily denied any such thing. Her hair had always been its present hue. Her skin flared into the angry color that often afflicts redheads when upset or embarrassed.

Turning to Lord Talbot, Clare sent a silent question. Ought they pursue this line?

'I suggest we all write a few letters to anyone we know who might have knowledge of those on this admittedly short list of marriages who could have produced a child in the required month. Let me see, if he was born in April, the wedding would have been no later than August?'

'Would the birth not be recorded?' Clare wanted to know.

'We have to have more details first. It is more complicated than I suspected. In Jamaica, it is a simple matter. Here, it is another thing entirely.'

Clare wondered about that island. She suspected he would have to return to Jamaica eventually. She longed to ask him if he planned to return soon nearly as much as she feared his answer. She forced her unwilling tongue to remain silent.

Not so Venetia.

'Tell us, Lord Talbot, do you plan to remain in England? Or does your future lie in Jamaica? I do so admire a man who travels. It is one of my fondest dreams to spread my wings and see something of this world.' Her demure smile was enhanced by a languid wafting of her painted fan.

Why, the little hypocrite, thought Clare. Could this possibly be the same woman who had forced Clare to travel at a snail's pace from London because of her sensitive stomach? She did not turn a hair at her outrageous words! All thoughts of exposure vanished as Clare realized that what she longed to know might be found in his reply. She listened with straining ears.

He toyed with the quill pen yet in his hand before answering. 'Perhaps. It all depends, you see. My father has left me some property not far from here. I shall study the matter and

43

see what appears to be the best prospect.'

Clare looked down at her lap where her fingers played with a silk flower. Whatever did he mean by those ambiguous words? Deciding she would be better off ignoring what she had no control over, she took a deep breath, then briskly said, 'I expect the sooner we write our letters, the sooner we shall get replies.'

She rose from her chair and hunted about for the rather nice hot-pressed paper she had brought with her from London. Gathering up a collection of quills, and after locating another pot of ink, she directed the others.

'Venetia, why do you not join me over at the card table? We can share this bottle of ink while Lord Talbot uses the desk.'

Quite happy to be of use while Lord Talbot was present to observe, Venetia settled at the card table, declaring, 'I shall write several ladies I met in London, now ruralizing at their country estates. They are all great gossips and know simply everything about everyone. Surely they will provide a clue.'

Clare exchanged a guarded look with Lord Talbot, then set to work at writing a letter to her sister and her brothers' wives. They might be well married, but seemed to be *au courant* with who was producing what.

She quickly scratched out a letter to her sister, being careful to inquire if Sarah knew anything of a young woman named Jane who had married the Earl of Millsham. Clare doubted that Jane might be recalled, but Sarah made a point of being well acquainted with marriages of the peerage.

Once they had finished their writing, Clare expressed her gratitude to the others.

'You found someone to write to, even though you have been gone for several years, Lord Talbot?' teased Venetia. Her fan was back in use now that she was able to set aside the pen and paper upon which she had neatly written her lines.

Clare darted an annoyed glance at Venetia. Really, for someone who set such store by propriety, she surely was inquisitive. Although Clare had to admit one did learn more that way.

Venetia, for her part, suspected Clare might be annoyed

with her for flirting with Lord Talbot. But the gentleman was far too handsome for Venetia's peace of mind. Were dear Clare to succumb to his good looks and manners, it would leave Venetia without a home, for her relatives had made it quite plain that she was to find another to take her in – they would not. Tiresome people. She had done her very best to help them all. Not every woman was as gifted as Venetia in knowing what was the best thing to be done at any given time. She had tried to point out the error of their ways in the nicest possible manner, and what gratitude did they show? True, she was not her best with children. She found them plaguesome brats at best. But she knew for a certainty the proper way to rear them. And as for household duties, while she might not have had the running of a house herself, she was a fount of information if they would only listen. She read a great deal, you see. True, novels were perhaps not the best source, but they were always so wise.

'I wrote my mother, for one,' said Richard. 'I have always found her to be knowledgeable when I least expected her to be. Since my father died, she has had little to occupy her time but to write letters. I received quite a stack of them filled with all manner of news.' He looked at Clare. 'She even mentioned you once. As I recall, you were an attendant at some rather glorious wedding she attended, and she thought you prettier than the bride.' He grinned wickedly at Clare's discomfort at this praise.

'Yes,' Venetia agreed, 'Clare has been a bridesmaid at a goodly number of weddings. Perhaps you ought to merely list them all, and we shall discover the missing parents from that, dear Clare.' She tittered a dainty laugh behind her fan, her eyes alive with delight in her wit.

'Oh, but I have, Venetia,' Clare responded, wondering what had gotten into her friend, who usually treated men as though they possessed some awful disease. The words reminded Clare that she had indeed served as attendant to many brides. Too many, it seemed. 'Since you were in the congregation at nearly all of them, I trust our lists match.'

Rising from the chair, she extended her hand to Lord Talbot.

'That was dry work, sir. Would you care for a glass of sherry while we send these off to the post? A celebration, if you like?'

Amused at her dry sense of humor and good grace at tolerating the snide remarks of her companion, Richard inclined his head with a deal of pleasure. 'If I do not keep you from your tasks.'

'The way dear Clare fusses over that baby, 'tis a wonder she has time for anything. I was taught that children should be seen and not heard.' Venetia swished from the study and began to walk up the stairs. Over her shoulder she added, 'We are not only plagued with his presence, but have to listen to him at all hours as well.'

Richard gave Clare a questioning look as she mounted the first step to follow Venetia. She squarely met his gaze with a troubled one of her own. 'I have the oddest fancy that he is in danger, you see. Rather than in the attic, I keep him closer by, a silly whim, I admit. The attic seemed too remote.'

CHAPTER FOUR

The tickets for the concert at the Octagon were obtained with no difficulty, and Clare looked forward to the outing with great pleasure.

She and Venetia joined Lady Kingsmill, Susan, and Lord Welby just outside the entrance, then strolled in to take their seats as though the gossips were not taking note of every movement, or who said and did what.

'The organ is in the other area, you know,' explained Lady Kingsmill in an amiable way. 'You may hear it quite plainly without any difficulty in the least. The soloist this evening is a baritone of some renown. I heard him once in London. You ought to be pleased with his performance.'

Clare was caught up in the atmosphere of the room. Casual glances about her brought home the interesting fact that not all the ladies of Bath found her beyond the pale. Perhaps it was the presence of Lady Kingsmill, as well as the genial approval of Lord Welby, that did the trick. But there were gracious nods and reserved smiles, which at this point was the best one might expect.

'I see that young fellow I told you about over there, Miss Fairchild. The one whose house you took? Fine gentleman. Look, he's coming this way.' Lord Welby nodded in the direction of Lord Talbot, a smile wreathing Welby's round face.

'So I see.' Clare felt sure her cheeks turned a bright rose beneath the scrutiny of the two men.

'May I join you?' The rich vibrancy of his voice feathered

on Clare's nerves, sending tiny chills down her spine.

She glanced up to meet that green gaze and sighed. 'We should be pleased, sir.' She edged her chair sideways just a trifle so he might draw another up if he so wished. It seemed he did, for he found a vacant chair, pulled it in line with hers, and thanked Lord Welby for making room on the other side.

'The weather has been lovely these past days, has it not?' She chided herself for mundane conversation, but if anyone listened, they would find it quite unexceptionable.

'Indeed.' He twinkled down at her as though he understood precisely what she was about. 'How nice to get a respite from the rains. I was told they could have snow here as late as April. Did you know that?'

'Really!' she exclaimed in horrified tones that she hoped would sound sincere. 'I shan't complain about a bit of wet, then.'

He bent his head as though inspecting his cuff for lint. 'Have you received any replies to the letters as yet?'

Clare touched the tip of her nose with one delicately gloved finger, thus concealing the movement of her lips. 'Two from nearby. Since my sisters-in-law are good to write, I expect more any day now.'

'Anything of interest?' He leaned toward her with polite curiosity, as though he had just uttered another word of wisdom about the weather.

'Yes. Best discuss it over tea when you are free to attend us.' She had not seen him anywhere the past several days, and it had surprisingly rankled her. Not that she actually was so vulgar as to search the throng of people strolling along Milsom Street or the crowd in and about the Pump Room. But she could not help notice his absence. After all, how many gentlemen were there around with his presence and looks?

He raised his brows in question, but as the concert appeared to begin, he could say little more. 'I shall be there tomorrow.'

'Fine.' She subsided in her chair, wishing, for some absurd reason, that she might dare move her arm a trifle so that it rested against his. She was far too conscious of him being next to her. This silliness must stop at once. It would not do to become enamored of a man who would in all likelihood sail off to Jamaica again, leaving her on the shores of England.

He shifted. Clare held her breath as his coat sleeve brushed her arm just where the shawl left her silk gown exposed. She could feel warmth and sense the firm texture of the excellent coat he displayed to such advantage, right through the thin silk of her gown. He must have patronized either Weston or Stultz while in London, for the fit was too perfect to result from the attention of a lesser tailor. In the confines of the room, she could faintly detect a spicy scent she had noticed before when near him. No doubt something from the Indies. Exotic and provoking. Like him.

The audience clapped, and Clare wondered what had happened to bring that about.

'I believe that was well done,' commented Lord Talbot. He gestured to the printed program in his hand. 'The next piece is a favorite of mine.'

Startled, Clare realized with chagrin that she had totally missed the first offering of the evening. Resolved to pay attention to the next piece, especially since it was one Lord Talbot recommended, she strained to listen with better awareness. Besides, it seemed that her nearness affected him not in the least.

Following the conclusion of the music, Clare was able to applaud with far greater enthusiasm, for she had actually heard it. She was impressed, as well. 'Bath has better entertainment than I suspected,' she said, turning to him. Others did such, and no one remarked. Surely it was permissible for a lady to offer a comment to the gentleman at her side?

His slow smile, lighting up those unusual eyes, did the strangest things to her heart. 'I am so pleased you like it. There is a play to be presented this coming week that I believe you might enjoy. Would you and Miss Godwin join me? Perhaps Lady Kingsmill and Miss Oliver as well? And Lord Welby, too, of course?'

'Delightful,' Clare managed to say before her wits deserted her. 'Simply delightful.' The next piece of music rescued her from making a total idiot of herself. Really, whatever possessed her? Her normal poise had completely deserted her.

Following the concert, Lady Kingsmill insisted they all repair to her house for a small, impromptu party. It was far too fine an evening to end it all just yet.

Venetia looked about to pout until Lord Welby beamed his affable gaze upon her, declaring her to be the prettiest thing he had seen in ages, reminding him much of his dear departed wife. Unable to resist such lovely words, she immediately urged Clare to join the group at Lady Kingsmill's.

Thus it was that Clare found herself sitting by Venetia while Lord Talbot and Susan sat across from them in the hackney for the jaunt across town. Lord Welby and Lady Kingsmill had each taken a chair to the house at Laura Place. The older lady stated she found the chairs got places faster in this congested little town with its streets that went up and down and curved everywhere.

Once established in Lady Kingsmill's drawing room, Mr Talbot drew Clare to one side. 'What is this you have received? News of value?'

Lord Welby interrupted them to offer, 'I have daily checked the papers at Duffields Library, and there has been nary a word about a missing child in any one of them.'

Admirably concealing her vexation at the intrusion of the kindly gentleman, who after all wished only to help, Clare nodded sagely. 'Most strange,' she replied.

'The letters,' prompted Lord Talbot. His eyes had taken on a green glitter to them that Clare found challenging.

'Well, my sister agreed that the girl, Jane, did indeed marry the Earl of Millsham. They were living at Millsham Hall until her husband died in a hunting accident. My sister did not know where the widow lived now.'

'Hardly a thing to force her to abandon a child in your coach, however.' The glitter in the green eyes dimmed, and Clare had the satisfaction of suspecting that he also had been annoyed when Lord Welby had joined them.

'Unless there were mitigating factors. But there are other

letters to consider.' She tossed him a defiant look, then turned away to speak to Venetia.

The housekeeper entered with a tray of delectable cakes and the inevitable macaroons for Lord Welby. He announced he preferred coffee to any other drink, and the group settled down to conversation and sweets.

Due to the general conversation and Clare's perverse desire that Lord Talbot be forced to call upon her on the morrow to obtain the rest of the information, the subject was not approached again that evening. He made no effort on that score either, leading Clare to wonder if he were merely bored, or wished to see her in private.

'I thought the concert last night at the Octagon quite fine,' Venetia said while marching up the stairs the next morning. 'Indeed, were it not for those tiresome tabbies who do their best to make our life uncomfortable, our time in Bath should prove most interesting.' Venetia flounced into the drawing room after a rather breathless trip up to the first floor. She had forgone breakfast in her room to join Clare for the morning meal. She seemed bent on keeping Clare company this morning for some reason.

'Lord Welby is such a dear man. He made quite a point of noticing us, along with Lady Kingsmill. Together I feel they did much to allay the nasty little gossips. It was a fortunate moment when we encountered Susan Oliver on Gay Street. She has proved to be a dear, kind friend.' Clare followed Venetia into the drawing-room, her energy undiminished from the exertion of the climb up the stairs.

'Do you intend to discuss the matter of little William with Lord Talbot today?' Venetia plumped herself on the nearest chair as though exhausted. She languidly fanned herself to cool her flushed cheeks while watching Clare with a careful gaze.

'Of course. If he comes, that is.' Clare paused by a window that overlooked the expanse of green that rolled down the hill across from the crescent. It was a serene view, one that never failed to please her.

'With your consequence?' Venetia blurted out. 'I think not. He will come, and you may discuss whatever was in those letters you did not show to me. Then we may perhaps settle the matter of the baby once and for all,' she said with surprising complacency, considering how she had rambled on about the matter for days on end, ever since the afternoon when they had written letters regarding little William.

'We shall see. This seems to be more and more involved. Have you had replies to your letters?' Clare turned to face Venetia, a cautious look settling on her face. 'A solution may not be that simple. What if we need to investigate?'

Before Venetia could sputter a reply to that outrageous remark, Bennison entered with the morning mail.

'I suppose you will retreat to read those letters. If I must reside with you and bear the arrows sent our way, the least you might do is to share the news with me.' Venetia assumed a petulant air, again waving her fan about her. That she was annoyed with her lack of mail was easily seen.

'My brother has done a bit of sleuthing on my behalf. It seems that the young Dowager Lady Millsham has utterly vanished!'

Further discussion had to wait until Lord Talbot presented himself at the house in Royal Crescent that afternoon. When Bennison ushered him up the stairs, Clare was nearly beside herself with impatience.

'At last you are here,' she declared far more passionately than was her wont. 'I have such news for you.' Then remembering her manners, she added, 'And have you had anything from your mail, sir?'

His grin was just a shade familiar as he slanted a look down at her once safely standing by her side near the window. He glanced to where Venetia watched them with her gimlet gaze and then turned to Clare. 'It can wait, I believe. What have you heard?'

'Putting all the items together, I have discovered that Jane settled at Millsham Hall with her earl, but her time there was short, indeed. It seems her husband met with a tragic hunting accident, leaving her a widow at a very tender age. And now she has disappeared.'

'No word about an infant?'

'Nothing,' Clare admitted reluctantly. 'However, they were married within the established time to produce William.'

Venetia erupted in a fit of coughing, and Clare crossed to ring for tea.

'Really, dear Clare, such a vulgar subject to be discussing. The matter of breeding should never be mentioned in polite society.' Venetia fanned herself with vigor surprising in one near fainting.

'But then, as friends, we need not subscribe to that, surely?' Lord Talbot crossed to chat at some length with Venetia until he saw her ruffled feathers had subsided. He turned to Clare as though in question.

The entrance of the tea tray complete with items chosen to please the gentleman forestalled any further mention of the letters. Clare was beginning to lose hope of ever having a quiet talk with Lord Talbot. Mercy, Venetia behaved as though a mere conversation with him would ruin Clare forever! To tell the truth, Clare was becoming a bit impatient with Venetia's dragonlike attitude. She was in Bath as a companion, not a chaperon.

Tea and cakes were consumed with utmost politeness, although Clare hurried with hers and bolted her tea in an unseemly rush. How fortunate it was not quite scalding.

Tea over, Lord Talbot rose from his chair, motioning to Clare. She followed him to the window where he pointed out a carriage being walked below. In a soft voice that did not carry beyond them, he said, 'I feared something like this might happen, so I came prepared.' In a louder voice he added, 'Will you do me the honor of a drive into the country, Miss Fairchild?'

Before Venetia could voice an objection, Clare beamed up a relieved smile at her rescuer. 'Yes. I should like it above all things. Let me send for my pelisse and bonnet, and we shall discuss the contents of the letters while trotting past the rural landscape.'

'Or perhaps a slow walk in the Sidney Gardens?' he

murmured as she floated past him to ring for Priddy.

'Admirable, to be sure,' she said in reply, her eyes lighting up with her pleasure in such a simple thing.

Venetia objected quite as Clare had expected she would. Clare slipped into her favorite blue silk pelisse, then tied the ribands of her neat Victoria hat of straw turned up around the front, lined with pale blue satin with dainty ostrich feathers on the side. All the while Venetia rambled on about proprieties and how she thought Clare to be far more circumspect than to behave thus. Her glare at Lord Talbot would have frosted a lesser man.

Picking at the triple fall of lace that cascaded over her full bosom, Venetia concluded, 'I think it vastly unfair of you two to go off and leave me in suspense.'

'But, if we told you everything, you could not in all honesty claim that you knew utterly nothing about it,' Clare replied. 'You see, dear girl, we are protecting your reputation.'

Clare bestowed a quick hug on her companion, then joined Lord Talbot downstairs where he had hastily taken refuge on the pretext of ordering the carriage brought to the door.

Venetia paused a moment in the middle of the drawing room, then hurried to the window to stare down at the open phaeton with a puzzled expression on her face.

'It is a lovely day out,' Clare said with satisfaction. 'The air yet has a hint of moisture in it, but it is not quite so sultry as yesterday. A drive will be most welcome.'

Clare thought she heard Lord Talbot murmur something about that not being the only reason, but couldn't be certain, as he was walking around to get in on the other side. The groom jumped up behind as the carriage pulled away from the house at a sharp clip. Clare didn't look up, but she was sure she felt Venetia's gaze upon her back as the carriage left the house.

Once the horse settled into a steady pace, Lord Talbot turned to study his companion. She ostensibly took in the pretty countryside. But her properly gloved hands twisting about in her lap revealed a concern for more than the sight of a few daisies and a rather prosaic view of ripening fields.

54

'What conclusions have you reached, if any?'

Clare turned to face him, glad she had worn a bonnet with a short brim so her vision was unobstructed. 'Would you think me utterly mad if I said I feel something is not right with this young Jane? Why should she completely disappear? I would like very much to visit Millsham Hall to see if the new earl can tell us anything.'

Richard nodded, slowing the horse to a walk, then finally pulling off to a side lane where they might turn around if so desired. 'I, too, have the sense that there is something havey-cavey here. My letters tell me the same thing as yours. My mother relates details of the wedding, and how happy the couple appeared. My brother wrote that Jane's husband was a splendid rider to the hounds, and that it seemed tragic that so excellent a man should make such a dim-witted fall.'

Clare's eyes had been fastened on a small bird that was hopping about on the verge. At the conclusion of his words, she turned her gaze upon Lord Talbot once again. 'That settles it. I shall take my coach to Millsham Hall.'

'I believe I shall go with you, Miss Fairchild. While I have no doubt you could do admirably on your own, for you have an inquiring mind and good sense, there are times a man is useful.

Clare tore her gaze from his, then looked back at him again to see if he was serious. 'Please do not feel obliged to accompany me. I would not for anything in the world put you to a deal of trouble.'

'I am already involved. I find my curiosity has grown. I would like to see the baby reunited with his mother.' His eyes seemed to add a message that Clare wanted desperately to believe. But it was far too soon for such, and she had been raised to more propriety than she had displayed as of late.

'Yes,' replied Clare softly. 'She must miss him dreadfully.'

He turned the carriage in the direction of Bath once again, then continued their planning. 'How soon can you leave?'

'Goodness, this has all the earmarks of something improper. I imagine I shall not be permitted to travel alone with you.' Clare said this with a small chuckle, but knowing she was precisely correct.

'According to the papers and the tabbies about the Pump Room, the latest scandal is of such great proportions that you have been relegated to stale news.'

'I must be thankful for small mercies.' She wrinkled her brow. 'And the latest *on-dit*?'

'A notice has been placed in the local paper to the effect that a lady has eloped from her husband, and that he warns he will not pay any of her bills in the future. She had run him into debt, and he cautions others not to trust her.'

'That certainly must have set the tongues wagging.'

'A decided hum hovered over the ladies at the Pump Room, I believe.' He grinned at her, and Clare found her pulse racing madly.

'I believe it is urgent we go as soon as possible,' she said to change the subject and calm that silly pulse. 'Do you agree? Although I shall not take Venetia along, no matter what she says. This calls for caution, and she is another not to be counted upon. Unruffled she is not.'

They entered Bath once again, and as he wove along the streets, noting the interested looks that followed them, Richard could only be glad he was to take Clare away from the city for a short time. Out of sight, perhaps out of mind and off the tongue? He detested the gossiping and knew it bothered Clare not a little.

'I am at your disposal.' He refrained from commenting about Miss Godwin. She was Clare's chosen companion, and as such, it was for Clare to decide their relationship. If he had his way, things would be vastly different.

Venetia reacted to the news of Clare's imminent departure exactly as Clare feared: lengthy lectures on propriety and virtue, challenges regarding motives, and impugning Lord Talbot until Clare thought she might explode.

At long last on the following morning, as her modest-sized valise was shut and placed by the bedroom door, Clare turned to face her companion.

'I have asked Priddy to travel with us. Lord Talbot has his

man and our Tom Coachman and a groom. You go too far when you cast aspersions on Lord Talbot. He has been the perfect gentleman at all times. His concern for little William, not to mention my good name, has been praiseworthy. Far better than some I might name, but shan't.' She paused to cast a significant look at Venetia.

Deciding it might be better to still her tongue for the moment, Venetia dropped her gaze to conceal her fears. If Clare found she might get along without her, it would mean that Venetia must find another place to live, and the number of options had dwindled severely as of late. She was down to Aunt Peasely, who was horridly deaf.

Clare regretted her words as soon as they flew out. Not that any of them were not true. But Venetia looked so shattered, like a frightened little bird.

'Forgive me, my dear Venetia. This is a necessary thing I must do, and I would not have you touched by it in any way. I pray you will understand?'

Venetia smiled like a cat who had just received a plump mouse. 'Of course, dear Clare. I feel sure Lord Talbot is just as he ought. I noticed he is most kind to Lady Kingsmill as well.'

A grim look flashed across Clare's face. Lord Talbot had seemed more than the perfect gentleman. His eyes and his hands touched her probably no differently than any other man's. It was merely her foolish reaction. Her years were beginning to affect her emotions, that was all. She had no business in longing for his touch, or wishing for a closer relationship. She scolded herself into propriety all the way down the stairs and out the door to the coach, while deep inside she was thrilled to know she would be in the same coach with him, partake of meals together – at least for a few days. As luck would have such things, it was highly unlikely he would return her regard. And that would be the end of that.

So, resolved to maintain a proper distance and determined that Lord Talbot should not think she was throwing herself at his head, she accepted his hand to enter the coach. They departed in a flurry of dust. From further down the crescent,

Mrs Robottom took stock of the departure, noting that Priddy was along and the baby left behind.

The trip actually went very well. Meals were no difficulty at all, and Clare told herself she was pleased that Lord Talbot failed to argue about the bills. Although he insisted upon treating her to an occasional meal, Clare paid for her lodgings and most else. It set her mind at ease. He remained the perfect gentleman.

The hours passed by in pleasant conversation and exploration of each other's interests. At least, as much as might be said with Priddy sitting across from them with her ears literally straining to catch every word.

Only when they rumbled through the front gates of Millsham Hall did Clare give Lord Talbot an anxious look. Could they pull this off? It seemed imperative they find Baby William's parents, or mother, as the case may be.

'Just follow my lead, promise?'

Clare gave Richard Talbot a startled look before facing the opening door. 'Very well.' She paused a moment before accepting the hand offered by the Millsham footman, then bravely set forth.

Curiosity gleamed in his eyes, and he watched the party march up the stairs with a speculative tilt to his head.

'Lord Millsham, please,' Richard said firmly to the butler at the door. 'Richard Talbot and Miss Fairchild to see him.' Richard took Clare's elbow with a gentle and proprietary hand as a slim, dark-haired man strolled forth from an adjacent room to greet them.

He waved a hand at the butler, effectively dismissing the man. 'Good day, Talbot, Miss Fairchild. I haven't seen you in years, Talbot. What brings you to Millsham Hall?'

Darting a nervous look at Lord Talbot, then back to the earl, who had suddenly assumed a disturbing mien, Clare hastened into speech. 'Actually, I am the one who sought your home. I hope I might find Jane, Countess Millsham,' Clare said, not certain if the earl had lately married and she did not know of it. 'The last I heard from the dear girl was from here.' He was not to know the two women were barely acquainted.

'I forget my manners. Come, we must not linger in the hall.' The earl flickered a glance at a nearby footman, then returned his bland gaze to them. 'Join me in my sitting room. It gets a lovely bit of sunshine this time of day.' He escorted them across the vast hall into a comfortable-looking room full of sofas and cozy chairs, tables piled high with books and magazines, and vases of summer flowers. In short, a place that was very livable and quite charming.

Clare studied their host. Odd that his eyes did not match the rest of him, for they contained a distinctly hostile look in their depths.

Richard noted that Millsham took an uneasy glance at the clock on the fireplace mantel before turning toward them again.

'Strange that you should come seeking Lady Millsham. I haven't seen her for some time. She never was one to socialize, and I fear she resented my moving into the Hall as quickly as I did. She seemed content to ruralize here, alone. I never could understand why Cousin Peter married the little drab.'

'You have no idea where she is? She does not reside at the Dower House?' Richard queried, wanting to press the earl for more answers. 'Forgive my curiosity, but I know how much Miss Fairchild wishes to see her.'

'I'm afraid I know nothing about her,' Millsham snapped, his composure cracking. 'My agent pays into an account for her, but that hasn't been touched the past few months.' Then getting himself in hand once again, he added, 'Tell you what, old boy, find her and let me know where she is, for I'd like to do something for the poor thing. Not proper to let the sixth earl's wife live in obscurity, now is it?'

His hearty laugh seemed forced to Clare, and she took a step closer to Richard. She permitted him to guide her onto a sofa at his side and drew comfort from his nearness.

The butler appeared at the door with a tray of tea and other refreshments suitable for a summer's afternoon. Clare sipped a cool glass of lemonade while wondering how Priddy was making out belowstairs.

The earl *seemed* all that was affable. That was the rub. Clare sensed he was uneasy, wary of them, though he had no reason to be, or did he? He sat with his back to the inviting sunshine as though wishing to conceal his expression from them. Or was she simply imagining things? Was she suspicious needlessly?

Sending Richard a searching look, she sipped the lemonade while wondering if Jane had decorated this room in such a charming style. What sort of woman would the new earl select? She shivered at the thought of marrying such a man as this, who appeared so outwardly smooth and unctuous. And inwardly?

Finally there was nothing to do but leave. The earl was like a block of stone, refusing or unable to reveal anything more.

As the coach rumbled down the immaculately kept drive, Richard turned to Clare and said, 'His request for news of Jane had all the earmarks of Caesar's order to the wise men to let him know if they found the babe they sought.'

'Murder?' Clare cried. Priddy looked well nigh to fainting.

CHAPTER FIVE

'Not murder, surely,' Lord Talbot replied, trying to calm both women with his voice and manner. 'But his concern did not ring true to me. What was your reaction, Miss Fairchild?'

'I, too, had the feeling our host was being less than truthful with us, for whatever reason he might have.' She glanced across to where Priddy looked more herself, then queried, 'Did you discover anything belowstairs?'

The abigail shot her mistress a triumphant look, then straightened her shoulders. 'Aye, that I did. After chatting some time with the cook, I found out that Lady Millsham, the poor little darling as cook called her, was with child at the time the late earl died! Although the cook said nothing direct, I suspect that she felt there was something smoky about the riding accident.'

Clare turned her head to gaze wide-eyed at Lord Talbot. 'I knew it. My instincts rarely mislead me. The sixth earl dies and his countess disappears sometime after. When you total up the baby in the basket, his belongings of the finest quality, and his red hair – you no doubt observed that the present earl has that dark red color? – you cannot deduce other than there is something decidedly fishy about the circumstances. I imagine his elegant lordship might be able to tell us a thing or two about that. Or am I jumping to conclusions on too little evidence?'

'May I make a suggestion? Why do we not stay over at an inn near here? It might be possible to do a bit of sleuthing about in the neighborhood, possibly set our fears to rest – or bolster our forebodings. As well, you know there are other possibilities. I should hate to think we overlook another prospect. What say you to that?'

Priddy had stiffened at his words; he could see her rigid figure in the periphery of his vision. He concentrated on Clare Fairchild. In the past she had possessed a reputation for propriety, a name without a hint of indelicate behavior. Her family was without reproach. While there would be nothing unseemly about staying over at an inn, what with her abigail to guard her, there could possibly be uncomfortable talk. She had already endured more of this than she ought, and it was not his intention to add to it needlessly.

'I imagine some might think it improper, but I would do naught to harm your good name.' He wanted to place a hand over hers to reassure her of his noble intentions, then realized that touching her was hardly the manner in which to proceed. Especially when she looked so tempting in her pretty pelisse and dashing hat, not to mention gentle blue eyes so widely imploring him.

Clare normally would have left for home immediately. She did not flout the rules of Society. Ever. But since little William had entered her life, everything had been topsy-turvy. What was it she had said to Venetia? That she had met every proper gentleman in the country? And that they bored her? Well, Richard Talbot did not bore her. She found being in his company stimulating and most desirable. For once in her life she was going to do the unconventional and dangerous!

'I believe that to be an excellent notion. With Priddy along to see to my reputation, there should be no problem.' She gave Lord Talbot what she hoped was an encouraging smile.

It took some time before they settled on a country inn at the next market town. While not of great size, the Star and Garter looked to be far cleaner than anything seen so far that day, and the aroma of fresh-baked bread hung in the air to tantalize even a jaded palate.

Country dinner was served early, so that Richard found

there was a good deal of daylight remaining afterward. He sought Clare out where she wandered about in the minuscule herb garden behind the inn. 'I believe I shall ride over to the village closest to Millsham Hall to see if there is any gossip to be found at the local alehouse.' He waited to see if she would rail at him for deserting her. He was not disappointed in his estimation of her character.

'I think that an excellent idea,' she replied with a resolute voice, damping the notion that she would have preferred his company for the evening. 'Perhaps you can pry out any details of the manner of the late earl's death, or maybe discover if anything is known about the poor little countess. I only wish I might go with you.' Clare gave Lord Talbot a rueful quirk of a smile, knowing full well that the less she saw of him the better it was for her simmering feelings. Personal matters must be pushed aside for the nonce. But later, she intended to explore them with intensity.

Richard arranged for a horse, then spoke briefly with his groom. Within a short time, the two men rode off in the direction of Millsham Hall.

The seventh Earl of Millsham was not pleased with the day's events. The visit from Miss Fairchild and Richard Talbot had upset the even tenor of his routine. Ever since their traveling coach rumbled off in the direction of Bath, he had prowled about his stately home with an uneasy mind, wondering if Miss Fairchild was one of those women who persisted in ferreting out the past. She reminded him of all the failures he'd endured in Society.

Just how insistent she might be about finding Jane, he could only guess. He wished he knew where the little drab hid. He had tried to find her without a shred of success.

Well, he reflected, even were she to suspect something a bit shady about her husband's death, there was nothing she might do about it now. He was in control of the situation. He had tied up every little knot, polished every detail. There was nothing to connect him with anything. Was there?

'Henry,' he said to the groom hastily summoned from the

stables, 'I wish you to make a check on those people who were here earlier. See if they decided to stop over some place nearby. Find out anything you can, then report back to me.'

Hours later, when the earl discovered that Miss Fairchild and Richard Talbot had elected to stay overnight at the Star and Garter, when they might easily have made it to Bath, although late in the evening, he chose to take action.

Crossing to his desk in what was gratifyingly now *his* library, he pulled out a small sheet of paper, then penned a few words in a deliberately disguised hand. He sanded, then folded and sealed the missive, omitting the use of his signet ring in the hot wax.

His groom hid an insolent grin from his master as he accepted the instructions for the next step. When the young fellow returned to the stables, he chuckled to the coachman. 'He's got an eye for the ladies, he has. Sending off a biyay doo to one of 'em. I'm off, but I fancy this won't be the first ride I take in her direction. I got a look at 'er. She's a rare beauty.'

The coachman, an elderly man who had been at the Hall for more years than the young groom could count, merely nodded and kept his thoughts to himself.

Clare found the hours dragging slowly once Richard Talbot and his man had ridden off. The landlady of the inn brought her tea in the garden, much to Clare's delight. For some peculiar reason, she wished to remain outside, not that the inn was unpleasant. Never would she confess that she eagerly awaited the return of the gentleman who had assumed the role of knight-errant on her behalf. Or was his gallantry merely for the infant? That she would likely never know, unless she might figure out a way to cleverly learn the truth of the matter.

With the fading light, Clare could no longer linger in the garden. She and Priddy, for the abigail had most properly taken a seat by a patch of grass to keep an eye on her mistress, went into the inn and up to the neat little room she was to call hers for the night.

'My goodness,' Clare exclaimed, entering the room in a

flurry of skirts. On her pillow lay a crisp, sealed note. Surely Lord Talbot would not have arranged to leave a note for her? Beyond anything curious, she hurried to the bed, sitting on its edge to tear open the paper.

'What is it, Miss Clare?' Priddy stepped closer to the bed at the sight of her mistress. Her face had paled; her hand trembled as she read the missive.

'Well, 'tis scarcely a love note. It seems that someone does not wish me in the area. I have been warned to leave here at once. But who would know my identity? Or why we are here? Merely to say that strangers are not welcome is silly. This is a market town and such people are here often.' Clare did not offer to share the rest of the contents with her maid. Rather, she tucked the note into her sleeve, then restlessly prowled about the room until Priddy made an excuse to go downstairs.

' 'Tis dizzy I'm getting, what with all that walking about. I'll fix you a posset to help you sleep.' Priddy was convinced that anyone who could not drop into an immediate sleep would surely sicken of some dire ailment.

'Thank you, Priddy,' Clare said absently. Oh, if Lord Talbot would only return.

It was another hour, during which Priddy tried to coax Clare into going to bed and drinking the bitter-smelling posset, not succeeding with either, before Lord Talbot came back.

Clare cracked open the door, waiting with anxious eyes until she saw his tall, powerful form making its way up the stairs to their floor.

'Psst.'

Richard frowned, knowing what he heard, and not believing it. He glanced at Miss Fairchild's door and blinked. There she was, still charmingly dressed and motioning him with a crook of her finger while peeking around the door at him.

Not saying a word, he quietly walked to her, standing before her with a puzzled look in his eyes.

'Come in, please. I must know how you fared.' Clare drew him in the room with a persistent hand. She closed the door behind him, then waited.

Catching sight of the disapproving abigail on the far side of the room, Richard half smiled. 'Nothing at all, I fear. I managed to bring the talk around to the young earl, his accident, but nothing of help came out of it. If there was any foul play, the locals either do not discuss it, or it was carefully done so that there could not be any talk.'

'Well,' she declared dramatically, 'I am more suspicious than ever.' She extracted the note from her sleeve, then handed it to him with a flourish. Instead of nattering on as some women might, she remained silent while he read. There was a faint tapping of a slim slipper on the wooden floor to indicate her impatience.

The frown returned as Richard read the note. 'Where did you find this?' He clasped the crisp paper in his hand, his eyes searching her face for a clue to her reaction to the threat.

'It reposed on my pillow, just as neat as could be. Priddy said the maid in the kitchen told her a groom had been here earlier, asking for me. Obviously whoever sent it gave him instructions on precisely where to put it to present the greatest impact on my tender nerves.'

'One does not get threatened with death every day of the year, that is true.' Richard admired the manner in which she calmly faced him, knowing there was someone who very much wished to put an end to her inquiries.

At those words, Priddy gasped and staggered to the nearest chair. 'Did he say death, Miss Clare? Oh, mercy! We ought to have left that baby at the inn in Marlborough. You'd be in no danger if he hadn't a come along with us to Bath. Miss Godwin was right.'

At the inquiring look from Lord Talbot, Clare demurely said, 'Miss Godwin is of the opinion that nothing good comes from associating with males, infants included.'

His low chuckle enchanted Clare. It was a pleasant contrast to the ugly thoughts that had haunted her since she and Priddy had returned to their room following the evening spent in the inn's garden. It had bothered her to know that someone had entered her room with intent of mischief.

'I refuse to allow this silly threat to discompose me. We shall depart for Bath in the morning, but that does not mean that I intend to give up the hunt. Indeed, more than ever I am persuaded that I must solve the Mystery of the Disappearing Countess.'

Richard longed to stretch out his hand to gently stroke her winsome cheek. Her smile looked a trifle defiant, with a touch of rueful whimsy about it. He well knew that were the abigail not present, he would yield to the temptation Miss Fairchild presented. What would it be like to hold that bewitching armful close to him? Or kiss those delectable lips? The charms of all the ladies he had known faded in comparison to this woman who so daringly stood before him, caring only for that little baby and the countess who most likely was his mother. She possessed a depth he had not encountered before. Caring, courageous, and resourceful, she appealed greatly to him.

'I suspect we shall learn nothing more by remaining here. Why do we not leave first thing in the morning? Once we return to Bath we can make further plans.'

'La, sir, I cannot involve you further. I am persuaded there is someone involved who is not all what he ought to be. You could be in danger.'

'True, people do not generally go about issuing threats of death . . . and mean it.' Richard had not meant to be so blunt-speaking. The thought of being dismissed from her life was not to be tolerated. He heard Priddy gasp, but concentrated on Clare. She paled slightly, then lifted her chin in a plucky tilt.

'I am far too tenacious to allow his little note to frighten me off.'

'I am equally stubborn, I fear. I shall remain at your side until there is no more need for your protection.'

Clare felt weak with relief. She had bravely prepared herself to go on alone, but she admitted quite readily that Richard, that is, Lord Talbot, brought welcome protection and wisdom. As well, men could go places and do things a lady simply ought not.

Their departure the following morning was not quite as early as Richard had hoped it might be. The abigail insisted on allowing Clare to sleep late, then eat a substantial breakfast, which the lady obviously did not wish. The hour was well advanced by the time the traveling coach rumbled forth from the Star and Garter.

Eventually Clare felt constrained to speak about the matter uppermost in her mind.

'What shall be the next step? I fear we have encountered a veritable brick wall in our search. Not a body knows where Jane went to following her husband's death. The present earl may call her a little drab, but I believe she is well up on how to protect herself.'

'Perhaps her family?' Richard suggested, not bothering to put forth other possibilities at the moment.

'I cannot recall her maiden name. Did your mother perchance mention it?' Clare turned her head to study the man at her side. In the morning sunshine slanting through the coach window, he looked remarkably handsome and strong, precisely the sort of hero a romantic girl would wish to come to her rescue or be her knight-errant. Except Clare was hardly a girl anymore, and her dreams seemed to be more prosaic nowadays. They were far more inclined to a husband and home than daring escapades and shocking villains.

'My, this road is surely worse than yesterday,' muttered Priddy from her side of the coach. 'My bones haven't been so rattled since I can't remember when.'

Clare had been so engrossed in her thoughts that she had failed to observe the truth of Priddy's complaint. The coach lurched and wobbled like a demented goose.

All at once the world abruptly tilted, along with a resounding thwack. Clare landed full upon Lord Talbot, squashing the gentleman most neatly against the door, which now appeared to have become the floor. Priddy had slid to the other side of the coach, wilting away in a dead faint.

'Good gracious! L . . . Lord Talbot! Do forgive me, I seemed to have quite crushed you.' Clare grabbed at the coach seat in an effort to right herself, ignoring the strange effect that being squashed against Lord Talbot produced on her. She was extremely conscious of the muscular form beneath hers.

Richard was concerned at the cause of the accident, but he could not fail to appreciate the delicious form that pressed against his so invitingly. He firmly resisted the desire to clasp her to him for at least a few seconds.

'I believe that under the circumstances you might be allowed to call me Richard. At least when we are alone.' He gave a significant glance at the unconscious Priddy, before succumbing to the temptation in his arms. 'Forgive me, Clare,' he whispered. And then he kissed her. And it lasted a good deal longer than one full minute.

Clare was roused from the shock of his kiss by the cries from without the coach. Tom Coachman and the groom, aided by Lord Talbot's man Timms, were calling to them. The groom climbed up the side of the coach to peer in the window just as Richard released her.

'Nice timing, Lord Talbot,' whispered Clare, valiantly trying to hide the impact of that kiss upon her sensibilities.

'Richard, or I shall repeat it.'

The warning brought with it a battle in her head. A rather scandalous part of her brain desired nothing more than another kiss! The sensible portion calmly said, 'Richard.' Her eyes twinkled with the absurdity of a spinster of her standing being placed in such a position.

His smile appeared a bit rueful to Clare's eyes, and she rather liked the notion that he wanted another kiss perhaps as much as she did. Even if the very notion ought to have shocked her into next Tuesday.

The following minutes were spent extricating Clare and the hastily revived Priddy from the coach, then assessing the damage.

Tom Coachman pulled Richard to one side. 'I don't think 'twas an accident, sir. There's somethin' right fishy 'bout the way the undercarriage came apart. Mind you, I ain't sayin' somethin' were done to it, but it 'pears right odd.' He motioned to where the wheel lay in the center of the road.

Richard walked around the coach to examine the point

where the axle joined the wheel. It could be that the force of the impact had bent the iron, but it seemed to him that the axle arm had been deliberately tampered with so as to cause the wheel to eventually come off. The binding action of the increased angle had done the trick without any obvious foul play. Upon inspection, the lynch pins looked to be different from the others on the vehicle, bringing the conclusion that they had been switched, an inferior sort replacing the sturdier original. He met Tom Coachman's concerned gaze with one of respect.

'Deucedly clever, I'd say.'

'Aye. More's to the point, how do we get it repaired out here in the middle of nowhere?'

Richard looked about him. A good-sized farm could be seen in the distance, and it was likely their best bet. He decided to inform Clare of his intention to ride over to inquire about transport.

Mindful of the ever watchful Priddy, he approached Clare with all due respect. 'I believe I ought to locate some means to get us back to Bath before nightfall if possible.'

'Excellent. It is beyond simple repair, I gather?'

He admired her practical acceptance of the situation. Her self-possession was indeed remarkable. Only that twinkle lurking in her eyes betrayed her possible feelings. And its very presence intrigued him more than words would ever have said.

'So Tom Coachman says, and I believe him. It will take an experienced wainwright to do the work. Clever bit of skul-duggery, though.'

'Am I to gather that it was deliberate?'

Richard tightened his lips in chagrin. That last remark had slipped out, no doubt due to her behavior. He was more accustomed to spasms and tears than poised composure from ladies in distress.

'I believe so.' He touched her arm in sympathy, for he suspected she was more upset than she allowed. With the maid, it was obvious, for she clasped her arms about her body, rocking back and forth while muttering words of distress.

At that moment, Clare turned to go to her complaining maid. The same second a report sounded and something whizzed through her bonnet. She stopped in her steps, a look of horror in her eyes as she whipped off the small headpiece to discover the hole. 'Dear heaven,' she whispered. She raised her eyes to Richard, her alarm quite clear on her face.

Richard whirled about, searching the woods beyond for a clue to who had fired the gun. If the man intended to repeat, he would have to reload . . . unless he had a second gun. Not a leaf stirred but what was tossed by a gentle breeze. No sound of galloping horse, no movement of any sort. The woods concealed whoever intended to murder Clare.

'That was a favorite bonnet, too,' Clare murmured. Then she sank down on the road, heedless of her pretty pelisse or the moanings of the maid. 'I believe I would rather you remained here and sent your groom on to the farm, Lord Talbot. Somehow, I find the thought of your departure more than a little disheartening.'

He stepped to her side, kneeling to study her pale face. She had sustained a severe fright, yet she hadn't fainted away. He nodded. 'That I will do, immediately.'

With a look from Lord Talbot, the groom took off as though a hundred demons were after him, which was surprising considering the coach horses were not from the racetrack. Only the skill of Tom Coachman and the groom had kept the horses from bolting in the first place when the accident occurred, followed by the shot. It seemed that horse was only too glad to get as far from all the ruckus as possible.

Hours later when a tired, unnerved, and somewhat shattered trio entered the house in the Royal Cresent, it was to the lament from Miss Godwin.

'Well, so you finally decided to return from your little jaunt. I must say, you show a shocking lack of sympathy for me, stuck here in Bath, wondering what is going on. That Mrs Robottom had the effrontery to stop in while you were gone, no doubt to pry into your secrets. No fear, I told her nothing.'

Clare turned anguished eyes to Richard. As if they had not

enough on their plates, they must now deal with the nosy neighbor?

'May I suggest that Miss Fairchild be allowed to retire for the night without any more chitchat? She has had an exhausting day of it.' To Clare he added, 'I shall see you first thing tomorrow. We must decide what to do next.'

'True. We never did finish that conversation.' She gave him a tired smile, then leaned upon Priddy's arm to go up the stairs to her room.

Richard failed to satisfy Miss Godwin's curiosity, and that young woman stomped up the stairs to confront Priddy. When denied access to Clare, Venetia was out of reason cross and retired to her room, blaming the entire situation on Lord Talbot and William, for you might know males were responsible.

Quite late the following morning, Richard entered the house in the Royal Cresent, ushered in by a most curious Bennison. When conducted into Clare's sunny dining room where she sat over a cup of tea and toast, he was most relieved to see how well she looked. Faint shadows lingered about her lovely eyes, and her mouth still looked a shade tired. But otherwise she presented an impeccable picture, and only one who knew what she had endured the day before would be aware that anything was amiss.

She rose in that swift, fluid movement that seemed to be so uniquely her own. 'Lord Talbot,' she cried softly, extending both hands toward him. 'I am relieved to see you are not the worse for the journey.' Then observing the rebuke in his eyes, she added in a very little voice, 'Richard, that is. But I am that glad to see you.' Then obviously embarrassed at her improper enthusiasm, she blushed, trying to conceal it by turning aside, gesturing to a chair. 'Will you join me in a cup of tea, or shall we adjourn to the study across the hall?'

'Finish your toast and tea. We can talk here as well as in there. You are alone this morning?' He glanced around the room, as though surprised to see her the sole occupant.

'Miss Godwin is no doubt exhausted after the worry of

yesterday. Such excitement required restoration to the spirit and body, you must realize.'

'How you can say that with a straight face, I'll never know.'

'Come now,' she chided while striving to keep her countenance. 'Have you thought more about what must be done next?'

'I am happy to be included after yesterday. I am aware I ought not have kissed you, Clare, but the temptation was more than I could resist.' His words were hesitantly spoken, as though he was not often given to this sort of apology.

'Irresistible? Oh, how can I scold you after that bit of flummery? You are a rogue and a scamp, sir.'

Her easy laugh broke any constraint between them. Richard joined her at the table, accepting the cup of steaming tea from her hand, while meeting her gaze with a very direct one of his own, a gaze he hoped contained his feelings well.

'If we desire to put a stop to the gabble-grinders and quidnuncs, we had best be seen in public, and together. It will jolt them, to be sure.' He exchanged a wry look with her in appreciation of the gossips.

'Where?' came her reply, swift and quiet.

'Remember what I said about a play? I purchased the tickets for a party this very morning. If it meets with your approval, I shall stop by to invite Lady Kingsmill and Susan, as well as Lord Welby.'

'Miss Godwin, too, of course.'

'I know a couple of gentlemen in town, respectable chaps. I thought to include them to even the numbers if that is agreeable?'

Smiling at the casually hopeful note in his voice, Clare nodded. 'I think that a splendid notion, indeed. Although I do not see how it furthers the cause of finding the Disappearing Countess.'

'One thing at a time. I'll write my mother, and you'd best do the same to your sister. Perhaps armed with the maiden name of our elusive countess, we shall have success.'

While wanting to find Willy's mother, Clare now discovered a most peculiar thing. She was not ecstatic about ending

73

this cooperation with Richard Talbot. The hunt had brought more real excitement into her heretofore proper life than she had dreamed might exist for a young woman just settling nicely onto the shelf. Perhaps she was destined for a different future than she had envisioned?

'Goodness, Clare! Entertaining so early in the day? Most improper,' Venetia snapped as she watched the highly suspect Lord Talbot leave the house following his obviously private chat with her hostess.

'Yes, he is all of that,' Clare responded. But her voice lacked any rebuke, sounding infinitely dreamy and fanciful. 'All of that and more.'

CHAPTER SIX

Venetia paced the floor of her nicely appointed room with a distracted air. The matter of Lord Talbot had progressed from worrying to alarming. She had seen that silly, infatuated look on other women's faces before. Clare was hardly the first to tumble into a disgraceful love affair with a totally ineligible man. Not that Lord Talbot was utterly beyond the pale. He possessed wealth and a respectable lineage. He was undeniably handsome and dressed with an exquisite attention to a detail and a restraint Beau Brummell would admire. His manners were a shade forward – witness his meeting with Clare in the dining room of all places – and he tended to an informality Venetia deplored. And he was a man!

She stopped by her window to look out on the vast green across the street from the Royal Crescent. Something must be done. What had precipitated the matter in the first place? Ah, yes, indeed. Baby William, that odious infant who occupied a pleasant room on the same floor as herself instead of a proper place in the attic. Who rent the air with his obnoxious cries at the most inconvenient times. And who apparently caught the heartstrings of Venetia's hostess much too ably.

How best to rid the house of the infant? 'Since I do not know the mother – and what a heartless soul she must be to abandon her child – I must contact the one other person who might possibly he concerned,' she announced to the view out her window.

A rather feline smile crept across her face as she glided over to the neat dressing table where she searched about until she found a sheet of paper. A quill and pot of ink uncovered among the clutter, she penned a short note, folded and sealed it, then took it down to be delivered with all speed. How satisfying to assure her continued stay under what she had to admit was a most pleasing roof. For all that dear Clare might do wrong, she was indulgent and did not quibble over little extras as some might.

'Venetia,' came a voice from behind her as Clare exited the study, 'you will join us this evening at the theater, will you not? Lord Talbot has purchased tickets and means to get up a party.' Her acute perusal of Venetia's face gave a deal of discomfort to the guest. 'He also intends to invite two gentlemen friends of his to complete the group.'

'La, dear Clare, he need not do such on my behalf. I wonder who they are?' Venetia narrowed her eyes, trying to imagine the eligibility of any man known to Lord Talbot. She followed Clare up the stairs, musing over the turn of events and how best to use it to her own advantage.

A short time later, Susan Oliver was ushered up to the drawing room, her pretty face alive with pleasure. The three settled down by the tea table for a comfortable ooze. It was not long before Miss Oliver brought up a topic dear to her fluttering heart.

'What a famous time we shall have this evening. Have you met either Lord Adrian Grove or Sir Henry Berney? Most acceptable gentlemen, I assure you, Miss Godwin. While a younger son, Lord Adrian is well to grass and possesses a tidy estate north of here. Sir Henry is a bit older, but a charming gentleman, and one with no need to pinch pennies, either.'

'Really,' drawled Venetia, as though to depress the younger woman. She concealed her distaste behind the unfurled lace of her fan.

'Quite true. I fancy the quidnuncs will be puzzled at this turn, for all our party will be the height of respectability.' Susan turned sparkling eyes on her hostess.

'How nice,' murmured Clare with true appreciation for the subtleties of the situation.

Venetia looked puzzled, but said nothing. She raised the question of what to wear, and the conversation turned to fashion and hairstyles, and whether or not it might rain.

When Lord Talbot entered the house on the Royal Crescent early that evening, it was to find two exquisitely arrayed ladies awaiting him with poorly concealed and pleasing impatience.

'La, sir,' fluttered Venetia from behind her fan, 'it has been an age since I have seen proper theater. I do hope the theatrical company is up to the mark.' She twitched the skirt of her pale blue sarcenet gown with nervous fingers. Perhaps the plan she'd considered quite fine this morning was now giving her second thoughts.

Richard repressed a grin at the rather odd notion of appreciation. 'I am told the production is of London quality. Bath is yet a desirable place for the theatrical circuit players, as the house is usually full.'

Annoyed with Venetia's quite unseemly remark, Clare tried to atone. 'We are vastly delighted with your theater party, Lord Talbot. A truly charming thought to bring together a group for a jovial evening. I trust we shall all be most amiable.' She darted a minatory glance at Venetia, daring her to behave with less than polite enthusiasm.

Venetia bowed her head sweetly in reply, causing Clare to wonder what the lady had been up to in the hours past. Each lady had spent time alone in her room, resting, fussing with her hair and clothes. When they had met for an early dinner, Venetia had worn a smug expression that Clare found a trifle odd.

Since they elected to travel in sedan chairs to the theater, due to the press of the crowd, she was not able to question Richard about any progress in their quest. Once they arrived at the theater – in good time, fortunately – she again found herself unable to speak with him. It was not that she did not trust Venetia to be privy to the conversation. It was merely her innate sense that such talk ought to be confined to privacy.

Now the delights of the play awaited them. Clare set aside her concerns and prepared to enjoy the evening. Her seafoam gown of sheer jaconet had drawn appreciative glances from Richard Talbot, and she felt assured she looked her best.

The theater on Orchard Street thronged with people. The narrow, curved street itself was a madhouse of sedan chairs and foot traffic, as the citizens of Bath descended upon one of the main cultural spots of the city.

'Two boxes, Lord Talbot?' exclaimed Lady Kingsmill, charmed to be included in this lively group. 'I declare, that is indeed generous, sir.' She led the way into the one closest to the stage, where a comfortable chair suitable to her girth had been especially arranged in advance.

'I wish to please, ma'am,' he said with a courtly bow.

'Ladies never take to having their gowns crushed, don't you know,' Lord Welby added sagely as he took up his position close to Lady Kingsmill.

'I trust that is true,' replied Richard with a glance at Clare's rosy cheeks, remembering one lady who hadn't seemed to mind overmuch.

Lord Adrian Grove and Sir Henry Berney entered the second box where Venetia and Susan Oliver sat in anticipation. Venetia fluttered her delicate blue lace fan with an energy Clare found amazing. The introductions were a revelation to her. Susan bloomed, while Venetia reminded Clare of a calculating huntress.

Susan dimpled a winsome smile, modestly conversing with Lord Adrian. She behaved with comely appeal. He obviously found her attractive in her pretty pink muslin, for she was in first looks this evening. Any protégée of the wealthy Lady Kingsmill must be of interest to a young man about town. If one were on the lookout for a proper wife – one who would be accepted in Society, yet be at home on a country estate – Bath provided good contacts. And the niece of a childless widow of means offered twice the interest.

On the other side of the box from Susan, Venetia wondered what to make of the quiet, elegant figure of Sir Henry. Suddenly she sat a trifle straighter, her eye catching sight of a man on the far side of the theater. 'Tell me, Sir Henry, who is that gentleman with the dark red hair, the one settling in the third box from the front across from us?'

Turning his gaze from the pretty lady at his side, he studied the man in question a moment. 'I believe that is the new Earl of Millsham. One thing to be said regarding riding, is that it so frequently provides Society with new faces. I confess I know little enough about the man. Have you heard anything?'

'Not a word,' replied Venetia, ignoring all that had been revealed in her hearing. She madly fluttered her fan, causing her companion to wonder what the lady would do when it became oppressively warm.

In the next box forward, Clare exchanged a guarded look with Richard. 'Do you see what I see?' At his faint nod, she continued, 'What do you suppose brings him to Bath?'

'Somehow I doubt it is the waters,' Richard replied a trifle grimly.

'We said nothing about a baby to him. There could be no connection between William and the missing countess that he could know. Could there?' Her voice barely reached him, she feared, for he leaned over to catch her words. His nearness made it difficult for her to think clearly. But then, she had not quite recovered from that shattering kiss of yesterday.

'I scarcely think so. I imagine we shall find out later if that is the case.' He watched the other man who sat alone in his box, disdaining the interest of those to either side of him. Then Richard turned to Clare again. 'At any rate, you have received no cuts since we arrived.'

'But we came early so as to settle Lady Kingsmill before the crush. Poor dear, she finds it shockingly difficult to move about at the best of times.' Clare glanced at the lady in question, who was complacently nibbling at a selection of comfits provided by Lord Welby.

'Indeed,' Richard said so reprovingly that Clare found it necessary to cover her mouth with her gloved hand to stifle a giggle.

The audience hushed as the curtains parted. The opening scene was well done. Clare found her attention totally captured to the exclusion of the displeasing man who reposed in the box directly across from them.

When the first intermission came, they were all, with the exception of Lady Kingsmill and Lord Welby, ready to stroll about the small area to the front of the theater.

Clare recognized a few of the faces in the crush of people anxious to get a breath of fresh air and exchange views of the performance with their friends.

'I vow this is worse than Drury Lane,' Venetia said with a sniff.

Hesitantly smiling in the direction of one of the ladies she had seen at the concert at the Octagon, Clare was distressed when that good lady looked straight through her, quite as though Clare did not exist.

'I perceive we have our work cut out for us,' Richard murmured just loud enough for Clare to hear.

Glad that the gentleman did not see fit to take to his heels from such a scandalous lady, Clare gave him a grateful look. 'I do not know what is to be done. And to think that all my life I have been a model of propriety. I do believe this is one instance where charity has been rewarded by malicious spite.'

Her neighbor, a Mrs Robottom, Clare had learned, sailed past her with her nose quite elevated. All in all, it was a humiliating experience to be snubbed, ignored as though she didn't exist, and given a decidedly cold shoulder by all but those in her party. With one exception.

'Miss Fairchild, Talbot. Fancy finding you here.' The smooth voice of the new Earl of Millsham as he greeted the Talbot party drew speculative gazes from all those around.

Drawing herself to her full height, Clare gave him a frosty nod. 'My lord, one never knows quite who will pop up next in Bath. 'Tis a vastly amusing place.'

'Indeed,' he murmured, taking careful note of the pretty woman with the shining chestnut curls before he bowed, then sauntered back to his box.

Susan Oliver walked next to Venetia as they hurried up the steps to resume their seats. 'I believe the earl seemed most taken with you, Venetia,' she said softly. 'He certainly studied you long enough. I hear he has no countess. Would you find him of interest?'

'La, Susan,' Venetia simpered, 'just because a gentleman looks does not mean he intends to wed. Otherwise the nymphs of Avon Street would all be respectable married women!' She spoke quietly but tittered a high laugh that could be heard in the next box.

Susan knew of the disreputable women of Avon Street, but she also knew a lady never mentioned them, even in jest. She cast a questioning look at Clare, wondering if that charming young woman had been wise in her choice of a companion. But then, one never knew about people. She was most pleased to turn her attention to the stage, with asides to the attentive gentleman at her side.

'How did you fare, my dear?' whispered Lady Kingsmill.

'I might have done better were you at my side,' Clare replied with a touch of humor. 'I fear my own consequence is sadly lacking. I vow it is most humbling to discover my family name means nothing here, only what some gossip has seen and reported.'

'There must be something that can be done,' Lord Welby said in an undertone so that others would not reprove him for creating noise while the play resumed.

The others nodded, each reflecting on the caprice of Society, not to mention gossips.

Clare decided to remain with Lady Kingsmill during the second intermission. 'It is not worth the effort, I thank you,' she replied in answer to the invitation from Lord Talbot.

'I believe I should like to stay with Miss Fairchild,' added Susan with a nice show of support. 'But I would welcome a glass of lemonade above all things.' She bestowed a dazzling smile on Lord Adrian, who hastened to obtain her desire.

Venetia seized the opportunity to separate herself from the others, declaring herself in need of air. She found the person she sought, then imparted her information with a succinctness Clare would have found amazing.

'Dear lady,' Sir Henry said in apology when he at last located her, 'I feared you had been carried away, for you seemed to disappear in the twinkling of an eye. I am relieved to find you safe and unharmed.' He took care to guide her back up the steps to where the others waited.

'Whatever could happen in Bath?' Venetia said with a dismissive shrug, her eyes alight with a pleased glow.

While the others had been off obtaining lemonade, Clare had sat utterly miserable in the Talbot box. She sensed the dark looks from ladies around the theater. The whisperings behind fans and gloved hands might be about others, but she felt the gossip directed at her, especially with all the nods and looks that went along with it.

Even the jolly company of Lady Kingsmill and Susan could not lift her spirits. If things did not improve soon, Clare would shake the dust of Bath from her feet and visit her sister. Sara might not be thrilled to have an unknown infant thrust upon her, but she would never censor Clare for doing her duty.

'That is what is so frightfully annoying,' Clare said to Richard in an aside as all were getting settled for the final act. 'I ought to be praised. Not that I feel insulted for being ignored rather than snubbed, if you know what I mean.' She gave him a confused grin.

'We shall think of something, my dear Clare,' Richard whispered in her ear under the pretext of adjusting her shawl.

Whatever the ending of the play might have been, it was good that Clare was not quizzed about it. The particular attentions from Lord Talbot had her in a flutter that would not be stilled. Could he be serious? A gentleman simply did not address a lady, even one nearly on the shelf, as 'my dear Clare' unless he meant it. She peeped at him from the corner of her eyes, wondering and wondering until she realized it had quite driven the other mystery and the resultant snubs from her mind. Was that what he intended? If so, she thought it vastly unfair for him to use such strategy. However, she couldn't utter a word, for no matter what, she would look a fool.

Lady Kingsmill insisted they all troop over to her house for macaroons and other delights following the play. Perhaps she intended to cheer Clare. They all agreed. Venetia entered her sedan chair looking remarkably pleased with her evening. At least she and Susan had seemed to enjoy themselves.

Clare and Richard were the last to depart. She watched the others heading in a line across the bridge, the linkboys carrying their torches of pitch and tow to light a path through the darkened streets. The fiery glow of the torches lent a festive touch to the black night. Each party streaming from the theater, whether on foot or in sedan chair, was led by a linkboy waving his torch high in the air as they fanned out across the city. 'Like a festival,' she commented to Richard as he saw her tucked into a sedan chair.

He had looked about the area, searching for the Earl of Millsham, wondering if his suspicions regarding the earl's sudden appearance in Bath might have foundation. But he had disappeared, leaving Richard no wiser as to his direction or plans.

At Lady Kingsmill's house, they gathered in her drawing room, which was lit with at least a hundred candles. Clare watched the others for a moment. She rather liked Lord Adrian Grove. He had the look of an eager puppy about him, that is true, but he also had a measure of resolve, with an air of maturity that could only please Lady Kingsmill. Clare suspected it was the elderly lady's fondest wish to see her beloved niece well settled. Lord Adrian would do admirably.

Sir Henry was another kettle of fish entirely. More a man of the world, he handled Venetia with an amused tolerance, as one might a spoiled child. That he saw her as nothing more than a slight dalliance was obvious to Clare. She wondered how Venetia felt. No doubt she would spout more of her man-hating nonsense. Nothing she said made sense in view of her actions. And as the proverb went, actions truly did speak louder than words.

Richard brought Clare a glass of excellent sherry, then drew her to a chair far from where Lady Kingsmill held court.

'I have been doing a bit of thinking about our problem.'

'As I see it,' Clare retorted politely after taking a sip of sherry, 'the problem is mine alone. I did not see you being cold-shouldered at the theater.'

'Clare,' he said with a warning glance. 'Or is it to be Miss Fairchild again? I thought we were in this mull together. I do want to help, you know.'

'Forgive me, I am a complete peagoose. I fear I have become addled in the brain. I have tried to seek a solution, but until we find our Mysterious Countess, I do not know what to do. Have you considered that if William is the son of Jane, Countess of Millsham, he is the true seventh earl? That would be good reason to do away with the child, and for her to wish him safe, if she felt him in jeopardy.'

'I agree. I have an idea. You will think it utter stupidity, I've no doubt. But think of it, please, before saying no.'

'Very well, I promise.'

'The worst of the gossips is that neighbor of yours. Correct?'

'Mrs Robottom? I believe so. I suspect the fastest way to get news about Bath would be to enlist her help. But we want the opposite.'

'We also want information. Who would be the most likely to know the previous Earl of Millsham and his dear little countess? I suspect she would. We can wait, but after tonight, I am hesitant to do that. Those replies may take an age to get back to us. I don't suppose you mentioned urgency in your letters any more than I did.'

'True,' she admitted. 'I would give a great deal to know what prompted the present earl to show his face at the theater this evening.'

'As would I,' Richard quietly added. He felt uneasy. It was a sensation he had observed before in times of danger, when something dire was about to happen. He had ignored it yesterday, believing them to be safe on an English country road. And Clare had nearly been killed. He would not willingly place her in that sort of danger again.

They were drawn into the general conversation the moment Lady Kingsmill observed their intimate and worried chat to be over. Although she said nothing directly, Clare sensed she sympathized, and that brought a good bit of comfort.

When the party broke off, Clare urged Richard to go directly to his place in the Edgar buildings, denying any hazard might be lurking in Bath. He would not hear of such a thing, which bolstered her spirits immeasurably.

'I shall see you safely into your house first. I could not sleep without being sure you arrived home unharmed.'

The linkboy's torch sputtered as Richard assisted Clare from the chair before her house. 'I shall see you in the morning, and we can proceed with our plan?'

'Actually, I am not certain what you intend, precisely. But I shall be here.' She slipped into the house, then peeped out the study window to watch him walk along the street. The glow of the link torch gave his figure an ominous look, and she shivered. Was she being fanciful? Or was he? Yet she had not imagined that hole in one of her favorite bonnets. She had taken a good look at the damaged straw and tossed the bonnet away in the ditch, not wishing to ever see the thing again.

What if she ended up with the same fate as her bonnet? Could the countesss be in hiding because she feared the same? Being done in? And had she possibly hidden her son in Clare's carriage because she suspected he was in danger for his very life?

Clare slowly walked up the stairs to her room, then on an impulse continued up to the next floor where she peeped in on little William.

Jenny was sitting in the rocker nursing the baby. A candle provided dim light so he would return to his sleep with no problem. Relieved, although she couldn't imagine he was in danger here in the house, Clare smiled at Jenny, then returned to her room.

The following morning, Clare paced the wooden planks of the study with uneasy steps. Thankfully, Venetia was off on some errands. She had insisted she needed no maid along at her age, and besides, she merely wished to pick up a book at the circulating library. And possibly an ell or two of coquelicot riband.

When Richard was shown into the study, Clare gave him a

guarded look. 'Good morning, sir.'

'Miss Fairchild.' His eyes mocked her prim behavior with a warm, teasing look, and Clare felt her resolve sail out the window.

'Very well. Richard. How do you propose we go about enlisting Mrs Robottom's help? And what makes you think she will even let us in her house?'

'Because of what she is, namely the greatest quidnunc in Bath. If she thinks she is to be privy to the scandal she perceives hanging over your name, hiding in your past, or whatever floats about in her mind, she will be eager to see us.'

Clare gathered up her light muslin pelisse from the chair where she had tossed it. She had dismissed Priddy for the day, urging her to see a bit of Bath while her mistress took care of pressing concerns.

Clare and Richard strolled along the walk toward Mrs Robottom's house fully aware of the twitched curtains as they passed various houses. It might have been comical had it been other than Clare's reputation at stake. And possibly William's life.

'Go ahead, knock,' urged Clare as they at last stood before the gossip's front door.

They were ushered up to the drawing room with amazing speed. The lady stood by the window, an indication, perhaps, as to why. 'Good morning.' Ice dripped from her words as sure as they hung in the air.

'I believe you know both of us,' began Richard politely. 'Miss Fairchild and I have a great favor to ask of you, if we may?'

Curiosity warred with hauteur within Mrs Robottom. She longed to know what they wanted of her. Yet she was very conscious of her place in local society. Could she actually condescend to assist these people? Of course, she would never know how improper their request might be unless she heard it. Curiosity won.

'Please sit down and explain your problem. If I am able to help you, I shall.' She graciously waved a hand to two chairs on the far side of the room facing the windows. She took a place on a settee not far away. 'Proceed.'

Clare was affronted at the lack of hospitality. The woman ought to have at least offered a dish of tea, or a glass of sherry, or something. Clare toyed with the cords on her reticule, failing to conceal her nervousness.

Curiously this very act pleased her hostess, for it made the elegant Miss Fairchild seem very human.

'First, we must beg your silence on this. It could be a matter of life or death, and we dare not take chances.' Richard leaned back in his chair, wondering if they were foolish to hope this woman might hold her tongue.

Mrs Robottom's eyes fairly bugged out. She urged Mr Talbot to continue.

'Miss Fairchild has had an exceedingly difficult problem thrust upon her. A child was left in her care, one she feels is in some danger. She dared not contact Bow Street, feeling the matter far too delicate for them.'

Mrs Robottom's mouth had gaped at his revelation and now she nodded vigorously at his words. 'Indeed, we all know what *they* are.'

'She is trying to locate his mother, and our trail has led us to Millsham Hall and the countess. But the present earl professes to know nothing of the countess's whereabouts, a fact we find singularly peculiar. Do you recall anything about the previous earl or his countess? Perhaps her maiden name?'

'Oh, my. Let me see.' Mrs Robottom considered the matter at some length before replying. 'I believe it was Caswell. Although I do not know where she lived for certain. I think it was not too far from here. Devizes, perhaps. The parents had a great brood of children, as I recall. Kept her mother at home most of the time. The girl's aunt gave her a come out and saw to it she met the sixth earl. They were a charming pair from what I heard. Odd, that he should die so soon after they wed. And you believe she had a baby? But why hide it? Is there something havey-cavey about the affair?'

'Indeed, Mrs Robottom, I believe there is,' Clare said, speaking for the first time since they had sat down in the enemy's camp, so to speak.

Suddenly aware of the menace in the air, Mrs Robottom gave them a solemn look. 'I shan't breathe a word of this, you may be sure,' she vowed.

Clare could only pray her promise held true. Their next step was to locate the Caswells. Time seemed to press on Clare, suspecting that every day brought William in greater peril for his life.

CHAPTER SEVEN

'I do not know what to say to Miss Godwin about our proposed effort to locate the Caswells. She is not best pleased to have the infant in the house, and I fear she resents my interest in him. I confess that I find her behavior odd at times. Am I foolish to desire this excursion be kept as quiet as possible?' Clare turned to face Richard as they neared her dwelling. She wished to settle their story before they entered the house just in case Venetia had returned while they were out.

Richard studied the young woman before him. Her eyes were deeply troubled, and the grave air that sat on her shoulders revealed her concern for the helpless infant. 'Why do you not tell her you travel to visit my mother? She is at Knowl Hill in the Dower House at this time of year. If Miss Godwin inquired, she would discover it to be not too far from Bath and a reasonable drive.'

'And if we find we must remain overnight, she would have no cause to think ill of us?' Clare inquired softly. 'Priddy will be with us.' Her wry expression brought a chuckle from Richard.

'Come. I suspect you could do with a cup of tea and some of those excellent tea cakes your cook bakes. We shall work out the details while we restore ourselves.'

'You do not hesitate to make yourself to home, sir,' Clare teased as they entered the house. Her heart raced at the warm look in his eyes. How strange, to be casually walking into the house like this with him, as though they had done it a hundred times together. There seemed a certain rightness in being with him. Strength radiated from him, and she felt even without touching him that she drew from its source to bolster her own.

She issued orders for tea and cakes to be served in the drawing room, then they strolled up the stairs side by side in great amiability.

'The lad will be safe with the maid?'

Jolted from her romantic musings back to the reality of the present, Clare nodded. 'I vouchsafe for Jenny, sir. She welcomes the chance to work here and has a fondness for the boy, I believe. I will caution her to use care.'

How silly, to be deep in fantasy while Lord Talbot dwelt only upon the problems to hand. It served her right, she fancied, the nonsensical wanderings of a spinster mind.

'I suggest you order a groom, or some man from the house, to go with her when she walks out with the baby. One never knows. And if there is trouble afoot, not that I feel there is any real danger, mind you, it is best to be prepared. We do not know for certain that the present earl is directly involved, you know. I feel obliged to point out that there could be another reason for his desiring to hush up the birth of an infant who appeared on the scene after his cousin's death.'

'I take it you think she might have had the child from some-one other than her husband? I cannot accept there might be an illicit love affair in Jane's past. She seemed far too proper for such.' Clare's eyes rebuked him for such horrid thoughts. But what did she know of the shy young Jane, now Lady Millsham? A chance meeting, casual sightings at a ball or rout while in London? Hardly the sort of thing upon which to base an opinion. Yet, she would have sworn the girl would never stoop to such unseemly behavior.

'Let us devise a plan for our coming expedition.' Richard sipped his tea, then picked up a dainty cake. It seemed a very domestic scene to his eyes. He had often thought about some-thing like this while in the heat of Jamaica, longing for the humdrum and dear rituals of English life.

He studied Clare while she poured her tea and selected a

cake. He probably knew her better at this point than most young men who took a wife. It was unfortunate that society deemed it improper for two people to truly get acquainted – to talk at length, perhaps differ in opinion, exchange philosophies – prior to being wed. There might be a greater number of happy marriages were it possible.

'I believe we ought to stop first at my mother's place,' he suddenly said. 'She would know the family, having attended the wedding and all. I feel sure she could give us their direction. She might be able to help us in other ways as well. I've always felt mother had a sound head on her shoulders.'

Clare offered him an amused smile. 'Why is it men so often seem surprised when a woman has good sense? If we are to manage the household and all that entails, it stands to reason that we ought to know a good deal about running these affairs and more. I do not imply she or any other who does well at that sort of thing is a bluestocking. But men can be shockingly bad at management of their estates. I believe both sorts can be found in both sexes.'

'Plain speaking, indeed, my dear Clare.'

His eyes mocked her, she reflected. Teasing and mockery were all very well, but she doubted there lurked any serious intent behind them. She took a fortifying breath and plunged into the preparations for the coming visit.

'Since my traveling coach is repaired and ready to go at any time, we may as well take it,' she offered, knowing his phaeton was not the thing for a journey – even a short one. 'Tom Coachman is a sensible person, and your man seemed to get along with him. With Priddy joining us, we shall be quite a respectable party.' Her eyes twinkled, and a hint of a smile lingered about her mouth. Then she sobered. 'This is a serious matter, and I ought not make light of it. What time shall we depart on the morrow?'

'Depart?' came a high, fluting voice from the door. 'Are you to go someplace tomorrow? Where?'

There was more than a hint of wishing to be included in Venetia's voice, Clare realized. And it would be only proper to do so, since Venetia was a guest in Clare's home. Indeed,

91

she knew she would be censured by her family for such wanting manners were she not to invite Venetia along. Yet, she couldn't bear to have Venetia, with her probing ways and nasty little barbs about men, in the coach and along for all the meals. Furthermore, Clare would have to bear the cost of lodgings and meals for Venetia. She was of a sudden loath to do so.

Richard Talbot took charge of the scene at once. 'I have invited Clare to Knowl Hill to meet my mother.' He strongly suspected the interpretation she would give his words, but it bothered him not one whit.

Eyes narrowing with the information, Venetia drifted across the room, her soft boots making little sound. 'My, this is indeed interesting, dear Clare.'

Annoyed at the coy insinuation ill-concealed in Venetia's tone, Clare sat a trifle straighter, giving her a cool look in return. 'Lord Talbot feels his mother may be able to offer assistance in our search.'

Richard broke in at that point. 'I would like Miss Fairchild to see Knowl Hill. If it were possible, we should ask you to join us, but I fear my mother's indifferent health makes that pleasure impossible. She has her good days and her bad. A deluge of people might send her to her bed.'

'I doubt we shall be gone overlong. Did you not say that Susan has planned a small party at Lady Kingsmill's house at Laura Place? I am sure you would not wish to miss that, especially if Sir Henry is to escort you.'

Venetia stilled in her wanderings about the room. Looking back at Clare to study her face, she finally nodded. 'Yes, I believe that to be preferable. I detest jolting about in a coach anyway, even though yours is quite well sprung, dear Clare.'

'Dear Clare' wondered if Venetia had totally forgotten that she had told Lord Talbot how she longed to travel.

Uneasy about the expression on Venetia's face, Clare resolved to ask Jenny to exercise even greater care, and request Susan to check on Venetia while Clare was away. Silly, foolish notions, she supposed. But the situation for William appeared to be more ominous each day.

'We shall be departing early tomorrow,' Richard now inserted into the conversation. 'I had best leave so you can set your plans in motion. I shall stop to have a chat with Tom Coachman as well. Is that agreeable?' His gaze sought hers with a wordless question in his eyes.

Wondering precisely what arrangements he intended to make with her coachman, Clare could only agree to this handsome suggestion. Whatever he had in mind was most likely sensible. She gave an inner sigh, to think she had reached the age when the gentleman whose company she was to enjoy thought about practicality first.

'Well,' tittered Venetia,' I have letters to write. I shall leave you to make all your tedious arrangements. Although you will only be gone a day or two?' Her eyes narrowed in sly speculation again, leaving Clare with the oddest notion that Venetia was not displeased in the least to be left behind.

'I will instruct Cook to prepare your favorite dishes, Venetia. Although I daresay that Susan will be offering a dinner as well as entertainment, so your time will be well occupied.'

A smile crept over Venetia's face. 'I feel sure it will.' She whirled about and soon could be heard whisking herself up the stairs to her room.

Dismissing her from her mind, Clare returned to the pressing matter of the trip. 'Is your mother truly unwell, Richard?' she whispered, knowing how acute Venetia's hearing was. 'I would not discommode her with our visit.'

'Never tell her I uttered that tarradiddle about her. She has an iron constitution. I believe you will enjoy her gardens, and the Dower House is an attractive place.'

Satisfied that they would not prove to be an encumbrance, Clare walked with Richard to the door, thinking all the while about what might prove needful on the trip.

Once the door closed behind him, she rang for Priddy, then began a list.

The following morning, before social Bath stirred, Clare and Priddy entered the traveling coach. Lord Talbot discreetly remained within, hoping to prevent any tittletattle about the departure.

He had joined Tom Coachman at the mews, observing his portmanteau placed in the luggage box under the boot with a keen eye. He noted with approval that the luggage Miss Fairchild intended to take along had already been brought to the coach and placed within. The lady believed in sensible precautionary measures, it seemed.

The road to the south and east crossed the Kennet and Avon Canal, then proceeded due east, passing carters coming to Bath with loads of merchandise and farm produce. It was not long before the coach rumbled through the small town of Claverton on their way south. Tom Coachman was not dawdling in the least. They paralleled the canal a short distance before turning from the main road and crossing the canal once again near the lockkeeper's cottage, just above one of the locks.

Clare glanced at Lord Talbot, or Richard as she more and more frequently thought of him, with curiosity. What would his mother be like? He had maintained a most proper conversation about generalities all the way, while Priddy had slipped into a light doze next to Clare.

'We are nearing Knowl Hill now,' he said quietly.

Hearing the restrained pleasure in his voice, Clare wondered how he felt about being a younger son and having his brother inherit everything of great value. Although she did not know what the estate bequeathed to Richard might be like, for he had not spoken of it to her since that first brief mention, she wondered.

Knowl Hill proved to be a truly beautiful site, as Clare had anticipated. Somehow she had felt it could be no less. A stately row of trees lined the well-kept avenue that led to the main house. A turning off from this avenue brought them to a cheerful-looking red brick home with an enormous wisteria vine climbing above the front entrance. Clare would have called it a manor house, for there was nothing small about the place, like some dower houses she had seen.

The many-paned windows sparkled, and a flower bed off

to one side provided a riot of summer color. It was a welcoming house. Clare hoped that the dowager countess would prove to be as well.

Mr Talbot exited first so that he might assist Miss Fairchild from the coach. Clare noted with approval that he lent a hand to her abigail as well, a gesture few men might have extended.

'She will think we are mad, to descend upon her with no warning like this,' whispered Clare, thinking that if her family knew aboout this harebrained scheme, they would believe she had taken leave of her senses. One simply did not plunk oneself down upon a dowager countess without so much as a by your leave, not properly, that is.

'It will be quite all right, you know,' Lord Talbot offered in the most comforting of tones. 'I'd not have suggested we visit my mother had I not thought so.'

Clare tossed him a grateful glance as the front door opened and a slender woman came out to greet them, followed by a lackey. She was dressed simply, yet fashionably, in soft plum mull with a sheer fichu across her shoulders. Her day cap of ruffled and embroidered muslin was most becoming to a face that, while much lined, beamed a welcoming smile to her youngest son and his companion.

'What a pleasant surprise, dear boy.' She gave Clare an inquiring glance, waiting for him to present his guest.

He performed the introductions with a minimum of fuss and with that gracious charm such a part of the aristocracy.

Clare greeted the older woman with proper modesty and an exquisite curtsy, confining her brief comments to the condition of the roads and the lovely summer weather. One did not chatter. She was well aware she was being studied with more than casual notice. Possibly Lord Talbot had not brought a young lady to visit his mother since his return.

Over a restoring cup of tea, Clare listened while Richard and Lady Knowlton exchanged pleasantries. Then the older lady sought the reason for her son's appearance, especially with a stranger along.

'Miss Fairchild has a rather peculiar dilemma, Mother. I

shall ask her to tell you the story as it has happened, for she does it quite well.'

After an embarrassed clearing of her throat, Clare launched into her tale, by now most familiar. She wondered whether to omit the shot fired at the carriage on their way back to Bath, when Richarad interrupted at her hesitation.

'I suspect Miss Fairchild has a reluctance to tell you how serious this has become. I can only imagine it stems from her desire to spare you worry. On our return to Bath, we sustained an accident to the coach. While we surveyed the damage, someone shot at her, creating a nasty hole in her bonnet.'

After a cautious look at Lady Knowlton, Clare added, 'Yes, it quite ruined one of my favorite bonnets, too.'

'Shocking!' Lady Knowlton declared in ringing tones, her hand flying to her throat in alarm. 'I gather you feel this was deliberate and not the result of a poacher?'

'It would seem so,' replied her son. 'You wrote that you attended the Millsham wedding. Can you tell us the direction of the bride? We wish to pay a call on her parents. If she is not involved, we must look elsewhere for the baby's family. There are one or two other possibilities besides the Countess Millsham.'

'Dear me, what a predicament for you to be in, my child,' she said sympathetically to Clare. 'One attempts to do one's duty without counting the cost, as it were, and occasionally one finds it far more than anticipated. Of course I know the bride's family. The Caswells live just south of Bradford at a place called The Folly. Most aptly named it is, too.'

Clare longed to know why, but hesitated to ask.

A twinkle entered Lady Knowlton's eyes as she added, 'I shan't explain that remark to you. You shall see for yourself.'

Which put Clare in a great desire to be on their way to Bradford without delay. She waited politely until the dowager countess rose, then, her poise wrapped nicely about her, Clare also stood.

Richard said, 'We shall drive on to The Folly as quickly as we are able, then return here by late afternoon. I have the feeling that Mrs Caswell will not detain us?'

'Quite,' Lady Knowlton said. Her eyes seemed to dance, and there was a naughty little smile curving her lips.

The traveling coach seemed horridly slow to Clare in her impatience to reach their destination. The distance from Bath to Knowl Hill was approximately four or five miles, not too long a drive. From the Hill, she learned it would be another six or seven miles to where the Caswells lived at The Folly.

'What an intriguing name for a home,' Clare said while peering out of the window at the passing scenery. Glancing at her escort, she chanced a smile. 'Your mother is a very charming lady.'

'Yes. I quite missed her while I was away. She adores my brother's children, and I can only thank your presence that she did not tease me about starting a nursery. She does so with great regularity.' He watched Clare's face with a sharp gaze to discover her reaction to his carefully chosen speech.

Clare could feel her face bloom with warmth at his words. He had an ability to disconcert her as no other. 'I expect mothers have that uncomfortable habit. I do not recall what my mother did regarding my brother. I expect I paid it little heed, as young as I was at the time.'

The horses had enjoyed their rest while at Knowl Hill. They drew the coach along at a good clip. How thankful Tom Coachman must be that Venetia Godwin was not along today. He could spring the horses at will.

They paused at the White House Inn once in Bradford to partake of a light meal. It was an adequate place with decent food. Fortunately Clare was not hungry and made quick work of her lunch.

The drive south to the Caswells' house was one of tense anticipation. Clare hoped they might meet with success. But what did that mean, precisely? The best of all would be that one of the Caswells would know where Jane was residing now. The worst was that Jane presently lived with them, which then meant that William belonged to someone else.

The mile took only a short while to cover, and within less time than Clare believed possible they were entering the road to the Caswell home.

The large house presented a neat enough, although most peculiar view. It appeared that a great number of additions had been made at various times, for the building sprouted ells and gables in the most unlikely spots. This assuredly was a folly. There were a great number of children playing about to the rear. Clare wondered if they had company visiting and was loath to intrude.

'I will have none of that,' Richard said firmly. 'We have come some distance, and I feel sure Mrs Caswell will see us.' He offered Clare his hand, then tucked it next to him while they approached the front door.

The housekeeper wore a harassed expression as she welcomed them into the cool, spacious hall. Considering the vast number of youngsters outside, the interior was amazingly peaceful. Which did not explain the housekeeper.

'We wish to see Mrs Caswell concerning her daughter, Lady Millsham.'

The housekeeper gave them an uninterested look, then bustled off to a room across and down the hall from the door. In moments she returned, requesting them to follow her.

They entered a room filled with shadows. Draperies were drawn nearly together, and the remaining sheer curtains hid what view there might have been. Reposing on a gray chaise longue on the far side of the room reclined a faded little woman who looked as though it would be beyond her to lift a finger. Her day cap drooped about a thin, lined face, and her eyes were curiously lifeless.

'Dear madam, I trust we do not find you ill,' Clare said in her softest voice. Considering the number of children outside, she was at a loss to explain the lack of people within.

'No, no, I daresay my days are all of a muchness. You wished to inquire about my daughter, Jane?'

'We do,' Clare replied, wondering at the lack of animation in the woman. 'Could you tell us where she is?'

'Why,' Mrs Caswell replied languidly, 'she is at Millsham Hall. Where else would she be?' It was the first time Clare had

heard a question asked with absolutely no inflection whatsoever.

'With the death of her husband, she ought to be residing at
the Dower House. She is not.' Clare found it difficult not to
rebuke this woman for her lack of interest or concern for her
daughter.

'Really?' replied the remarkably incurious voice. 'Then I
fear I cannot answer your question. For I felt sure that was
where she would be.'

'Could you tell us if Jane had a child a few months back?'
Clare asked with great patience.

'I do not actually know for a certainty,' came the slow reply.
'She wrote me that a babe was expected. When I heard not a
word, I supposed the birth did not go well. Some do not, you
know,' she added with a faint frown. 'Not that I ever had such
happen to me. I had ten births, all well and growing, thank
the good Lord.'

Clare tried to keep a serene face in view of the remark from
Mrs Caswell, for it seemed to Clare that the pious conclusion
was more of a complaint than thanks.

Mrs Caswell lifted a dainty glass of rather dark red liquid
that Clare suspected might be blackberry cordial, and
downed it in one swallow. An enormous sigh was followed
by an application of a huge white cambric handkerchief to her
brow, as though in utter weariness.

'We visited Millsham Hall recently, and the present earl
could give us no direction for Jane. You know nothing?' Clare
normally would never repeat a question, but she found it so
difficult to accept that a mother could be so ignorant of her
daughter's whereabouts that she felt she must try again
before leaving.

'Nothing?' drifted back the answer.

Clare met Richard's gaze in the dim light, trying to fathom
what he was thinking. Ought she reveal a possible child and
heir to Millsham to this poor, indifferent woman? Somehow it
seemed to Clare that the less this woman knew, the better.
Besides, it looked highly unlikely that she would do anything
one way or another.

'Forgive us for intruding upon your peace, Mrs Caswell,' Clare concluded, rising from the hard chair where she had sat during the conversation.

'Quite all right,' Mrs Caswell replied in the most die-away air Clare had ever heard.

Both Clare and Richard blinked in the bright light of a summer's day when they left the house. Clare turned to look beyond to where at least a half-dozen children rolled hoops, swung, and played at games. 'At least they appear to be healthy and normal. Poor woman. What a pity she cannot tell us anything of use. I fear the journey was quite wasted.'

'Not totally,' Richard said as he assisted Clare into the coach. Priddy darted a glance from one face to the other, looking for clues to their success or lack of it.

'How so?'

'We know why Lady Millsham did not return to stay with her parents. That mother would scarce be welcoming to any young woman with a baby.'

'I see what you mean,' Clare replied thoughtfully. 'So where does that leave us?'

'On the way back to Knowl Hill, for the moment.'

Clare left him to his thoughts while she softly explained to Priddy what they had found at the Caswell house.

'I can see why it was named The Folly,' Richard said of a sudden.

'Why?' Clare dutifully replied.

'Well, architecturally it is all of that and more.'

'I declare! What a terrible thing to say,' she sputtered, trying not to give in to the laughter that bubbled up. She utterly failed, and they shared a delighted laugh.

Once past Bradford, Clare turned her mind to finding Jane, if she still lived, that is. 'Lord Talbot,' Clare said with a quick look at Priddy, 'you do not think she is dead, do you? Killed, that is?'

Instantly perceiving the line of thought Clare pursued, Richard immediately shook his head. 'No, if she were dead, I doubt if the present earl would be so curious as to her where-abouts, or so concerned.'

Clare fastened her eyes on his, a shock going through her as she realized the great danger that Lady Millsham might be in, wherever she presently lived.

'I feel she took refuge when her husband died. Perhaps she suspected her husband's death was not an accident, and sought to protect her son from a like fate? Something must have happened to frighten her recently, however. A peril great enough to force her to place her dear son in your coach, hoping you would care for him until that danger passed.'

'Pray that we find her before that danger becomes a reality. I feel as though it presses in on us. Let us return to Bath immediately,' Clare cried.

'I fear it is too late to do so today with safety. I promise we shall leave first thing in the morning.'

'I hope all will be well,' Clare murmured, full of forebodings. The pleasant hours she had spent with the baby had increased her affection for the lad. She would allow no harm to come to him if she could help it.

CHAPTER EIGHT

'I had feared that it might be the case,' Lady Knowlton said with a twinkle in her kindly blue-green eyes. She welcomed the two travelers into the drawing room while Priddy hastily went up to the room assigned to Clare to work magic on a crumpled gown for dinner.

Clare wondered where Richard Talbot had come by his eyes, the color of rich malachite. His mother's hair was the same lovely chestnut, hers artfully laced with silver. Not that all that much might be seen of it, but what peeped from beneath her exquisite day cap gave a clue.

If she had the ordering of the decor in the Dower House, she also had fine taste in furnishings. The inherited evidence of her taste, Clare supposed, could be seen in Richard's elegant, yet never foppish clothing. He always looked as fine as fivepence, yet did not give Clare the impression he spent a great deal of time before his looking glass. Still, she could see a resemblance to his mother.

She wondered about his easygoing, yet firm character. He was enormously complex when she compared him to the gentlemen she had met in London. His curiosity matched her own, and he was as unhesitating in the pursuit of the missing countess as Clare might wish. Not quite obstinate, or precisely mulish, he possessed a resolute nature she truly admired. Perhaps too much. When she chanced to get a trifle too close to him, she sensed it with every fiber of her being, a most uncomfortable feeling, she thought. It was one she'd never had to deal with before. There was not a thing she might do about it other than withdraw, unfortunately.

'Indeed, Mother, we found The Folly quite lived up to its name,' Richard replied, pulling off his gloves while he escorted Clare to a chair near his mother. 'Whatever prompted them to add on all those ells and gables? The place looked as though it had sprouted in every direction.'

'Ten children, my dear.' The countess placed her needlework on her lap, a hint of a fond smile in her eyes as she studied her youngest son. 'I was told the house was not particularly large when they bought it. They simply added on as they needed the space. I suspect they did not hire an architect to assist them. Tell me, Miss Fairchild, you found out nothing of help?' The countess turned a polite gaze toward Clare, who shook her head sadly in reply.

'No, ma'am. I confess I found it vastly difficult to understand how a mother could be so unconcerned about her eldest daughter. But then, I miss my dear mother dreadfully at times. I am fortunate I have an elder sister I may confide in, if I feel the need. But to have a mother and not be able to turn to her in time of trouble . . .' Clare shook her head.

'You are close to your family? I remember Viscount Seton, your father, that is, and your mother. Charming couple. Pity they died so relatively young. A fever as I recall?' Her interest, though courteous, seemed genuine. Her eyes revealed warm sympathy.

Remembering the dreaded fever that carried her parents from her within weeks of one another, Clare merely nodded. It had been a nightmarish time for her, one she tried to forget. She had nursed them, when no one else would enter their rooms. It was a wonder she had been spared, considering how close she had been to them, and how exhausted she became before the end.

'It has been a tiring day. I trust one of your excellent dinners will be forthcoming shortly? If we may be excused, we shall go up to change.' Richard had observed the shadows that entered Clare's lovely blue eyes at the mention of her parents. He wished there might be a way he could quickly wipe them away.

Brightening, Clare rose from her chair, dipping a lovely curtsy to her hostess. 'I hope we do not cause too much trouble for you, ma'am.'

'Not at all,' murmured Lady Knowlton in reply as she walked with them to the hall. She instructed Clare on her room, then watched her glide up the stairs, graceful and fluid in her carriage.

Once the girl had turned the corner, Lady Knowlton glanced at her son, and commented, 'Charming girl. Comes from a fine old family. Interesting that you should champion her cause, as it were.'

'I could not like the manner in which the tabbies of Bath were shredding her name, all because an unknown person had placed an infant in her coach and she was too kind to ignore it. She is a young woman of great character. I could scarce believe that she did not suffer a spasm when a shot went through her bonnet, as most young ladies might have. She did look a trifle pale, however,' he said, his eyes grim, recalling how Clare had sunk to the road, her eyes wide with apprehension.

'Remarkable, indeed. There will be no gossip from this visit?' They strolled up the stairs together, then paused at the top.

'We enlisted the aid of the greatest quidnunc in Bath, a Mrs Robottom, to lend us support. I fully expect that when we return, we ought to see an improvement in the atmosphere. She will put it about that Clare is caring for the infant of a friend who has taken ill. I trust Mrs Robottom will make a great tale of it. I only hope we can recognize ourselves.'

'You think that it was a wise thing to do?'

'I had to do something.' He patted his mother's shoulder, then hurried off to his room to freshen up for dinner.

Lady Knowlton stood a moment, then she too went to her room, a wistful smile on her face. It seemed very much evident to her that her youngest had at last found his match. Now if only some way might be found to persuade him to remain in England.

*

104

The following morning, Clare joined Lord Talbot in the breakfast room, her best bonnet in place and ready to eat a light
meal before taking off for Bath. She well knew the earlier they
reached the city, the better.

'Mother shan't join us. I expect she reclines on her pillow
until a more respectable hour.'

Clare nodded, not displeased she wouldn't have to face
that shrewd study from Richard's mother this morning such
as she had endured last evening. Lady Knowlton evidently
labored until the delusion that an understanding existed
between Clare and Richard. That they were merely friends
was a fact that did not particularly cheer Clare. She had left a
most proper letter of thanks for her hostess, and would write
again once they reached Bath, expecting it to be the last time
she communicated with the countess.

When they had sipped their last of tea and coffee, they
went to the coach where Priddy and Tom Coachman awaited
them. The groom stood by the coach door, giving Lord Talbot
a nod as he entered.

'All's ready, sir.'

Clare caught that remark and raised her brows in inquiry.
When only a bland smile returned her way, she settled back
against the cushions to idly inspect the view from the
window. Ready for what? she wondered.

They drove along the avenue that led to Knowl Hill rather
than the way they had arrived. Clare turned questioning eyes
to Lord Talbot.

'I wished you to see where I grew up. It's a rather charming house.'

It was that and more. They paused some distance away,
because of the early hour and not wishing to disturb his
brother and family. The early sun shone on a lovely Georgian
structure of impeccable taste set on a grassy slope with stately
oaks and hornbeams as accents.

After they had turned about, Clare took another wistful
peek at the house. 'It is a handsome building, standing high
on the hill, and in such a very beautiful situation. You must
have enjoyed growing up there very much.'

105

Richard engaged to relate a few tales of his boyhood, suitably edited, to entertain Clare. He found her interest all he could want, and her enjoyment of his boyish pranks delightful.

'I can't believe you did all those naughty things and lived to tell about it,' she said, chuckling at the last of his stories.

Just then the coach rumbled to an abrupt halt not far from the lockkeeper's cottage on the Kennet and Avon canal. Richard stuck his head out of the window at once, while Clare regained her upright pose once again. He pulled back, then glanced at Clare before leaving the coach. 'There seems to be a tree across the road, or some such thing. I shall see what is to be done.'

'Do be careful,' she remonstrated, a tiny frown of worry creasing her brow. Odd, the road had been fine yesterday and there had been no wind to speak of last night.

Curious, she slipped from the coach to see what had actually stopped them. The scene appeared peaceful enough, with a tranquil sun hazily beaming through light clouds. A gentle breeze tossed the willow branches, and long summer grasses danced to-and-fro. Harebells and small scabious poked their blue heads from among the green. To her left, a canal lock could be seen in the distance.

The three men labored to pull a downed tree from the road. Clare was about to walk over to see what had caused the hornbeam to fall when she saw a glint of metal among the shrubbery. She froze in her steps, longing to call out, only finding her voice was also stilled. Was that a gun? Or something innocent? Feeling slightly foolish, she turned to see what Lord Talbot was doing.

Then a shot rang out, and she felt a tug at her bonnet. She vividly recalled when she had felt just such before. 'Richard . . .' Her terror could be heard, even though her cry was faint.

'Clare!' Richard dropped the limb he had picked up and dashed to her side, alarmed at her pallor. He had heard the shot, and was thankful Clare had not been touched. Then he caught sight of the hole in her bonnet, and dragged her toward the safety of the coach. Another shot might not miss!

'I have b-been a pattern card of respectability all my life. N-nothing ever happened to me that was daring or out of the ordinary. And to think I believed Bath would be dull and uneventful,' she whispered in an aside, as they stood leaning against the coach, trying to catch their breath. She was winded from their mad run, and rested her head against his chest while waiting for her legs to return to normal.

The pounding of his heart against her ear lessened a trifle, but he must be as apprehensive as she felt. 'I shall be enriching the milliners of Bath at this rate,' she added. 'Perhaps one of them has taken to drastic measures to improve her business?'

How comforting it was to cling to his solid form, to absorb the scent of costmary from his linens, and feel his strength as he clasped her in his arms.

'Somehow, I doubt it.' Richard tightened his hold to her, grimly searching the area for signs of anyone. Deciding Clare would be safest inside the coach, he thrust her within, then with the help of his man and Tom Coachman, he investigated the area around the crossroads. They found nothing more than some bent grass where a person might have crouched for a time. Nothing of help.

'Our plans have changed.' Richard stuck his head inside the coach to study Clare. She looked as calm as if she had been at a tea party instead of being the target of an armed man. Her bonnet dangled from her hands, the hole much in evidence. 'I espied a boat, and my man is now arranging for the fellow to take us to Bath via the canal. Your maid will stay in the coach. We shall be underway as quickly as might be. Let us hope we can foil our pursuer by this little trick.'

'Priddy, I'd not have you stay here if you are afraid,' Clare whispered to her redoubtable maid.

'I am afraid of nothing,' Priddy replied, while thankful she was not required to stand up.

Leaving all her things but her indispensable reticule, Clare crossed to where the small boat waited for them along the bank following the trip through the lock. It was about the size of a wherry, and carried a load of produce going to Bath, or so the lad said. His eyes were round with amazement at the sight of these folks who were willing to pay a great sum just to have a boat ride.

'You will go as fast as you can, my lad? There is another guinea in it for you if you can get there quickly.'

'Aye, sir. I'll do my best. There's another lock on the way, you know.' But he was as good as his word. He signaled his partner, who set their tow horse into a gallop, and the narrow boat shot off along the canal. The high banks concealed them from the road; only someone who peered over the edge might discover them.

Clare huddled in her pelisse, thinking this trip had to be the wildest she had ever taken in her life – next to the one to Millsham Hall. Richard joined her on the clean sack spread out on the bottom of the boat. He took off his jacket, then wrapped it about her in spite of her protests.

'I observed how you trembled, my dear. There is a sun, such as it is through the clouds. I shall be warm enough.' He leaned back against the hull of the boat, watching her as she settled as well. They were close, the lad at the front had his back to him. Richard felt the strain of the near distaster, but he felt something else as well. He was honorbound to keep his distance, but he longed to hold her in his arms once again, and not to ward off her terror.

Yet that firm chin, tilted up in defiance, indicated she was pluck to the backbone. He truly admired her spirit, that tenacious yet serene ability she had to plunge ahead with what she deemed right. The sun picked up golden threads among her curls, now free of the ruined bonnet.

'My dear girl . . .' At her questioning look, he realized he had spoken aloud. 'Is it possible he shot and missed deliberately, to discourage you from looking for Lady Millsham?'

Clare shivered in spite of the morning sun and the warmth of Richard's jacket about her. 'That seems so utterly fantastic. Why? What would we uncover if we find her? I am far more suspicious now than if he had not shot at all. For, if you think about it, it points a finger to Lady Millsham. I think a madman must be behind this scheme.'

'Will you give up your search?'

'I cannot. That innocent baby needs his mother. And I begin to believe she needs a champion almost as much as we need to find her.'

'Were you not terrified?' Richard drew closer to her so she might lean against his shoulder if she chose.

Clare nodded. 'Of course.' She was very aware of that shoulder so close to her. If she were to lean her head just a trifle, she'd be able to take advantage of it. She ought not do such a thing, she knew. She looked again. Then she tilted her head to rest upon that wonderfully firm and comforting shoulder, and sighed very softly. 'I suppose it was the same person who shot before. Odd, how he knows where we go and when.'

'Only Miss Godwin knew where we planned to travel.'

'Do not forget Mrs Robottom.'

'So that means there could be countless others? I pray not.'

Clare turned her head to study his face at close range. It was an opportunity a woman rarely got, unless during a dance, and that was usually a hasty glance. One did not spend time staring at one's partner on the dance floor.

'Clare,' Richard said in a deep tone that thrilled her right down her spine all the way to her toes.

The approach to the next lock brought a stop to any further tantalizing words. Clare looked apprehensively at the gates that allowed the little boat to enter the lock, then the others that permitted it to continue once the water level was attained.

'Mister, you playing games with someone? There's a fellow that's watching you from the near side of the lock.' The squeaky voice of the young lad interrupted Richard.

'Quick,' he ordered. He pulled a rough woven sack from the produce and tossed it over them. He tugged at Clare to scrunch down in the boat, hoping that they could manage to skim past with no more shots fired.

'Perhaps he is merely checking to see how we go?'

'I did not think he had remained behind to watch our

departure, but you never know,' whispered Richard against her ear. 'We certainly saw no sight of him.'

Clare turned to reply and discovered her lips against his cheek. His skin was clean-shaven and smelled of that exotic spice she had noticed before. Before she knew what she was about, the tip of her tongue darted out to taste of him.

All thought of the danger that possibly lurked ahead of them faded, as he swiftly gathered her close and united their mouths in a most splendid and satisfying manner. She tentatively slid a hand up his arm to twine her fingers in his hair, admiring the thick texture of it. He crushed her against him, and Clare offered not the least resistance. Not, that is, until the voice of the young lad reached her ears.

The boat jerked forward as the lad called back softly, 'I don't think it was anyone who meant you any harm, sir. More likely someone who wants to watch the boats.'

Clare heard and stilled in Richard's arms for a few moments before sanity returned. She hastily recalled herself and pulled away, becoming aware of the dusty sack and their cramped positions.

There was an uncomfortable expression on Richard's face when he tossed the rough woven sack aside. Under the circumstances, he ought to be offering marriage to Clare, for they had been together in a highly improper situation. Yet he wanted a wife because she truly cared for him, not because he must make the proposal as a result of propriety dictating such. He did not know quite how to handle this complication.

Clare caught his fierce scowl, brief as it was. Was he regretting that impetuous kiss of moments ago? She wasn't sure quite how she felt about it now. It had been so wonderful, then Society's decrees reminded her of what might be said and expected. She drew herself up, wrapping her arms about her, feeling defensive. Along on either side of the canal, now without a deep wall, trees dipped and bowed in the breeze. The scent of meadowsweet and the call of the moorhens reached through her preoccupation.

'It seems we near Bath.' She struggled to find a calm voice. 'Perhaps he can let us out near the first lock so that we may find our way up from there?'

Richard darted a dismayed look at the woman next to him. Clare had withdrawn from him so abruptly, though he thought not in anger. But if not in anger, then why? 'I shall so request.' They would leave the boat before it was to enter the short flight of locks where it descended to the Avon.

Thus it was that two slightly disheveled figures shortly scrambled out on the towpath, then made their way up the bank to find a couple of chairs not far away. Richard joined her, wanting to make sure nothing happened to her during the short ride to her house.

Upon reaching the Royal Crescent, Clare entered the house with a thankful heart, followed by a determined Richard. What else would she have to endure before reuniting little William with his mother?

The sight of that quick scowl on Lord Talbot's face was engraved on Clare's heart. So often those unguarded expressions revealed what was truly within. She chose not to consider what it meant at the moment. That could come later, when she retired to her room for the night. Now she wanted to have her tea. That Lord Talbot stood studying her anxiously did not escape her. She wished he would leave.

'Clare! Well, gracious me! You look as though you were pulled through a hedge backward!' Venetia cried in horror at the spectacle her hostess presented. 'What has happened? A highwayman?'

Grasping at the offered excuse, Clare nodded. 'He may have been. A tree had been dragged across the crossroads, and we were shot at. Were it not for the quick thinking of Lord Talbot, heaven only knows what might have happened. Where is the baby? I must reassure myself that this has all been worth the trip. For you must know that we found not a trace of Lady Millsham.'

Venetia turned away from Clare, slowly strolling to the window of the study. 'He is out with Jenny. She thought a bit of air would do him a world of good.'

Clare examined her once favorite bonnet, wondering what she could find that she would like half so well, and absently inquired, 'You ordered the groom to go with her, of course.'

'I did not consider it necessary. Who would bother a maid, after all?' Venetia tittered a high little laugh, sounding disdainful, almost offended.

Clare dropped the poor bonnet and whirled to face Lord Talbot. 'The baby!' she exclaimed. 'He might be in danger!' She rushed past him to the door, throwing it open to venture out to the street. A scandalized Bennison hurried after her, beckoning to chairmen who were on their way back to the central part of town with an empty chair.

Richard hurried after Clare, walking at a rapid pace to keep up with the men. He had not failed to catch her exceedingly formal tone of address, and he suspected it was not merely for Miss Godwin's benefit. Blast it all, he had alienated her, most likely beyond reparation.

Leaning toward the chair, he queried, 'Where would she be likely to go?'

'The Sidney Gardens, and hurry!' she ordered the chairmen.

The chairmen took the less traveled streets to speed their path, dashing through the Circus, then down Broad Street to rush across Pulteney Bridge with great haste. Clare took no notice of a number of people she knew, concentrating on Jenny and the baby. Pray they were safe and she was overreacting following her own harrowing experience.

At the end of Great Pulteney Street the chairmen came to a breathless stop before the Sidney Gardens' entrance. Clare pulled several coins from her reticule, not even bothering to see what they were, thrust them at the chairmen, then walked with deceptive speed into the heart of the walkways that wound through the lush gardens.

'Cor!' exclaimed one chairman, after looking at the largess in his hand. He smiled broadly, winked at his partner, then settled down to wait for another fare.

'Clare, have a caution,' demanded Richard at her side, wondering how any woman could look so unruffled while skimming through the park at such a rapid pace.

'It is my instincts. They never fail me, you see, and I fear for the baby.' She ceased speaking to save her breath, then checked her steps as she saw Jenny and the baby not far ahead. She was about to give a sigh of relief, when she noticed Jenny was backing away from a man who had apparently sidled up to her.

'Wait here,' commanded Richard, hoping the intrepid Miss Fairchild might actually do as ordered for once. Tossing his hat aside, he ran toward the man, thinking if he approached the villain from the rear, he'd not be seen.

'Now see here, gel, just you don't let out a peep. I'll take this little fellow and be gone in a trice.' The man grabbed for William.

Jenny clung to the baby with all her strength. She screamed just as Richard dashed from behind to spin the man around. One punch on the jaw felled the assailant in a heap. Richard stood breathing heavily, absently massaging his knuckles as he studied the man at his feet. Nothing distinguished about him. Looked to be a groom or the like. Middling height and coloring, the sort to blend into a crowd, go unnoticed most anywhere, yet Richard memorized those features. He would not forget them soon.

Clare ignored her knight-errant to rush to Jenny's side. The maid looked about to faint, and Clare did not wish the baby to be dropped to the ground.

She competently gathered the infant into her arms, then spoke soothingly to Jenny. 'There now, it is all over. That nasty man shan't bother you again. Lord Talbot will dispose of him. Is that not correct, sir?'

Clare finally met Lord Talbot's inquiring look with her own. She was well in control of her emotions now. Her gaze was politely appreciative, cool, and most formal. Had they been in the middle of the Upper Assembly rooms, she could not have been more correct.

Barely resisting the urge to give vent to his frustrations, Richard bowed. 'I shall most gladly remove your dragon from your path, dear lady.' He bent over to pick up the man, then added, 'I shall talk with you later, Miss Fairchild.'

Murmuring a vague reply, Clare swept from the park with

Jenny close to her side. Blond curls a tumble, her bonnet in ruins back at the house, she ignored the stares of the few in her path and hunted for a hackney.

Once they reached the Royal Crescent, Clare marched past Bennison to the study. Not finding her quarry there, she charged up the stairs to the drawing room, the baby still clasped in her arms. Espying her target, she halted inside the door.

'Had it not been for the courage of dear little Jenny, this child would now be only God knows where. Some horrid man attempted to wrest the babe from her arms while she innocently walked in the Sidney Gardens. Had it not been for our fortuitous arrival,' and it slightly galled Clare to give due credit to Lord Talbot, 'we would most likely never have seen William again, nor would his mother.'

Venetia sniffed and waved a handkerchief in the air. 'How do you know his mother did not intrigue to recover the boy?'

'Rubbish,' exclaimed Lord Talbot from the doorway.

Clare whirled about, noting with dismay just how devilishly handsome Lord Talbot looked. Those malachite eyes of his glittered with strong emotion, and he seemed not the least undone by all that had transpired. Amazing man. And, she reminded herself, he did not appear to cherish the least desire to unite with her in any proper manner.

'I must agree. She would know that she has only to appear here and be welcomed.' A sudden thought struck her. 'Or did you by chance see her while we were gone and deny her access?'

'Clare, *dear*, how can you think such a thing of me!' Venetia cried, utterly aghast at what her impetuous words had wrought.

'Forgive me,' Clare replied, appalled at her thoughtless accusation. 'My wits have gone begging what with all this excitement.' She patted the baby on his back to soothe him.

Venetia nodded her acceptance of this apology, then subsided in her chair.

Richard was enjoying the little contretemps between the two women. It appeared high time that Clare saw her

114

companion and guest for what the woman was. Or had she, and allowed Miss Godwin to remain anyway?

He admired the way Clare looked with the baby in her arms. Very maternal, he mused, wondering how he might extricate himself from her bad books. 'You look very well with the child in your arms, Miss Fairchild.' He hadn't intended to speak his thoughts, but at the becoming blush that bloomed on her cheeks, he was almost glad he had. 'Why hasn't some man married you long ago?'

Venetia cooed a dainty chuckle at her friend's obvious discomfiture. Not forgiving the slur cast at her regarding the child, never mind the truth of the matter, she fluttered her lashes at Lord Talbot and said, 'Perhaps she has turned them all away . . . if there were any?'

Not terribly surprised by the defection of her guest, Clare drew herself to her full height and replied in a clearly amused tone, 'Well, it was not because I was never asked, for I was. A goodly number of times. I cannot recall why I rejected them, and it would scarcely be good manners to reveal them if I did, would it? Perhaps,' and she flicked a glance at Lord Talbot, 'they disappointed me in some way. Or maybe I simply did not care for them as I felt I ought. Not being required to marry because of the usual monetary necessity, I have had my leisure to consider the proposals offered. I daresay, had my father been here to insist I be wed, I would have made a choice.'

Clare handed the infant, who now looked most out of sorts, to Jenny, sending her along to her room with a gentle smile quite at odds with the caustic bite in her words to Lord Talbot.

'I believe I would far rather be a spinster than to marry without love,' Clare stated firmly, giving Lord Talbot a resolute look directly into his eyes.

CHAPTER NINE

'It never rains in Miss Austen's novels. Did you know that, dear Clare?' Venetia offered while warily watching her hostess, who stood by a south window of the drawing room. Clare had stared out at the fitful showers for some time without any comment whatsoever. It made Venetia nervous.

'How interesting. At least it is quiet and utterly peaceful, today. I doubt if any shall hazard the wet to pay a social call in this inclement weather. After the past few days, I welcome the inactivity.' Clare released her hold on the corded tassel, allowing it to swing gracefully down before she turned to face her guest.

'I thought you wanted to shop for a new bonnet?'

'Yes, well, so I did. I have depleted my bonnet supply to a shocking degree. My most favorite ones, too,' Clare said with a sigh. 'It is a good thing I can manage the price of new ones, for they are horridly dear, are they not?' she said lightly, wondering what was going on in Venetia's mind to bring such a guilty expression to her face.

There was a noise downstairs, and both women turned toward the door to see what was amiss. Clare walked to the top of the stairs to discover the stout figure of Mrs Robottom, her hand on Bennison's arm, puffing her way up. A pair of wooden pattens, their iron rings hidden from view, sat neatly on the flagged entry floor, and a great red oiled-silk umbrella reposed nearby, dripping onto a cloth hastily set down by Bennison.

'Good day, Miss Fairchild,' wheezed Mrs Robottom as she neared the top of the staircase. 'Lovely weather for ducks, I daresay.' Then she chuckled as though she had uttered words of original wit.

Giving the woman who had been the originator of a great deal of her grief since coming to Bath a wary look, Clare politely replied, 'And good day to you as well. I confess I am surprised to see anyone out in such rain.'

'She just said not a minute ago that she doubted we would have any company, and now here you are,' Venetia said with surprising satisfaction.

Clare wondered if Venetia merely preferred to avoid direct conversation, for Mrs Robottom was no particular friend of hers. Ushering the stout matron into the drawing room, Clare bade her sit down. Bennison paused by the door, a brow raised in inquiry.

'Tea and cakes, I believe,' Clare ordered, figuring that her caller would appreciate such. Then she crossed to take a chair close to where Mrs Robottom perched.

'I heard there was a near disaster yesterday,' began her visitor.

Nodding cautiously, Clare decided to allow Mrs Robottom to do most of the talking, as which near disaster she meant was beyond Clare.

'That poor baby,' continued the caller, 'must have been frightened nearly to death. You are a very brave woman, Miss Fairchild.'

'La,' Venetia inserted, 'she is quite intrepid. I wonder that she dare do half the things she does, for I should faint, I am sure. My mama thought it vastly unladylike to be so bold. But then, ladies of a certain age may do as they please, I suppose. I have cautioned Clare time out of mind that she must show more discretion.'

Darting a glance at her guest, Clare merely smiled. 'You really ought to use spectacles when you do your needlework, Venetia. You are beginning to show the signs of incipient wrinkles about your eyes.'

Horrified at the very notion of such a frightfully dreadful

thing, Venetia jumped up, 'Oh, dear, I'd best see to it at once.'

Mrs Robottom watched the flutter of Venetia's muslin skirts as they went around the doorway, then smiled at Clare.

'That was unkind, I fear,' Clare said ruefully. 'But I believe I have heard quite enough of my naughtiness of the past few days. I warn you, dear ma'am, that if you have come to ring a peal over my head, I shan't listen for a moment.'

A hearty laugh echoed about the room. Mrs Robottom took Clare's measure with shrewd eyes. 'You have spirit, my girl. Ladies of a certain age, my eye. You are far from being in that lot. Now,' she settled more comfortably onto her chair, 'tell me precisely what has occurred in your latest efforts to find William's mother. I might add,' she added with a shade of uneasiness, 'I feel badly about the misunderstanding I had regarding you, my dear. I am truly embarrassed. I ought to have sought the answer instead of flapping my tongue. It shall be guarded more closely in the future, you may be sure.'

Not knowing quite how to respond to such a handsome apology, Clare merely nodded her head and said, 'I confess I felt dismayed to think my family name meant nothing in Bath. However, I am sure you expended your best efforts to right the mistake. My brother would be vastly amused at my pretensions, I believe.'

'And he is?' Mrs Robottom asked, her face assuming a wary mien.

'Viscount Seton,' Clare answered with just a hint of pride in her voice. The urge to let her guest know that her family was most respectable had proved irresistible.

'Oh, my!' the matron replied in near comical dismay.

Deciding that Mrs Robottom might possibly find a missing clue in what Clare had learned to this point, she elected to reveal more than originally intended.

'Now, to tell the tale. You see, it was like this,' she began. What followed was a carefully edited version of the trip to The Folly and the interview with Mrs Caswell. The sympathetic clucks and tuts from her listener prodded Clare on to reveal more, although keeping well away from the matter of Lord Talbot wherever practical.

'And you visited Lady Knowlton as well,' commented Mrs Robottom, noting with interest the delicate pink that flared in Miss Fairchild's pretty cheeks at the mention of that part of her story.

'Indeed, she is a charming lady, all that one might wish,' Clare answered demurely.

'I cannot like that you have been shot at,' continued Mrs Robottom. 'Although, I expect you like it even less,' the lady chuckled, then sobered as she recalled that such a shot could very well have proved fatal.

'It has been rather hard on my bonnets,' Clare said in reply, her eyes reflecting that in spite of her light words, her memories of those awful moments still haunted her.

'I wonder if there might be a clue overlooked at that inn in Marlborough?' Mrs Robottom mused after Bennison had set the tea out for Clare to pour.

'The Castle Inn? Yes, I have wondered at that, but I questioned everyone about and learned nothing of value. It was as though that infant simply dropped from the sky.'

'And we know that infants do not come in that manner, do we not, Miss Fairchild?' said a masculine voice from the doorway, rather too full of amusement for her liking.

Tea sloshed over into her saucer as Clare raised shocked eyes to meet those of Lord Talbot. How dare the man come up here unannounced! She needed time to compose herself before facing him again. 'Good day, Lord Talbot. I see you join the ducks in the rain.'

Mrs Robottom chuckled as she keenly observed the two who faced each other across the width of the drawing room. The tension between them could have been cut with a butter knife.

Turning to Bennison, who revealed nothing of his thoughts, Clare merely ordered, 'Another cup for Lord Talbot, if you please. Or would you prefer sherry, sir?'

'Tea would be welcome on such a day.' He strolled across the room and bowed to Mrs Robottom, then took Clare's limp hand in his to place an almost lingering kiss on it.

She gave him a stricken look, quickly concealed beneath

119

lowered lashes, but not before, she feared, he had observed it. Hastily, she rushed into speech. 'I just confided the story of our search to Mrs Robottom. She is of the opinion that there may be a clue at the inn in Marlborough that we somehow missed.'

'It is possible.' He accepted a cup of tea from Clare, taking note with great interest of her faintly trembling hand, and her reluctance to meet his gaze. 'Not having been there at the time, I cannot vouch for what explorations were made. Your coachman noticed nothing? I still find that hard to accept, for he is an exceptional man. I cannot fathom anything slipping past his eyes, particularly something as large as that basket. You examined the infant's garments, I fancy.'

Drawing herself up exceedingly straight, Clare nodded. 'I did.' She rose from her chair and swiftly crossed to the hall where she called for Jenny. A word with that young woman, and Clare returned to join those by the tea table.

'Tom Coachman informed me that he was called to the stables by the ostler for a brief look at a horse with a problem. The ostler sought his opinion. I gather it was time and enough for someone to pop that basket into my coach from the far side where no one in the inn yard would be the wiser. No, whoever did this was rather clever about it.'

'You still feel the lad is Lady Millsham's child?' Mrs Robottom turned to see Jenny enter with the baby in her arms.

Walking to her mistress, Jenny gently placed the boy in Clare's arms. 'Shall I wait, miss?'

'Yes, please,' Clare replied while smiling down at the baby in her arms. She reached out a tender finger to stroke the downy cheek. He clutched at her finger with surprising strength, and she chuckled softly. Her eyes crinkled with amusement as she glanced up to find her two guests watching her with vastly different expressions. Mrs Robottom looked on with fond delight. A polite mask concealed Lord Talbot's thoughts.

'See? Note the fineness of his clothing. I believe I have found a coronet cleverly incorporated into the embroidery of his gown.' She unwrapped his shawl, then held up the lower part of William's dress, indicating the center of the delicate design with a steady finger. She had her emotions well in hand now, thanks to the bundle in her arms. If Lord Talbot thought she might quail before him, he could think again.

Mrs Robottom fumbled for a pair of spectacles in her reticule, plopped them on her nose, then studied the design. 'I see what you mean. It seems to me there is an elaborate *M* in the pattern as well, just below the coronet. I can see this is thee work of a skilled needlewoman.'

Lord Talbot spared a glance at the neediwork, his mind clearly occupied elsewhere. Clare wished he would take himself off. With Mrs Robottom sitting at her side, she could scarcely ask him why he was here. That polite mask he had assumed shortly after arrival hadn't cracked once. Although those eyes of his, now deep emerald, were ever watchful, she reminded herself.

'Jenny, isn't it?' queried Mrs Robottom. At the shy nod from the girl, the matron continued. 'Are you certain you remember nothing unusual from that day? Not the least little thing? A person who did not belong where she was, perhaps? Or an event just a trifle worth noticing?'

Jenny shrugged, then frowned as she considered the lady's words. 'I don't likely know, ma'am.' She scrunched up her face in deep thought, then brightened. 'There was an old woman shufflin' around the kitchen garden. I never seen her before, come to think on it.'

Lord Talbot sprang to life once again. He leaned forward, setting his teacup and saucer on the table as he fastened his gaze on the maid. 'An old woman, you say? Can you recall any particulars? Was she perhaps a nanny with one of the parties at the inn?'

' 'Twarn't no people travelin' with babies, sir. I dunno where she came from, and that's the truth.'

'Take care,' murmured Clare, 'or you will frighten the girl with that intense look of yours.'

He opened his mouth to reply, then glanced at Mrs Robottom. Obviously changing his mind, he paused a moment, then said more gently, 'How was she garbed?'

Jenny shrugged. 'A simple blue dress with a white apron, sir. A white day cap on her head as is proper. She didn't ask for nothin'. Cook took pity on her and offered her a cup of tea, which she drank like a lady.'

'Which tells me she must have been a nanny or the like. Manners never lie, you know,' Mrs Robottom exclaimed.

William elected to fuss, waving his arms about in distress. Clare eased him up on her shoulder, patting his back expertly to soothe him. Peering over her bundle, she stated, 'I believe I shall return to the Castle Inn at Marlborough to continue my investigation.'

'Excellent idea. I shall inform Tom Coachman to be prepared to depart once the weather clears.' Richard leaned back against his chair, his hooded eyes watching Clare's sudden stiffening in reaction to his words. 'We ought to have no trouble if word of the trip does not leave this room.'

Annoyed beyond belief, Clare wondered how to tactfully inform this impossible man that she wished to avoid his company now after enduring it for two journeys. Well, she admitted to herself, perhaps 'enduring' was not precisely the best word to describe her feeling. But it had become too draining for her to be with him. Facing him across a table at all meals required fortitude. Sitting next to him while in the coach was worse than facing him, for frequently she was jostled against his body. It was impossible not to be terribly aware of him in every fiber of her being at such proximity. And the memory of those kisses seared her mind, haunted her sleep, and dogged her footsteps most unrelentingly.

'I planned to go alone, with only Priddy to keep me company,' she explained at long last.

'Rubbish,' he tossed back at her with a twinkle creeping into his eyes. 'You shall need a man to scout about in areas where you cannot go, Miss Fairchild.'

She did not trust that twinkle in the least. His words mocked her even more than his eyes.

Any further discussion of the proposed trip to Marlborough broke off when the sound of feminine chatter reached their ears from downstairs.

Miss Oliver glided into the room with a jolly smile on her face, her cloak having been handed to Bennison, and quite dry by virtue of a hood and umbrella. 'I wondered whose pattens those were in the entranceway. How lovely to see you, Mrs Robottom, Lord Talbot as well. You look well, Clare, considering all I have heard.'

'Heard! Goodness, people get about more in the rain than I suspected.'

'Well, the streets have become virtual rivers, and one must be exceedingly careful where one puts a foot. Is that not correct, Lord Talbot? But then since you come but from the Edgar buildings, I fancy it was not too difficult for you?'

'What tale has reached your ears at Lady Kingsmill's drawing room?' Lord Talbot carefully inquired.

'Only that you and Clare foiled an attempt at kidnapping. It is fearsome how so many children have been snatched for one reason or another the past year.' She studied Mrs Robottom a moment while Clare ordered another tray of tea to be brought, then said, 'And what of your visit? Did you learn anything useful?'

'Nary a thing,' Clare responded before Lord Talbot could say a word. 'The countryside was lovely this time of year, and we found the Caswell's home with little difficulty. Lord Talbot's mother, Lady Knowlton, kindly furnished us with their direction. Mrs Caswell is encumbered by ill health, not to mention a strong lack of curiosity,' she added to general laughter. 'I fear she seemed to know nothing of her daughter or if she had even borne a child.'

'Mercy!' Miss Oliver said, aghast at such a woman.

'I intend to return to the inn at Marlborough to see if I can uncover anything missed before.' Clare darted a minatory glance at Lord Talbot, one he seemed to totally ignore, much to her annoyance.

'Leaving again, dear Clare?' Venetia sauntered into the room, wafting her fan before her. Though her face was bland, Clare detected a furious glint in her gray eyes. 'I shall go along this time?'

123

First darting a glance at the dismayed face of her dear friend, Susan said, 'Oh, and I had so hoped you might be of assistance to me, Venetia.'

'You wanted me? But *I* do not intend to travel. Why Clare bothered to lease this house, I shall never understand. She is away more than she is here.' Venetia gave Clare a petulant glance, then returned her attention to Miss Oliver. 'Why do you seek my company?'

'My aunt is planning a rather grand party, and I just know that you would be the one to assist me. I have had so little experience at this sort of thing. Please promise you will help?' she said with appealing grace. When Venetia gave her a dazed nod of agreement, Susan enthusiastically continued. 'Clare, you must promise to attend, for I shall not take a refusal. And Mrs Robottom as well. Naturally Lord Talbot, as hero of the hour, will be with us.' Susan gave him a mischievous smile, then primly looked at her lap.

'Well,' Clare said, as though the wind had just sailed out of her, 'that is something to look forward to, indeed.'

Venetia rose, gave Clare a simpering, superior look, then motioned to Susan Oliver. 'Perhaps we should find a place to begin our work, for it requires a good many lists, you know.'

At the door, Susan paused. 'I shan't fail you.' Then she disappeared from sight.

Considering what had just happened for a moment, Clare said, 'I do hope that Lady Kingsmill does not mind discovering that she is to give a rather grand party all of a sudden.'

The softly shared laughter broke what tension had been in the room with Venetia's entrance.

Before Clare knew what was about, Lord Talbot, Mrs Robottom, and she had planned the excursion to Marlborough to the last detail. And to Clare's chagrin, Lord Talbot included himself, with Mrs Robottom's genial urging, while that dear lady announced her intention to make the rounds of all the gossips during their absence.

The following morning, Clare managed to get out to Milsom Street, where she went to the same shop Venetia had patronized. The milliner seemed delighted to serve her, sympathizing over the loss of beloved bonnets while eager to sell any of several utterly ravishing creations in her shop.

'There you are. I was just on my way to your house.'

Clare turned, totally dismayed at the sight of Lord Talbot filling the shop's front door. He closed it behind him and strolled forward to view the bonnet Clare was trying on.

'Good morning, sirrah.'

'Sirrah, indeed,' he said indulgently, as one might to a rather beloved child. He reached out a gloved finger to flick a rather frivolous riband that decorated the bonnet.

Knowing she was far too adult to stamp her foot or indulge in a tantrum, Clare graciously gave him a glacial smile, then said, 'What are you doing here?'

'Looking for you.'

Ask a stupid question, Clare reminded herself. 'I am attempting to replace my ruined bonnets.' She turned back to the image in the looking glass, wondering if that delectable bonnet of minutes ago still appealed to her.

'I shall be happy to give you the benefit of my vast experience,' he offered amiably. 'My sister thinks I have impeccable taste.'

Clare didn't trust the look in those green eyes of his. 'I daresay she does. Sisters are inclined to be doting, I have noticed. Possibly blind as well,' she added, unable to resist the chance to tease him.

'Now, what would my mother say to that? Hm? I assist her as well.'

Clare knew when to retreat. 'What do you suggest, then?' She waited for him to select some horror of a hat, or affliction of a bonnet. What did men know about such things? She soon found out, when he selected an elegant bonnet of fine pale straw lined with deep blue satin and decorated with delicate zebra feathers to one side of the brim. It was undoubtedly one of the most fetching bonnets in the shop.

'I am impressed, Lord Talbot,' she reluctantly admitted while studying the effect in the looking glass. How she hated to acknowledge that the bonnet was exactly what she wished.

'I believe this might do to replace the second one. As I recall that one went rather nicely with your blue pelisse.' He handed the amazed milliner another dashing bonnet, this of navy curled silk, lined, edged, and trimmed with the palest cream satin. Two dear bows decorated the front of the high crown, and the narrow brim enabled Clare to see to either side without difficulty. She tied the riband beneath her chin while trying to come to terms with this side of Lord Talbot.

She found it remarkable that he recalled her pelisse, much less the color of it. That he could choose a bonnet so exactly right for her was more than a little unsettling.

'I warned you I am a dab hand at this, my dear Miss Fairchild.'

'Lord Talbot,' she scolded, then rose to pay the milliner, longing to flee to her house and away from him.

They exited the shop, Lord Talbot carrying the two hatboxes for Clare in one hand, his other placed firmly beneath her elbow. As though she might dash off? 'I am hardly likely to disappear whilst you hold my new bonnets in your hand, sir.'

'You look well today. Are you ready to depart for Marlborough?'

Glancing about to see if anyone was close enough to over-hear his words and possibly misconstrue them, she nodded. 'Now I am. I simply couldn't face any of my old bonnets.'

'Typical woman,' he murmured as he ushered her across the Circus on the way back to the Royal Crescent. 'I gather Miss Godwin is more than resigned to remaining at home.'

'As long as I take Priddy along with me, she says nothing. I confess I feel a bit guilty at leaving Miss Godwin at home once again. I am a shockingly poor hostess, I fear.'

'I trust Miss Godwin will survive far better than you can imagine. Do you have any notion as to what she does when she is out and about on her own? Why does she not require a maid with her, when she insists you have one?'

'I did not take Priddy today,' Clare pointed out.

'But how well do you know Miss Godwin? I heard that she meets a gentleman at Duffields Library. Heaven knows what they discuss, but I am informed that he wears his cravats incredibly high, so that one can scarcely see his face, and that he does not remove his hat, even though speaking to a lady.'

Clare mulled over this bit of information as they entered the house she had hired. Handing the boxes to Bennison to send up to Priddy, Clare beckoned Lord Talbot into the study.

'I find this rather disturbing,' Clare said, turning to him while gesturing he sit down by the secretary. She joined him nearby, unbuttoning the neck of her muslin pelisse as she sank onto a chair. Giving him an earnest look, she went on, 'I have wondered from time to time. For example, it was she who ordered Jenny to go without a groom to attend her. I have spoken about that with Jenny, so it shan't happen again. But what next? Dare I leave? Goodness knows I cannot take the baby jauntering about with me. And we can witness that traveling is not the safest, can we not?'

Her gaze collided with his, and for several moments she totally forgot the topic under discussion. Instead, the exotic scent she associated with Richard Talbot returned to her as she remained tangled in that green gaze. His face had felt so firm, so good. She had enjoyed being close to him, finding comfort, among other things, in his nearness.

'The babe shall be safe. I hired a man specifically for the purpose of guarding the child and his nurse.'

Bennison cleared his throat at the doorway, and Clare snapped back to full consciousness. Whatever possessed her to be so taken with the state of Lord Talbot's eyes! Or what might lurk behind them? Not to mention scandalous memories!

'Tom Coachman said to inform you that he has things ready whenever you wish to depart, Miss Fairchild.'

She thanked him, then sought Lord Talbot's gaze, this time only fleetingly. 'You still intend to go along?'

'I do,' he said judiciously. Rubbing a well-manicured hand across his jaw, he appeared to study Clare as though she were a rare specimen of something he coveted. It made her feel vastly uncomfortable.

At that moment Jenny coughed to gain her attention. Clare rose, breaking the tension that seemed to flare up whenever

Lord Talbot came too close to her. 'Yes?'

'Begging your pardon, miss. I remembered something else.'

Richard narrowed his eyes, as though wondering if the girl told the truth.

'The woman I saw at the inn, the one I said Cook gave a cup of tea to? Her name, it was Mrs Dow.' Jenny curtsied after giving this report, then ruefully added, 'I fear that's all, miss.' She bolted from the door, leaving Clare standing in the center of the room clasping her hands together.

'Mrs Dow. A very unprepossessing name, I must say,' grumbled Richard as he walked to Clare's side.

'We must find her, sir.'

'I thought you once promised to call me Richard when we were alone?'

'Did I, indeed? I fear a spinster must use care, sir. I would have no one get the wrong idea.'

'And do you know the right one, yourself?'

Ignoring his provoking question, Clare turned slightly from him, merely saying, 'We had best be prepared to leave early in the morning, sir.'

'I shall be prepared, never fear, Miss Fairchild.' With that, he took himself off, leaving Clare to wonder just what he meant by that last sentence.

CHAPTER TEN

'I feel as though I had spent the last few weeks in my coach. And do you know, it does not improve with time?' Clare grumbled. The vehicle hit a rut, and she was most thankful she had braced her foot against the opposite seat.

Actually, Mr McAdam had improved the roads a good bit. The use of small angular broken stone, packed down by the passage of traffic, greatly facilitated the comfort of travel. Something must have caused that rut, she reflected.

No cloud of dust rose in the air behind them, witness to the rains that had fallen this past week. Clare was grateful for that as well, knowing that otherwise they would have arrived at Marlborough covered with gray from head to toe, what with the number of vehicles coming and going on the road.

The carriage rocked sharply again. Clare grew alarmed. A little curl of fear rose within her, and she wondered if she ought to leave her bonnet in the coach this time should they have to stop. Then she wondered what part of her might be hit if she did. Memories of the previous times they had been forced to halt came back to her. She turned her head to catch Lord Talbot's gaze.

'I suspect the rains have created small ruts,' he offered by way of response to the apprehension in her eyes. 'I doubt it is anything to worry about. We ought to arrive at the inn shortly, as I told Tom Coachman not to spare the horses. He's a good man.'

Lord Talbot had been most aggravating this morning, she

reflected. Oh, he exhibited the most perfect of manners. She could not fault his attire, for those biscuit pantaloons fit like a second skin, and his coat of deep blue Bath cloth could serve as a tribute to Mr Weston's skill as a tailor. His cravat looked a perfection, and that discreet waistcoat, as much as she could see of it, reflected fastidious taste. His chestnut hair became him arranged *à la Titus*, as did the benignly devilish smile that lurked about those firmly chiseled lips.

Oh, it was nothing obvious, but Lord Talbot was slowly driving her mad. His green eyes teased and mocked her, by his posture he tantalized her. Those wicked glances held remembrances in them that were best left unsaid. From the very first thing this morning, when he had held her hand a trifle too long while assisting her into the coach, to the occasional touches, due, he apologized, to the rocking of the coach, he contrived to make her aware of nothing but him. Her senses reeled! Blast and drat the man! Why would he grimace with distaste one day and behave like this today? She felt lost and confused, and not merely because they were having little success in locating Lady Millsham.

'Pity we cannot take the canal to Marlborough,' Mr Talbot said blandly. 'We parted with it at Devizes, I believe. It was a very agreeable passage, if one does not mind the odor from produce. Did you not find it agreeable, Miss Fairchild?'

Clare stifled a gasp as she darted a glance at him before she could stop herself. How dare the man refer to that trip! And the effrontery to ask her if she found it agreeable, of all things. Those green eyes were dark and lively, denying the innocuous tone of his voice. That she had discovered she cared far more than she ought to for this odious man during the excursion on the little boat she would never confess to him.

Twice he had kissed her, made her heart nearly take flight within. But she could not forget his grim visage that second time. She would force no man to marry her, nor compel him to follow the silly dictates of Society when it scarcely seemed necessary. She would recover. It took some effort to return his wicked smile with a frosty one of her own, but she thought her attempt went creditably well.

130

'We are slowing down, Miss Fairchild. Do you suppose we are to be free of this bone-rattling coach for a while?' That mocking brow slanted, as though he knew how well he was getting beneath her guard, riling her interior.

Her coach was the latest design, with the finest spring mechanism to be found. Clare smiled sweetly and replied, 'Yes. One's bones can be so easily rattled, it seems.' Then she wondered what she had said to make him grin.

She turned to view the outskirts of Marlborough. The Castle Inn lay on the east edge of the town. They ought to enter the inn yard within minutes, if memory served her correctly. A horseman galloped up toward their coach, obviously intending to beat them into town.

'Look out!' Richard pushed Clare over to the seat, knocking the breath from her. Her face pressed against his chest; his body covered hers with distressing familiarity.

At that precise moment, a shot rang out once again. Only this time Clare's bonnet remained intact. Her heart thudded with horror as she realized a bullet now lay embedded in the cushion behind Mr Talbot. His splendid coat began to turn a dark red where his arm had been grazed. Had she remained upright, who knows if her bonnet or her head would have the hole!

Priddy quietly swooned away, sliding to an ungraceful heap on the opposite side.

The nick in Richard's arm stung a bit, but otherwise was of no great concern to him. Clare was. He ignored the slowly spreading stain to chance his stake in his future.

'You might have been hit. I shall claim my award, I think, for saving your life.' Ignoring her faint protest, he gathered her a bit awkwardly in his arms, then proceeded to kiss her with every ounce of his expertise.

It lasted but briefly, for once Tom Coachman got the horses under control he slowed the coach to a stop. Richard lifted his head to order him on to the Castle Inn, then returned his attention to Clare.

She pulled back, aware of far too many things – his wounded arm, her insensible maid, propriety, not to mention her questions about this man and his intentions toward her.

'Oh, no, my dear Clare. No retreat. I have waited for just this opportunity.' He gave her no chance to escape, for indeed, he had captured her beneath him, pinned her down with his body. He was acutely aware of every little squirm and wiggle she made, the softening of her resistance. He felt so certain she had welcomed his previous advances. Surely she knew the importance of his taking her to meet his mother? Waiting not another second, he claimed his lady.

With this kiss Clare felt the struggle within her failing. His lips cast a wondrous spell on her. Her arms crept up to slide about his muscular form. Only the need for a breath of air drove them apart. She opened her eyes, feeling languorous, confused, a glowing riot of sensation flowing through her body.

'It is as I thought,' he murmured. 'I knew I could not have imagined your response. Whatever maggoty notion you have acquired in your head we shall deal with once this venture is over.'

The world returned with Priddy's moan and the slowing of the coach. Clare eased herself up as Richard withdrew. The blistering words she intended to hurl died as she took note of the way he compressed his lips and the slight pallor detected on his tanned skin.

She resisted the desire to soothe him, rather she braced herself for the jolt as the carriage left the main road. Priddy took some comforting and reassurance that her mistress was in one piece. A look at Mr Talbot's arm nearly sent her into a second swoon. Only a bolstering word from Clare kept Priddy alert.

When at last they drew to a halt, Clare fearlessly met that clever gaze, refusing to blush. 'Lord Talbot, you'd best have your wound attended to, while I explore the kitchen. Priddy, perhaps you may learn something from the maids.' Clare refused to give the man mercy, for he looked capable of dealing with his predicament on his own, with his man for assistance. As well, she knew she dared not touch him again. It had shaken her to discover her feelings for him were stronger than ever. She might appear heartless, but it was better than making a fool of herself over the man.

Priddy clucked her tongue as the trio marched into the inn, Lord Talbot clutching a handkerchief to his arm. She observed the landlord's shocked attentions to the gentleman while she grumbled along behind Clare.

It was most clear Priddy thought the entire expedition to be harebrained and rackety, doubly so with the shot. Even though she was fond of the baby, she maintained the parents knew where he was and could get him if they wished. They quite obviously did not wish, and Miss Clare ought to find someone else to take the lad. It was not her responsibility. Two ruined bonnets was as nothing compared to a ruined heart, and Priddy was not half so blind as Clare assumed.

Clare fixed Lord Talbot with a stern eye, admonished him to take care of himself, then headed to the rear of the inn. Glancing back, she caught sight of the men making their way to a private parlor, where Lord Talbot could strip off his coat and have that graze attended to properly.

She felt guilty, although she probably would not have been allowed near him. She found it necessary to create barriers between herself and Lord Talbot, to the point of thinking of him as Lord Talbot, not Richard. His Christian name seemed too intimate to use, even in her mind. Since it appeared that there was no hope for her with the man, she had best make the distance grow, not lesson. What those kisses meant, she hesitated to guess, but from the wicked gleam in his eyes, she suspected it was not matrimony. She could not stoop to being any man's mistress.

'Priddy, nose about as best you can, corner a maid if possible. I shall do what I can.'

Within short order, Clare located the cook that Jenny had talked about. A step into the vast kitchens of the inn revealed them to be somewhat quiet now that it was between mealtimes. Not that they weren't required to fix a bite to eat on a moment's notice, mind you. Clare suspected that were she to poke her nose in here around the hour of dinner, she would find a far noisier place.

The woman wore a polite, but off-putting, expression Clare found rather daunting. Summoning her best lady-of-the-house expression, she moved into the center of the room.

'Do you recall an old woman who stopped here not long ago? You gave her a cup of tea, I believe. Jenny said her name was Mrs Dow,' Clare prompted. She noted with a sinking heart that the cook gave no sign of recognition. 'Jenny said she dressed like a nanny in blue with a white apron and white cap.' As she gave the description, Clare realized how hopelessly common it seemed. There must be any number of women similarly garbed. Then Clare had an inspiration.

'You see, she performed a great service to me, and I wish to reward her for it. It seems a shame she not be remembered, for I feel certain she has need of a bit of money.'

A flicker of something Clare could not identify crossed the cook's face. 'A reward, you say? Aye, like as not she could use a bit of help, that one. She hung around here fer several days afore you came, now that you mention it. Always clean and polite, she be. Wouldna' tell me what it was she looked for. So it was you? Right nice of you to remember her. Not all the gentry pays any attention to what's done fer 'em. But I never asked where she came from. It don't pay, you see. Would she wished me to know, she'd have told me.'

'I see,' Clare murmured.

A maid scurried in for a basin of water to wash the gentleman's wound. Clare noted its cleanliness and approved the soft, spotlessly clean cloths the maid snatched up before rushing away.

Rejecting the image of Lord Talbot having his bare arm cleaned and treated, she forced herself to admit she had found a blank wall. She requested a cup of tea for herself and her maid, then chatted a little longer, hoping to draw the cook out on the matter of Mrs Dow. Finally, thanking the cook for her time, Clare slowly made her way back to where Priddy waited outside in the inn's garden, followed by a maid with the tea and cake.

'I see you didn't learn much more than I did, Miss Clare,' Priddy said sourly. She poured the tea and waited for her mistress to help herself to a piece of seed cake.

'Let me assure you, I have not given up as yet,' Clare admonished. She sank down on the stone bench, feeling dejected, yet not totally defeated. She sipped at the hot, restoring tea, ignoring the cake.

'I have great doubts, ma'am,' Priddy said, her voice revealing every bit of it. 'Oh, Lord Talbot got fixed up right fast. Did you speak with him to see if he discovered anything from the landlord? I saw him leave the inn to go down to the stables. I suspect he and Tom Coachman are there even now, chatting away with the stable hands.'

'I would like to listen in to what is said.' Clare drained the last of the tea, then set the cup back. 'I fancy he wishes to ask Tom about the rider who shot at the coach. I thought at first it must be a mistake. Why would anyone wish to shoot at me now? Unless, perhaps, to warn me away. I vow, it makes me all the more curious,' Clare said, twisting her hands in her lap as she considered possible ramifications of the deed.

Refusing to let her thoughts dwell on Lord Talbot, she impatiently popped up from her seat next to Priddy to pace back and forth along the narrow paths.

'That poor baby,' she said to urge her thoughts along a different direction. 'What agony his mama must endure to be without him.'

'Do you think she knows that young Jenny has the care of him now?' Priddy filched a second piece of uncommonly good cake. Her nerves needed shoring up.

Clare paused in her perambulations to stare at Priddy. 'If that old woman was a nanny, it would stand to reason that she would be with the mama, and that where one is the other is as well. And . . . I strongly suspect that they are not far from here, for I doubt the elderly nanny would travel very far. Come, let us go inside to see if the landlord has a good map of this area.' She bustled off to the inn, finding their host in the cool interior.

Priddy brushed the crumbs off her hands, then her lap, loath to leave the rest of the tea behind. Her reluctant but faithful feet followed Clare into the inn.

Her request brought forth a much creased and worn copy of a fairly recent map, which she took along to the private parlor where Lord Talbot had been treated.

'There are vast forests to the south and east, and the downs to the north look scarcely encouraging. I believe they are somewhere along the main road. My instincts tell me they are in a town between here and Bath.'

'Very clever, Miss Fairchild. I suggest you always follow your instincts. I recall you said they rarely let you down.' Lord Talbot peered over her shoulder at the map, reaching out to trace their route. 'I wonder where we ought to begin?' His jacket revealed a slight bulge where the bandage wrapped about his arm, but other than that, there was not evidence that he was in great pain or distress.

'At the beginning, I fancy.' Clare just barely kept her tongue from stammering at his sudden appearance. 'That is, Manton, Fyfield, West Overton, and East Kennet for starters. They are but villages, so it ought not take overlong on our trip back to Bath. You know how it is in a small place; everyone knows everyone else, and a stranger sticks out a mile.' She glanced up to see his reaction to her suggestion. She sensed it far better to ignore his wound and check her desire to pamper him. If he seemed certain of himself now, what would he be like were she to fawn and fuss over him?

'Very astute.'

Clare turned away from that penetrating gaze, not to mention the lazy grin. He seemed to see far too much, and she had much to conceal. 'I somehow doubt she would hide herself in Devizes. There is too great a chance for her to be spotted by someone who knows her. And besides Devizes is a good many miles away. No, I feel sure she is close by.' A rising excitement grew within Clare, a sense that they were drawing close to their aim.

'You did not ask what I learned.'

'Nor did you, sir,' she retorted tartly.

'I suspect you found out little from the cook. The men in the stables were able to tell me that the old woman appeared here several days before you arrived. They have not seen her since.'

'I am aware of that,' she stated primly.

He cleared his throat, then continued. 'The day the babe was left in your coach, she caught a ride in a wagon. The groom heard her ask if she might be put down at West Overton.'

'I told you West Overton might be a likely place,' Clare said, unable to resist inserting that little barb.

'Miss Fairchild, may I say you have developed a most distressing tendency to interrupt. If I am to lead this expedition, I wish a bit of respect.'

Had it not been for the hint of laughter in his voice, Clare would have picked up the pitcher of ale from the large oak table and poured it slowly over his head. Rather, she sniffed, ignoring the scandalized stare from Priddy. 'As you wish, sir.' Her meek reply obviously surprised him, and she was delighted she had been able to throw him off balance at least once. He did the same to her all the time.

'When do we leave?' She wanted to find Lady Millsham and return to Bath to assume a quiet life again, away from this provoking man.

'Following the light repast the landlord agreed to bring us, the coach will be waiting and we may be off.'

Knowing it was a mark of respect for the landlord to wait upon anyone in such a large and well-known inn, Clare subsided onto a Windsor chair to anticipate their meal. She said nothing while the hot food was set down, but took the opportunity to give Lord Talbot a cool look for daring to make arrangements without consulting her. But then, Lord Talbot dared a great deal.

Richard studied the subdued young woman across the table from him. She had invited her maid to join them, something that startled Richard, thinking Clare would prefer to be alone with him. Well, it ought to serve to put him firmly in his place, wherever that might be.

What had happened to the promising relationship was beyond him to figure out. She changed so suddenly that his head had reeled with the unexpected impact of it. One moment they were comfortably settling in to a loving intimacy that he fully expected would lead to the altar, when the next she froze up on him like a pond on a winter's night. His most recent attempt to reestablish a better relationship looked promising, but she still retreated when he neared. It was like hunting a particularly clever fox.

For the moment, he intended to bide his time. He would watch and wait until he deemed the moment right to approach her again, and he would not do the thing gently or meekly. Oh, no. He quite proposed another style altogether. Quite. He smiled at her, hoping to touch her confused heart, for it stood to reason that she be mixed-up. The elegant, cool, and exceedingly proper Miss Fairchild seemed to him to be acting like any lovesick girl unsure of her direction. He hoped. That he had shamelessly taken advantage of the shot bothered him not at all. He had found what he hoped, that Clare cared for him. Now to find out what else was bothering her.

'I suggest we drive over to Manton, even though it is a bit off the main road, to see if there is any chance our lady might be there,' Clare offered between bites of an excellent pigeon pie.

'What makes you think she has made her name known?'

Clare's fork paused in midair while she considered his statement. 'Well then, 'tis a good thing I have seen her before, is it not?' She popped the last morsel of pie into her mouth, and once it was safely in her stomach, patted her mouth, then prepared to depart.

In spite of her genteel protests, softly spoken in an undertone, Richard settled their accounts with the landlord, then ushered her out of the door with an efficiency Clare had to admire, albeit reluctantly.

Once settled in the coach again, her gaze fixed on a distant point out of the window, Clare concluded, 'I desire to cover my share of the expenses, sir. 'Tis not proper for you to do so, especially when you have suffered an injury on top of it all, and in my defense.'

When he took her beautifully gloved hand in his to study the slender fingers encased in finest leather, Clare's gaze jumped to meet his. She tugged at her hand to no avail.

'When you speak to me, I would see those lovely eyes, my dear Clare.' He held his breath, aware he had overstepped the boundary she had established.

She dropped those long golden lashes with a hint of smoke tipping the ends before raising them to reveal penitent eyes. 'Forgive me. My manners are sadly lacking. I shall blame it on the hectic pace of the past week or so, if I may?'

He flashed her a derisive look, but released her hand, for she had apologized so handsomely he could do no less.

In Manton they found no evidence of a stranger in the area. Clare admitted it might be best for Lord Talbot to investigate the tavern while she prowled a bit in the village shop. It was a curious place, a repository for everything from bread, shoes, and tea, to cheese, ribands, and bacon. There was a pleasant smell of spice and other intriguing aromas in the air. She suspected that little went on in the vicinity that missed the eyes and ears of the proprietress.

'Nothing?' Lord Talbot inquired as he joined Clare in the coach.

'Not a clue,' she replied, offering him a small paper twist of comfits she had decided to purchase as her excuse for venturing into the shop.

Fyfield offered no better fare, though slightly larger in size. The Bell Inn proved a substantial place, clean and neat, with fresh muslin curtains at the windows and excellent home-brewed ale. Lord Talbot partook of the latter, while Clare enjoyed another of her comfits and wondered if the day was degenerating into a total loss.

West Overton was by far the largest of the villages between Marlborough and Devizes. The coach jounced and jostled over the cobbled streets to the inn at the center of the town. As before, Clare went to the village shop, while Lord Talbot took himself off to the Rose and Crown.

'A true gentleman,' Priddy said as she admired his stride across the road and along the far side.

'Come, we have better to do than admire such as him,' chided Clare, refusing to admit she found the sight appealing.

If Priddy knew how far from a perfect gentleman Lord Talbot truly was, she would be shocked to the core of her spinster heart. Clare paused before entering the shop, wondering if that was what ailed her – a spinster heart, whatever that might be. Then she doubted if the longings and aches she endured differed greatly from those of any other young woman and went inside. Within a brief time, she returned to the coach and Lord Talbot.

'I believe we have found her. A young woman answering to the description I gave the shopkeeper lives not far from here. If we go left at the next lane and five houses down, we shall find a pretty cottage with foxglove and daisies to either side of the door. That is where she will be.' Clare faced Lord Talbot with a triumphant expression, not displeased to report success before he could say a word.

'Shall I tell you what I discovered or keep it to myself, I wonder,' Richard replied.

'Come, let us not waste a moment. You may explain as we go.

She bustled him off along the street to the next corner, then marched him along to the fifth house, where a lovely little garden bloomed just as promised.

Along the way, Richard rapidly told that he had found similar news, of a young woman come to live with her old friend and the sad news of the loss of her baby. Although one old fellow said it was a blessing, seeing as how the two women scarcely had two pennies to rub together.

'I hope we are in time to offer some relief,' Clare said, frowning at the thought of Lady Millsham in abject poverty.

The cottage might be tiny, but it proved to be spotlessly clean. The white-haired woman who answered the knock at the door studied the three before her with shrewd eyes. 'Come in. Come in. People to see you, my lady.'

The elderly nurse turned to face a door at the far end of the little room. A rustle of muslin accompanied a young woman into the room, her look of dismay revealing a great deal to those who watched.

'Mrs Dow, I asked you not . . .' Her voice faded away to

nothing as she halted after she discovered the identity of those who had come. 'Oh, dear.' She bowed her head and burst into a flood of tears, murmuring something to the effect that all was lost and her efforts for naught. Some moments passed before Mrs Dow soothed her into a chair.

The nurse gestured to the guests to seat themselves while Lady Millsham composed herself, her hands twisting the damp handkerchief she had used to blot her tears.

'Jane, Lady Millsham, that is, we are come to fetch you to join your son. He is safe for the moment, but I fear for him. He needs you. We think it best if you come with us to where he is in Bath.'

Lady Millsham fainted dead away.

CHAPTER ELEVEN

'Lord-a mercy!' exclaimed Mrs Dow, her several chins all quivering with horror. She wrung her hands anxiously as Clare rushed to Lady Millsham's side.

'Water,' Clare demanded while chafing the young woman's wrists. She inwardly scolded herself for revealing her own fears so abruptly. How foolish to frighten a girl who must be already terrified, if Clare's conjectures were correct.

'I believe this will be more the thing,' Lord Talbot said as he held a small glass of cordial, all that Mrs Dow had to offer in the way of restoratives.

Impatiently taking the glass, Clare held it up to Lady Millsham's lips, pleased when the young woman sputtered and opened her eyes once again.

'Oh, I am so sorry,' Lady Millsham murmured. 'I had so hoped that if I hid and provided a place for William, all would be well. I thought the new earl would take himself off to London or the Continent, and I would be safe.'

'I see,' Clare said, glancing at Lord Talbot, her eyes steady and worried. 'Suppose you sit over here in this comfortable chair and explain how this situation came to be.' She helped Lady Millsham to a small armchair, easing her down, then insisted she finish the cordial before attempting to relate her tale.

Richard sipped the glass of cordial he had poured for himself, retreating to the background and watching the women's faces.

'Sometime after I married,' Lady Millsham began, 'my husband's cousin came to pay us a visit. On the surface he seemed a nice enough person. But as time passed, I noticed little things about him, unpleasant things that I won't bore you with, but that gave me reason to believe he was someone I wished far away. My husband laughed at my fanciful notions.'

She stared out of the window of the tiny room, as though seeing once again the vast acres of Millsham Hall, the rooms where she had lived so briefly. A shaft of sunlight caressed her face, revealing the grief that had etched itself around her eyes. She dropped her gaze to her lap, studying her folded hands.

'I thought his cousin became overly friendly with several of the grooms, yet my husband considered my fears nonsense. And then one day they went out riding. The weather was excellent, the horse my husband's favorite. There was no reason for the accident. I strongly suspect the gear was tampered with in some manner. I was never allowed to see the saddle or anything to do with the horse. It was considered far too upsetting for a new widow. Only later did I come to suspect foul play. When I eventually made my way to the stables, the saddle and gear had disappeared. I thought that exceedingly odd.'

'Is that why you fled Millsham Hall? That you feared the new earl would do away with you as well?' Clare perched on the edge of a small chair close to Lady Millsham's side.

'I was breeding at the time of my husband's death. At first I expected to live at the Dower House. Then the earl became far too interested in me and my condition. Oh, he did not know for certain, mind you. I imagine he wished to make sure that there would be no issue to threaten his position. Perhaps I was fanciful again, but my suspicions forced me to find another residence. The only person I dared to trust was my old nurse, Mrs Dow. I feared the housekeeper and the other servants had all transferred their allegiance to the new earl.'

'And you had the baby here?'

'Aye,' Mrs Dow said in a final tone, more herself now her darling girl seemed restored. 'A fine healthy boy, he was and is, I trust?' Her fears for the baby were relieved by Clare's smile and nod.

'William is still healthy and growing fast.' Clare wondered how she might persuade Lady Millsham to come with them to Bath.

'He is a good baby? It near broke my heart to part with him. I had felt I was safe here. Then I saw one of the grooms nosing about the village. Recalling how he had seemed to be under the new earl's influence, I hid away, not taking the baby out at all. I feared it but a matter of time when someone would discover us. I thought and thought about what to do.' She took a deep breath and glanced at Mrs Dow, as though seeking strength.

'That was when I conceived the idea of placing him with someone I could trust. When Mrs Dow told of seeing you at the Castle Inn, I felt it was my chance to keep William safe. I remembered that you have numerous nieces and nephews, and heard that you spoke of them in a loving way. We had been planning this for some time, you see, waiting for the right moment, the proper person.'

'You must have been quite terrified,' Clare said in a soothing voice, noting absently that Lord Talbot had maintained a peculiar silence all the while. She glanced his way, seeing only that his color seemed off, that he sat rather rigidly in his chair. Turning back to Lady Millsham, she urged her to continue.

'You see, if the earl did come here, he would find me alone, but for Mrs Dow. I could say that I found the Dower House too drafty, or dark, or not to my liking, and that I far preferred the quiet life of the village. He could not really argue with that. Once he was satisfied that there appeared to be no child, he would leave me alone.'

'But, my lady,' Lord Talbot said, speaking for the first time, 'your son is the new seventh earl. It is wrong for this impostor to take his place.'

'I do not care a fig for "place." If William were acclaimed the new earl, I suspect he would not live long. I prefer a live son to a dead earl, sir.' Her spirited words brought a nod of approval from both Clare and Lord Talbot.

'I hesitate to frighten you further, but the Earl of Millsham is in Bath at the moment. And someone tried to take William from Jenny – she's the wet nurse, as I suspect you may know – while she walked with him in the Sidney Gardens. Thanks to Lord Talbot, the attempt failed. I had ordered a groom to be with Jenny whenever she left the house, but this was countermanded while I was off to see your mother.' Clare reached out to cover Lady Millsham's trembling hands with her own.

'How did you know who was involved?'

So Clare explained the series of events that had brought them to the cottage in West Overton, severely editing the account. The visit with Lady Knowlton, the attacks on Clare, as well as the subsequently ruined bonnets, and the conversation with Mrs Caswell were either omitted or sharply abbreviated. The moments spent in Richard Talbot's arms Clare tried not to think about.

'I beg you to pack your things and come with us to Bath. The time has come for you to be with your son. If the Earl of Millsham harbors some fool notions about doing away with little William, the more of us around the baby, the better. Please, come with us?'

Lady Millsham exchanged a long look with Mrs Dow, then nodded. 'I shall come with you. I can see that leaving him alone will not do. Indeed, my heart leaps with gladness at the very thought of seeing his dear face once again.' She rose from the little chair, taking Clare's hand as she, too, rose. 'I shall pack and be prepared to depart whenever you say.'

They made arrangements to return in two hours, then Clare joined Lord Talbot on a slow walk back to where Priddy and the others waited for them at the Rose and Crown.

As they strolled along, Clare grew increasingly uneasy about the man at her side. He seemed far too silent, and each word appeared to be reluctantly dragged forth from him as though he were in. . . .

'Are you in pain, Lord Talbot?'

'No.' He winced when he stumbled on the uneven cobbles.

The Rose and Crown lay directly across the street, none too close in Clare's estimation. She guided him across the threshold of the inn, noting as she did that he looked shockingly pale and a trifle unsteady, as though that tiny glass of cordial had put him in his cups. Firming her lips, she gently pushed him toward a chair, then nudged him down in spite of Priddy's disapproving glare.

A brief conversation with the landlord, and she returned to Lord Talbot's side bringing his man, Timms, along with her. Between them, with Priddy clucking away in the background, they managed to get the protesting man into a private parlor where Clare urged him onto a stout chair.

'Take off his coat,' she ordered the apprehensive Timms. 'Clare,' began Lord Talbot, totally ignoring the propriety she had insisted upon.

'Never you mind, sir. I have a suspicion you suffered more from that simple graze, as you called it, than you are willing to admit.' She stood glaring down at him, her arms akimbo while she watched the disrobing.

At his wince when Timms removed the coat from his injured arm, Clare pounced. 'Aha! Now I shall see for myself just how much you endured when you knocked me aside to take the bullet intended for my bonnet.'

Timms decided it was impossible to pull the shirt over Richard's head, the pain would be too much and needlessly. He accepted the small embroidery scissors that Priddy took from her case to cut the sleeve from the shirt. Ignoring Richard's dark look, he pulled the sleeve off, dropping it to the floor.

Clare removed the bandage from Richard's arm, inhaling sharply as she saw the angry look of the wound. It festered and looked raw. What ought to have been a simple scratch had become far worse.

Turning to Timms and Priddy, she gave a number of softly spoken orders, then faced her nemesis. 'We are not traveling back to Bath today, I fear. To do so would jeopardize your health.'

Richard bestowed a narrow look on her. 'What about the baby?'

'Yes, well, perhaps I can think of something. You, sir, are

getting into bed.' Her no-nonsense attitude seemed to amuse him until she touched his arm, just below the wound. He sucked in his breath, closing his eyes.

'Ah, you grit your teeth, close your eyes, and tell me you feel no pain?' She accepted a bowl of water from Priddy, then with a clean cloth proceeded to wipe his wound again. By the time she finished her ministrations, beads of sweat stood out on his forehead. She liberally dosed the area with basilicum powder, then proceeded to cover the wound with clean gauze. Fastening the new bandage, she motioned to a grim-faced Timms.

'I shall help you take him to the next room. It is clear to me he needs bed and sleep more than anything else.'

Richard shook his head. 'We need to go.' He tried to rise and found he was clearly outvoted in his efforts. Before he knew what was happening, he found himself sitting on the edge of a high four-poster with a dragon who resembled Clare Fairchild standing over him holding a bottle of evil-looking stuff.

'Just a spoon and you shall feel much better, sir,' the dragon coaxed.

With Timms, Priddy, and Clare Fairchild all standing over him, and feeling the very devil, Richard did the only thing he could. He swallowed the wretched liquid and shuddered even as he allowed Timms to remove his boots.

In spite of the way she had treated him, he was sorry to see the back of Miss Fairchild as she blushingly hurried from his room.

Back in the parlor, Clare whirled about to face Priddy, hands clasped in distress. 'I shan't allow him to get into a coach to be jolted home this evening, and I doubt if he will be much better come morning. There must be another way we can solve this dilemma. It is imperative that Lady Millsham get to Bath as soon as can be. And yet I fear Lord Talbot needs a night's rest before continuing. All this jostling about has done him ill. Poor man.' That Clare felt horridly guilty was not said.

'That is true, Miss Clare. What will you tell Lady Millsham

when she expects to be collected?'

Clare cogitated on this all through a light repast brought by an inquisitive servant. Once Clare finished, she popped up to roam about the room, casting worried glances at the bedroom where silence reigned. Timms had reported that his master fell asleep, and that all was quiet.

Pausing in her anxious perambulations about the room, she placed her hand to her face, rubbed her chin a bit, then turned to her maid, a determined look Priddy knew settling on her countenance.

'You will drive in the coach when it goes to pick up Lady Millsham. Have Tom Coachman place her trunks in the boot, and then you all go to Bath. Anyone who might be watching the house in Bath will see you with someone who appears to be me! Give her my shawl to wear, perhaps a bonnet? You will explain as little as necessary to Miss Godwin. Then you come back tomorrow for me. It is so simple, I cannot think why it did not occur to me immediately.' Clare clapped her hands together, delighted with her plan.

'But Miss Fairchild,' objected Priddy, ' 'tis most improper. ' Her starched back grew even straighter at the thought of more scandal attached to her mistress.

'Priddy, the man saved my life. This is the least I can do for him.'

Reflecting that her mistress was correct, and that she would undoubtedly do as she pleased in the matter anyway, Priddy nodded, then walked from the room in a huff to inform Tom Coachman of the change.

Sometime later Clare stood by the window, watching her coach as it rumbled off in the direction of the cottage where Lady Millsham waited. She had sent a message to Tom Coachman to hire two outriders and an extra groom for the trip. Her fears for the young Jane, Countess of Millsham, were great.

Now that her fears were confirmed, Clare felt the danger for all of them far more than originally believed. It seemed to her that only a madman could conceive such a dastardly and murderous plan.

Leaving the window, she crossed to open the bedroom door. Her patient was fitful, shifting about, restlessly moving his head. Swiftly going to his side, she placed her hand on his brow. It was warm, but not exceedingly hot. Thankful for small mercies, she took a cloth from a basin of water, wrung it out, then began to wipe his forehead. Not satisfied, she found a bottle of lavender water in her case, and emptied a portion of it into the basin. Then she resumed her task, all the while studying the dear, exasperating face of the man she cared for too much.

How ironic. She had turned down countless offers of marriage with highly eligible young men, men who had only been allowed to hold her hand. Richard Talbot had kissed and caressed her nearly senseless, taken a shot intended for her, but he had not asked her to marry him. Indeed, he had looked rather grim confronted with the very thought.

Yet she felt impelled to be with him. She well knew she might have gone with Lady Millsham and Priddy, leaving Timms alone to care for his master. She couldn't.

'How is he?' Timms whispered at her shoulder.

'Not as bad as I first feared. How stupid of him to pretend he was scarcely hurt. See what it got him?'

'And you, Miss Fairchild? It would have been better had you gone with the coach, I think.'

Clare gave a rather inelegant sniff and grinned at Timms. 'I can scarce believe my reputation could be worsened. It is considered vulgar for a young unmarried woman to go dashing off to a rescue, you know. To go dashing off on anything, for that matter. I daresay I shall manage to cope. If Lord Talbot survives this, he will undoubtedly wish himself back in Jamaica where the ladies are most likely a languid lot and not given to mad starts.'

She turned her attention back to Richard, bathing his forehead with the lavender water in an effort to reduce his fever. Sometime later, she removed his bandage again, noting with dismay that the seepage did not look good.

'Best send for the apothecary. The remedies I carry with me are not good enough.'

'I'll have no quack tending me,' came a low murmur from the bed behind her.

Clare spun about to see two heavy-lidded eyes fixed on her. Though barely conscious, he had willed himself to say that much.

'And what do you know about it, sir? We shall see what he says.'

It turned out that except for cupping Richard, the apothecary had little to offer Lord Talbot other than what Clare had already done for him. She paid the man, then returned to the bedside, thinking herself a fool at the very least.

Yet she refused to cease in her efforts. If keeping the wound cleansed and dosed with basilicum powder offered the best hope, that is what she would do. And she would try not to dwell on the ramifications of her nursing.

There was little doubt as to what this mad affair would do to her name. And she would say nothing about it to Richard, nor would she allow him to offer himself on the altar of propriety. Stuff and nonsense. Her eldest brother was unlikely to force the issue, being far up north and more involved with raising sheep and other interesting things. The rest of the family had long since learned to permit Clare her way and would not interfere. However, she could count on her sister, Sarah, giving her a harbor should she want it. And that offered much comfort at the moment.

Yet she owed this man her life, and she did not take such a debt lightly. She wrung out the cloth again to bathe his forehead.

Mr Timms lit the oil lamp, placing it on the table not far from her side. He met Clare's intrepid gaze with a lift of the eyebrow.

'Go get something to eat,' she urged. 'I suspect you will need to spell me later on.'

Seeing the wisdom of this, Timms nodded, then quickly left for the common room.

'You ought not be here,' Richard murmured, finding himself able to speak once again. The wound in his arm was not nearly as bad as Clare made it out to be. Yet he had allowed himself to be cosseted and fussed over like a babe. Why? He studied her face as she hovered over him, the tip of her tongue showing as she concentrated on wiping his brow. She was such an appealing armful, and he ached to hold her, though he knew full well he dare not make a move.

'This is where I must be. You are a foolish man. Do you know how even a simple scratch can poison the blood? It is nothing to be taken lightly, I assure you. Once that begins, there is nothing to be done for you.'

Richard knew she was right; he had seen a man die from a mere broken blister that got infected. When those red lines had run up his leg, it had not been long before he was gone aloft.

'I purchased more basilicum powder, for my supply was low. I confess I do not understand why it is effective, but it does seem to help,' she said in an effort to comfort him.

There was a knock on the door. Clare crossed to see who it was. Mrs Dow entered the room, carrying something wrapped in snowy linen.

'Once I knew what was the trouble, I set about finding a remedy to help this brave man, here.' Mrs Dow took a step closer to the bed. 'We need all the heroes we can find.' Boldly she pulled the bandage from his wound, shaking her head in obvious consternation at the sight she found. 'With your permission, I shall put on my best remedy, Miss Fairchild.'

Clare noticed the annoyed look on Richard's face and hid her momentary amusement. 'Please, if you have something that is beneficial, we ought to try it.' She hated and feared the angry redness that surrounded the spot where the bullet had grazed Richard's arm.

Unfolding the linen cloth, Mrs Dow removed what appeared to be a very moldy piece of bread. Clare frowned, thinking this a strange manner of healing anything. She watched as the old nurse gently placed it over the wound, then lightly bound it to the arm.

'You shall see, sir. Tomorrow your arm will be looking far better. Mark my words.' Then she turned to Clare. 'And as for you, missy, you best get to the other room, for this man needs some sleep, and you look as though you could do with a meal.'

Instead of arguing, Clare meekly went to the private parlor. Here she found Timms waiting to serve her a simple but nourishing supper. She ate automatically, her mind in the other room, wondering how that bread could induce a cure. Yet she knew that often the old nurses knew of medicines that doctors refused to consider, condemning them as old-fashioned.

Reluctant to venture far from the inn to stay in Mrs Dow's neat cottage, Clare allowed herself to be persuaded to sleep in a bedroom down the hall while Timms and the authoritative Mrs Dow ruled the sickroom for the night.

Come morning, Clare found all her problems returned. As she pushed herself up to lean against the headboard, she sorted out the worst of them. Venetia would undoubtedly make a great fuss, for one reason or another. Yet Clare felt sorry for the woman, and hesitated to ask her to leave.

As far as Lady Millsham went, her presence brought danger to the household and Clare, yet it was unthinkable to send her elsewhere. Clare would find a solution. Or perhaps Richard, that is Lord Talbot, could think of a clever resolution to the threat imposed by the new Earl of Millsham, impostor though he be.

It did no good to dwell on the matter of Lord Talbot. Once he realized that Clare had no intention of forcing him into the parson's mousetrap, he would take himself back to Jamaica and she could forget him. And then, the sun, moon, and stars might stop their path in the sky, and the world stop spinning as well. She sighed, then put her unpleasant thoughts aside to rise and prepare for the day ahead. Goodness only knew what it might bring.

Returning to the private parlor in her crumpled dress of yesterday, she found Timms bringing in a basin of steaming water with clean towels draped over his arm. 'He wants a shave, which I consider a good sign, miss.'

The dark shadow that had covered Lord Talbot's lower face had intrigued Clare last night. All the men she had observed were clean-shaven, and she suspected they tended to the task often if dark-haired. Knowing she would never be allowed to view the process, she merely nodded and murmured approving words.

Mrs Dow entered the parlor, closing the door behind Timms with a decided snap.

'How is he this morning?' Clare inquired with a breathless voice.

'Much better, Miss Fairchild. Now sit you down while I see to a good breakfast for you. None of this toast and tea for you this morning.'

Guessing that Lady Millsham had requested such fare and failed, Clare merely smiled and nodded, watching the good woman bustle from the room.

Following a small bowl of porridge, Clare surveyed a plate of buttered eggs, several rashers of bacon, and a pile of toast. A pot of marmalade sat on the table to tempt her.

Timms came out of the bedroom wearing a harassed expression, rolled his eyes, then hurried out the door without saying a word.

Chewing her toast consideringly after succumbing to the lure of the marmalade, Clare wondered what prompted that peculiar look on Timms's poor face. Moments later she found out, when the bedroom door flew open.

'Well! I believed you to be in bed, sir,' Clare said, rising from her chair in protest. The man before her stood dressed with care, and no sign of the shadow of a beard remained. His coat had been brushed and pantaloons restored to their usual state of perfection. She felt a dowdy by comparison.

He ambled across the room to stand at her side. 'Feel my forehead if you please. Please note there is no fever. That obnoxious application Mrs Dow put on my wound appears to have done the trick. The redness is gone, or so they tell me, and healing seems to have set in. Are you content? Or would it have been better had I popped off?'

Unable to stop herself, Clare put a hesitant hand to his forehead to see if he told the truth. He did.

'What utter rubbish you speak, sir. As if I could wish the

hero of the hour to his grave. Have you eaten anything?' she said, hoping to ease the sudden tension that had sprung up between them. They were alone in the room, and she was too conscious of his proximity for her liking. She sank down onto her chair with surprisingly weak knees.

'Timms is to bring me a tray.' Lord Talbot pulled up a chair to the small table, settled himself, and proceeded to disconcert Clare by staring at her with a very steady gaze. 'When Tom Coachman returns, we shall travel back to Bath and not spare the horses, my dear.'

'I am not your dear,' Clare objected. 'As to the other, I daresay that since you are so much better, we might go, if Mrs Dow gives you leave.'

'That woman shan't forbid me.'

'No? We shall see what she says. I place far more confidence in her than in your spoutings. You have an ulterior motive.'

'And what might that be?' He leaned over the table to fluster her even more with his attentions. His voice contained a dangerous note she ought not disregard.

'Why, to be safe in the Edgar buildings again and away from this hazardous female who brings you nothing but trouble.'

The door flew open to admit Timms bearing a tray of food. Clare watched with astonished eyes to see a plate heaped with a rare steak, veal-and-ham pie, and poached eggs on toast as well as a pot of coffee set before her table companion.

'You do not intend to eat all of that!'

'I do if someone does not keep chattering at me to depress my appetite.' The narrow look he gave her silenced her more than his words. One did not chance that if one was wise.

When Tom Coachman pulled up before the Rose and Crown, he found Timms waiting for him with a number of small parcels in his arms. Informed that his mistress and Lord Talbot would be out directly, the coachman settled back on his bench and grinned that his estimation of the gentleman had proven right. He was a rare one and make no mistake.

CHAPTER TWELVE

'La, Clare, I do not know how you could do such and at this time in particular. I vow I am most vexed. Can you not see the danger of harboring that woman in your house?' Venetia met Clare at the top of the stairs, dressed in a round gown of fine black bombazine trimmed with crimped crape and elegant little roses. Her attempt to look melancholy and annoyed at the same moment failed dismally in Clare's estimation.

'What has happened, Venetia, to upset you so?' Clare said as she reached the landing, then turned to enter her bedroom. 'And why are you wearing black, pray tell?' Clare had found the trip back to Bath fraught with difficulty, the least of which was having to put up with the odious Lord Talbot. The man had allowed the cosseting at the Rose and Crown to go to his head, demanding Clare's constant attendance and care.

'Are you fatigued? I must say, you look terribly pulled.'

'Venetia,' Clare inserted, the tone of her voice revealing just how little of her patience remained.

All at once Venetia crumpled on the little chair before Clare's dressing table. 'My Aunt Peasely died.'

Not quite seeing how this could put Venetia in such a pelter, Clare muttered suitable words of sympathy while she divested herself of her pelisse and bonnet, then sank upon her bed. She wished Venetia would go away so she might throw herself down to vent her feelings as she longed.

'You see,' Venetia confided, 'she was the one relative I counted upon to take me in.'

Somehow chilled at the import of those words, Clare merely nodded, then said in a bracing voice that was far from how she truly felt, 'I trust that if you apply yourself, you might well find a gentleman to wed. You are a lovely woman with many fine attributes that I feel certain would please.'

'Well,' Venetia said, somewhat appeased, 'I confess I have not met a gentleman who indicates a partiality for me. Although I have met one man who rather interests me.' Then she abruptly rose from the chair, just as though she had said more than intended. 'I had best leave you for the moment so you may change from that horridly rumpled gown. Shall I order tea in the drawing room? For I am certain you must be perishing for a good cup of tea by now, what with your journey and all,' making it sound as though Clare had come from the west of Scotland rather than West Overton. 'I fully intend to hear an explanation for all this nonsense about Lady Millsham, you may be certain. Men,' she grumbled as she languidly strolled out the door. 'You might know that the problem rests with them.'

Then pausing in the act of shutting the door, she added, 'Did you not consider that if they had shot at you in the carriage that someone might attack this very house? Really, dear Clare, I had not believed you to be so inconsiderate.' With that sweetly said complaint, she closed the door and Clare was left in blessed silence.

Swiftly crossing to the door, Clare locked it, then hastily pulled her crumpled gown off, dropping it in a heap by the door. Next she removed her underclothes. From her drawer she extracted the clean clothing she wished to wear. She dressed as far as her petticoat, then at last threw herself on the bed, soaking her tears in the largest handkerchief she owned.

Her bout of self-pity did not last long. Never one to indulge in a fit of megrims, she wiped her eyes, then went to her looking glass to see if the damage might be repaired.

'What a peagoose you are, to be sure. Just remember that expression on Lord Talbot's face and you shall be put in your proper place – firmly on the shelf, my girl,' she admonished herself as she stroked a bit of Denmark lotion on her face, then dusted lightly with rice powder. Deciding the ravages of her tears might well be accounted to her fatigue, she selected a simple blue round gown of jaconet with a double ruff of ivory lace. Surveying the results, she pinched her cheeks, brushed her curls, then stuffed her feet into a pair of soft shammy shoes the same blue as her gown.

In the drawing room, she found Venetia standing by the front window watching a carriage that had come to a halt before the house. 'I wonder who that can be?'

'I trust it is someone we may welcome.'

'Lord Talbot? But that man was with you in West Overton. I wonder what he wants now?' Venetia said skeptically. It was evident that Venetia had decided the gentleman might be tolerated, but no more than that.

Clare sank down on the closest chair. If that dratted man said one thing about her looks, or tears, or anything, she would explode.

Bennison ushered Lord Talbot into the drawing room with kindly ceremony. The butler murmured words about tea, then disappeared.

'Are you feeling more the thing, Miss Fairchild?' Lord Talbot strolled over to where Clare took refuge, peering down at her with that knowing gaze of his.

'Quite, sir. And you? I am persuaded you ought to be reposing on a bed, rather than out calling so soon after a trip, even if it was a short one.' Clare gave him a frosty look before gathering up a piece of needlework she had caught sight of tucked along the side of the chair. Pretending a great interest in the state of the work, she ignored her guest until driven by her normally good manners to face him. 'Has Timms checked your wound?'

'Wound?' Venetia cried in alarm. 'Dear Clare, you did not mention an accident. What happened? I cannot fathom what might occur to give Lord Talbot an injury!'

Clare decided she imagined the faint sneer in Venetia's voice. 'I have scarcely had time to do so, Venetia.' Turning back to Lord Talbot, Clare persisted. 'The travel might have done it harm. Did he have a look at it?'

'Your concern does you credit, ma'am. Timms pronounced it progressing nicely. Mrs Dow sent along more of her remedy, so we have it well in hand.'

Venetia had joined the two sitting so quietly by the tea table, supposedly waiting for Bennison to return. 'Are you going to tell me about it, or must I have mild hysterics?'

Clare chuckled, even though she knew it would irritate Venetia. 'As we neared the Castle Inn at Marlborough, a man rode along the coach and took aim, and I fear the bullet most likely intended for me – or my bonnet – grazed Lord Talbot. You see, he realized what the man was about, and pushed me out of harm's way. I am most grateful to him, although I dare-say my milliner would welcome the sale of yet another bonnet. I am not totally persuaded that this is not a ploy by the milliners to gain more business.'

'How can you joke about such a serious matter,' Venetia rebuked in a horrified tone.

'It is either that, dear girl, or join you in mild hysterics, and I doubt I am really quite the sort.' She turned a curious pair of eyes on Lord Talbot, like Venetia, wondering what had brought him here now. It was enough that they had spent hours together in the coach. What could be on his mind? If he thought for one moment that she would continue the cosset-ing, he was mad.

'After Timms changed the dressing and I cleaned up, as I notice you did, I realized that what is needed is a plan.'

Bennison elected that moment to enter, bearing a tray loaded with the required hot beverage, little cakes, and lemon biscuits. He placed it before Clare with all due ceremony, then left.

Clare frowned as she began to pour the cups of steaming Bohea tea. 'A plan? What for, may I inquire?'

Venetia intruded to peer at first one, then the other of the two so absorbed in their quiet conversation. 'I trust it is to do with removing that woman from this house.'

'Venetia, dear, you overstep yourself,' Clare replied in a dangerously serene voice. 'Lady Millsham is a guest of mine, and as such will be accorded all hospitality. I am glad she cannot hear your words. When she feels up to joining us, I hope I shall not hear anything that might displease my ears.' Clare's gentle rebuke was softly spoken, however, she suspected that Venetia well knew that every word bit true.

'Of course,' Venetia muttered, 'I am only concerned about you, dear Clare. Your heart is far too tender.'

'She is all of that, I feel certain,' Lord Talbot added. 'Indeed, you ought to have seen her tending to my wound at the Rose and Crown. Quite the ministering angel.'

Clare blushed while Venetia clucked her tongue at this new evidence of Clare's shocking behavior.

'I do not know what her brother would say to this.'

'And you shan't, either. If one word of all this reaches his ears, I shall know who is responsible.'

Since Venetia had intended to write a lengthy epistle to the man in question, she flushed and bit her lip in vexation.

'Truly, Lord Talbot, I am concerned for your good health,' Clare continued, as though Venetia had not brought up an unpleasant subject. 'You ought to be resting.'

He shook his head to reply, taking a sip from his tea before explaining what he had in mind. 'There must be some way we might lure the person in question to tip his hand, so to speak.'

Noticing how Venetia seemed to be avidly listening to his words, Clare decided to intervene. 'My dear, would you be so kind as to see if Lady Millsham will join us? I am persuaded it would be good for her. You are so clever at coaxing people to your wishes. She must not be allowed to dwell on her misfortunes.'

A look of annoyance was quickly followed by a superior smile. 'Of course I shall. Surely she must have had enough of that baby by now,' Venetia said, then swallowed the last of her tea, taking a lemon biscuit with her before leaving the room.

Clare held up her hand to silence Lord Talbot, then when footsteps on the stairs could be heard, she turned to him. 'Now,' she whispered, 'what do you have in mind?'

The gleam in his eyes disconcerted her momentarily until

he lowered those absurdly long lashes – really too long for a man – to look at his hands.

'We must find a way to entice Lord Millsham into revealing himself for what he is.'

'What if someone is injured? I'll not have another shot do greater damage. Are you absolutely positive you ought not be at your apartments in the Edgar? Safely in bed?'

That gleam surfaced once again, and she found herself blushing, although she wasn't quite sure why. 'I am fine. My arm does not give me great pain. Do not distress yourself, Miss Fairchild.'

She stiffened at the rebuke in his voice, and vowed she would not ask about his condition again.

Bennison paused in the doorway. 'Miss Godwin, is she not here? There is a letter for her.' He held a crisp white missive in his hands. Clare wondered who might be writing to Venetia, for she was an abominable letter writer and rarely answered the odd note that came.

'The letter's for me?' Venetia breathlessly snatched it from the butler's hand, broke open the seal, and rapidly scanned the contents. 'I . . . I must go see Miss Oliver. Right away. Enjoy your tea.' In a flurry of black bombazine, Venetia whirled about to return to her room. Lady Millsham was just sipping her tea when Venetia could be heard rushing down the stairs to the ground floor. Moments later the front door slammed shut, and she was gone.

'Well,' Lord Talbot said, 'I cannot say I am sorry to see the back of her. Now we may discuss my idea without wondering if it shall reach another's ears forthwith.'

'I know precisely what you mean,' Clare murmured, frowning at the disloyal thoughts she harbored.

'I would urge caution on both of you,' Lady Millsham pleaded. 'The news that Lord Talbot had been injured greatly upset me. What a monster he is!' Lady Millsham exclaimed.

There was no need among the three to identify the man in question.

Clare said lightly, 'Sir, you shall not take any more chances.' Her minatory look was somewhat lost at the sound of steps on the stairs once again. She turned to the door to see Mrs Robottom enter on Bennison's arm. Clare rose to greet her guest. She introduced her to Lady Millsham, and Mrs Robottom professed herself honored to meet the young countess.

'Delighted to see you safely home again, Miss Fairchild, Talbot. Traveling is dangerous. I daresay you will not wish to venture out soon.' Mrs Robottom took the chair closest to the tea tray and plate of cakes. When pressed by Clare, she agreed to sample one with a cup of Bohea tea.

'We were about to work out a plan whereby we might lure the earl into unmasking himself. Or at least revealing his part in this mad plot. I daresay it will be difficult to prove he murdered Lady Millsham's husband, however.' Lord Talbot gave Lady Millsham a look of apology for introducing a delicate subject bound to upset her sensibilities.

'Hm, I had no idea he was such a rum sort. Nasty business, I fear. Yet, I suspect there is a way,' Mrs Robottom mused aloud.

'Without any tears or bloodshed, if you please,' added Clare.

The quartet explored ways and means to draw the earl into the open, so to speak, but no one had a really good plan by the time tea drew to a close.

'I suspect he has one of his men keeping a watch on your house,' Lord Talbot said to Clare.

'If that is the case, Lady Millsham had best stay inside for the time being. He may possibly have put two and two together, deducing that the child I shelter here belongs to Lady Millsham. Of course he cannot prove that the baby is in actuality the true earl, but we dare not take any chances.'

This statement required a full explanation for Mrs Robottom, who was further scandalized by the actions of the dastardly earl. They agreed to consider the matter at length, then meet on the morrow to discuss it again.

'We must not be foolish, nor underestimate the mad desires of this man. If he is desperate, he may do dangerous things.' Mrs Robottom nodded her head, the puce plumes on her bonnet quivering with her efforts.

Lady Millsham begged to be excused to return to her baby. Clare smiled, her eyes wistful as she watched the young mother hurry up the stairs, then she joined her guests in the stroll down to the front door. Lord Talbot lingered, and Mrs Robottom gave him a sly glance before her departure.

'You do have a way of putting me to the blush, sir,' scolded Clare after the door closed behind the older lady.

'I wanted to talk with you, and I did not wish that old prattlebox to listen.'

'She has been helpful,' Clare reminded.

'If it were not for her rattling tongue, you doubtless would not be in this fix today.' He studied Clare a moment, then added, 'I wished to see if you will go riding with me in the morning.'

'I do not have my horse here, and besides, ought you be doing something so strenuous?' Clare longed to have a good dashing ride along the gently rolling hills that surrounded Bath.

'You have a riding habit with you?'

Clare nodded reluctantly. 'I do, for I hoped to find a decent mount while here. I have not had the time.'

'Be ready in the morning, about nine if that is agreeable. I fancy you are out of bed by that hour?' He stared down at her with that wicked gleam dancing in his eyes once again. It made Clare feel all trembly inside.

A genuine smile lit her face for the first time in days. 'I should like that above all things.' She wouldn't ask if his arm was well enough, for it seemed to vex him. 'I may only trust you will not do something exceedingly foolish.'

'Oh, I daresay I shall before we are done.'

With that enigmatic remark, he was out of the house and down Brock Street.

Clare ran to the study window to watch him, noting how straight was his carriage, and what a jaunty step he had. One would never know he had been subjected to a nasty wound that must still plague him. If Lord Millsham saw Lord Talbot, it would annoy him greatly to see his man had missed. If indeed that had been his intent.

Clare was not convinced. Nothing in this entire business made one whit of sense, which further served to persuade her that they were dealing with someone who was not quite right in his upper story.

When Venetia returned looking pink-cheeked and flustered, Clare was too preoccupied to quiz her about the reason for Susan's message. She concentrated on the ride tomorrow with Lord Talbot, all thoughts of perilous matters far from her mind. A call to Priddy was followed by a search for her blue riding habit.

On Milsom Street, Lord Talbot paused before the window of the premier milliner in Bath, surveying a dashing top hat with a gauzy veil, most suitable for riding. He entered the shop and money exchanged hands, with the assurance that the hat would be delivered to the lady at the Royal Crescent promptly. Satisfied, he left the little shop, continuing on his way until he espied Miss Oliver parading toward him with young Lord Adrian Grove at her side. The two were totally engrossed in each other, and scarcely aware of the maid who dogged their footsteps.

He stopped before them, intruding on their world with a hearty good day.

'How lovely to see you, Lord Talbot.' Miss Oliver beamed up at him with great goodwill. Even the young man beside her seemed not to mind they were interrupted.

After a few minutes of general chatter, Lord Talbot inquired of Miss Oliver, 'I trust you completed your business with Miss Godwin? She passed me all aflutter on her way back to the Royal Crescent.'

Miss Oliver gave him a blank look. 'Miss Godwin, sir? I fear I have not seen that lady in days.'

'Odd. Perhaps I misunderstood.' But Richard knew full well he had heard correctly. And it made him exceedingly curious. He bowed most elegantly to the young couple, then sauntered down Milsom Street, his mind occupied with thoughts of tomorrow morning's ride. He stopped in a gun shop, after a number of inquiries as to the location, to inspect the merchandise. He had no intention of facing the following day unprepared or at a disadvantage.

Clare surveyed her dark blue velvet riding habit with satisfaction. Although not new, it fit her well and was frightfully comfortable. It had military frogging marching down the front of the jacket and clever little epaulets on her shoulders. At last she plucked the very dashing top hat from its box and stood a moment admiring the beautiful creation. The veil swirled about in enticing abandon.

'Dear Clare,' Venetia exclaimed as she poked her head around the door. 'A new hat? I must say it is vastly becoming, although a shade daring for someone your age.'

'Amazing how well it goes with my habit,' Clare replied before thinking.

'Did you not select it for just that reason?' Venetia inquired, her eyes narrowing.

'Of course,' Clare said hastily. 'But I did not have my habit along when the hat was purchased. One never knows,' she concluded obscurely. Clare wondered how Lord Talbot knew her taste so precisely. She ought not accept such a gift from him. Indeed, it was scandalous that she allow it. But one look at the smart hat set in place on her blond curls, and she was beyond hope.

'Are you going riding alone, with just your groom along?' Venetia asked while studying Clare's sparkling eyes and flushed cheeks.

Clare gathered up her gloves and crop after adjusting her habit shirt one last time. The collar was wont to go askew, and that would never do when she was riding with Lord Talbot. Without examining her reasons, she wished to look her very best for him.

'Actually, Lord Talbot has asked me to ride this morning. He sent a note that he has found an acceptable mount for me. I vow it seems an age since I last rode out.' Pausing at the head of the stairs, she added, 'I am remiss in not inviting you to accompany us, but I recall you said that riding gives you the megrims.'

The vexed expression sitting on Venetia's pretty face fled as she ruefully nodded. 'True. I shall go for a stroll, I believe. Perhaps I shall see Miss Oliver.'

Clare again paused, this time part way down the stairs. Looking back at Venetia, she frowned. 'Did you not call on her yesterday?'

'Oh, yes, so I did.' Venetia's agitation was slight, but noticeable to Clare, who knew her guest well by now.

When she joined Lord Talbot before the house on the Royal Crescent, she was pleased to see a sleek chestnut with fine lines.

'La, sir, you have an excellent eye.' She permitted him to toss her up on her horse, settled herself in the saddle, and gathered the reins in her gloved hands. 'How good it is. The air is fresh, and I believe these horses wish themselves gone.' With a gay laugh, she signaled her horse to proceed. Lord Talbot joined her.

The curtains in the study twitched, Venetia checking to see which way the riders went, then fell into place. Shortly the door opened, and Venetia skimmed along Brock Street, down Gay Street to Queens Square, where she rapped sharply on the door of one of the more elegant homes. In moments she was let inside.

Once beyond the confines of the cobbled streets of Bath, Clare and Lord Talbot cantered along until they reached a pleasant knoll with a view of the city. Sunlight dappled the gray stone buildings, picking out the abbey and several sites Clare recognized.

'Such a lovely day,' Clare exclaimed, feeling at peace with the world. She reined in her horse, then turned to face her companion. 'I have not properly thanked you for my hat, sir. I fancy it is highly improper for you to give me such a thing, but I confess I quite adore your gift.' She peeked at him, her eyes shining with happiness.

Casting his gaze about them, Lord Talbot replied, all graciousness, 'I am pleased you like it, for when I saw the hat, I knew it was you.'

Provoked he paid more attention to the scenery, Clare was about to complain, then thought better of it. After such a handsome gesture, he was entitled to appreciate whatever he wished. Perhaps the hat was Lord Talbot's way of repaying her for her care of him. Although the accident need not have happened if he had remained in Bath instead of tagging along in spite of her cautions.

'At any rate,' she continued, ignoring the lack of attention, 'I believe it goes quite well with my habit. Indeed Miss Godwin thought I had ordered it.'

'You saw her this morning before you left?'

'Yes. She usually sleeps in, but this morning she joined me at breakfast. Perhaps she had plans to see Miss Oliver again.'

'I happened to meet Miss Oliver and Lord Adrian on Milsom Street just after I purchased that handsome hat. When I asked Miss Oliver if she had successfully concluded her business with Miss Godwin, she declared she hadn't seen the woman in days. What do you make of that bit of news?'

'That is rather strange conduct.' Clare nudged her horse and the two jogged comfortably along the ridge, weaving in and out of trees to capture a bit of shade, for the day was growing warm. 'I wonder what my dear guest is up to, with all her devious behavior. Do you suppose she is having a clandestine affair? And she so proper.' Clare exchanged an amused smile with Lord Talbot.

'If it is nothing more than that, I should be glad. I have a number of suspicions about Miss Godwin, none of them, I fear, good.'

'You are not alone there, my friend,' Clare began, about to reveal the reservations she had collected over the past days, when Mr Talbot drew a pistol from his coat and fired toward the stone ridge. A bullet whipped past him about the same time.

'What?' Clare cried, terror piercing her.

Lord Talbot didn't answer her, rather dashed off in a gallop up the hill and over the ridge. Clare nudged her horse, tearing after him, her heart in her throat, fearing for his life.

At the top of the ridge, she slid from her horse and took

cover behind a large boulder, peering over it to scan the fields below. Trees dotted the area, and a rough lane cut across where she could make out two figures. Stepping forward, she could see it was Lord Talbot in hot pursuit of whoever it was who had shot at them. Him, actually. Her hat was safe. Perhaps, she mused as she used a handy rock to assist her return to the saddle, the man was a connoisseur of bonnets and hers had not met with his approval.

By the time she reached the foot of the lane, she found Lord Talbot waiting for her, a look of pure disgust on his face. 'I have the feeling he eluded you.'

'Fellow rode like the wind. Hadn't a hope of catching the man. What is worse, I fear I could not get a good look at him, so there is no hope of identification.'

They rode back to the house on Royal Crescent discussing the attack, deciding not to reveal it to Lady Millsham, poor dear. She endured quite enough grief without adding to it.

'I must thank you for the ride, sir, not to mention the hat. It was most, ah, eventful. The ride, that is,' Clare said, giving him a worried look after sliding from her horse into his arms while Bennison held the horses, a task that he obviously deemed beneath him.

'One can only wonder what the fellow is about.' He studied Clare a moment, then continued, 'We must do this again . . . without the fireworks, one would hope.' He bestowed one of his gleaming looks on her that made her heart beat rather more quickly.

'I vow I shall never accuse Bath of dullness. One only wonders what will happen next,' Clare said, waving at him before entering the house.

He remounted then ambled toward the stables.

CHAPTER THIRTEEN

Venetia lay in wait for Clare as she entered the house. At least that is what it seemed to Clare when she surveyed her companion where she stood in the center of the hall. Venetia peered out the door before closing it, apparently taking note of the retreating horses and the figure atop one of them before turning back to Clare.

How much of a companion Venetia had proved to be was slightly beyond Clare at the moment. It seemed as though they saw little enough of one another. Clare decided that once the present trials were over, she would suggest her guest visit somewhere else.

'La, dear Clare, you are home. No ruined hat?' Venetia said archly.

'No.' Clare glanced up the stairs to determine whether Lady Millsham might be within hearing. 'We had a delightful outing. Frightfully lovely morning. Really, my dear, you ought to take it up, riding, that is. I understand it does wonders for the complexion.' Darting a glance at Venetia, Clare could see that slender figure stiffen. The number of bottles and jars of lotions and creams on Miss Godwin's dressing table bore testimony to her reliance on them rather than healthful exercise.

In a faltering voice, Venetia said, 'Nothing happened? How . . . how fortunate.'

Pausing in her ascent to her room, Clare glanced back to see Venetia biting her lip. In vexation, no doubt, flashed through

Clare's mind. Just why did Venetia believe something uncommon had occurred during Clare's morning ride?

Sounds of the baby crying drifted down from upstairs. Clare smiled, knowing Lady Millsham would be at his side in seconds, so devoted was she.

'When is she to leave, Clare?' demanded Venetia in a petulant voice. 'That baby is giving me the megrims.' She entered Clare's bedroom behind her, without so much as an invitation.

'Do come in, Venetia,' Clare said, knowing her irony would be lost on the woman. Clare tossed her whip on the bed, then carefully removed her lovely new riding hat, placing it back into the pretty chintz-covered hatbox it came in yesterday, gently tucking the filmy veil in about it. 'You well know that Lady Millsham will remain here as long as needful.'

Priddy entered, taking the hatbox from Clare to place it on top of the wardrobe. She sniffed with disdain that Miss Godwin did not take the hint that Clare was to change her clothes after her ride.

Quickly removing her jacket, then her habit shirt, Clare stepped from the full, trailing skirt, handing it to Priddy before picking up the lavender muslin gown she intended to wear the remainder of the morning. The highwaisted gown had a little ruff at the discreet neckline that Clare thought becoming to her age. An embroidered flounce at the hem and delicate embroidery at the wrists of the long sleeves pronounced it the first stare of elegance.

Annoyed that Venetia would remain, although it must be said that Venetia spent her time staring out the window at the green across the way, Clare permitted Priddy to do up the back of the gown while listening to Venetia's running series of complaints.

'I am sorry you are so unhappy, Venetia. Perhaps things will improve.'

'Not with Aunt Peasely dead, they shan't,' grumbled Venetia. Then espying a footman making his way to their door, she scurried from the room, leaning over the stair rail to see who was to receive the missive.

Bennison glanced up to where he observed the lady waiting. 'It is a message for Miss Fairchild.' He marched up the stairs with a stately tread, refusing to relinquish the letter to Venetia.

'I could take it in to her, for she is dressing.'

'I should be remiss in my duty if I did not hand it to her personally, miss.' The butler stared down at Venetia with a purposefully blank look that made her drop her gaze, then retreat to the drawing room, her resentment evident in every line of her figure.

'What is it, Bennison? Ah, a letter,' Clare said as she left her room, accepting it with pleasure. She broke open the seal, then unfolded the parchment. 'Only see, Venetia! Lady Kingsmill is giving a ball for Miss Oliver. They doubtless will announce her betrothal to Lord Adrian Grove. Lord Talbot said he saw them on Milsom Street utterly engrossed in each other to the point of seeing no one else.' She waited to see if Venetia would explain her so-called visit to Susan Oliver that never occurred.

'I loathe betrothal parties. It is so depressing to see chits barely from the schoolroom waltzing off to the altar.' Venetia flounced about the room, picking up a vase, then putting it down, then doing the same with another object.

Clare began to fear for the safety of the decor. She walked to Venetia, taking her restless hands in her own. 'You ought to be happy for Susan, for I believe she is very much in love with Lord Adrian. He has an excellent competence, and she stands to inherit a goodly sum from Lady Kingsmill, so the marriage is off to a good beginning.'

'That is as may be,' Venetia snapped, pulling her hands from Clare's, then drifting over to the window to stare out with moody eyes.

'What shall you wear for there is to be dancing? Lady Kingsmill will take over the Upper Rooms for the party. It is a charming place. Since there are no assemblies this month, I imagine it is easily possible.'

'If one has enough money, nothing is impossible,' Venetia said, laughing at her wit.

'You seem in a peculiar frame of mind today. Do you feel well?' Clare stood by the sofa, toying with the invitation in her hands.

'Will Lady Millsham attend?' Venetia said with a petulant sniff.

'Oh, I hardly think she will wish to, given the circumstances. Although, I feel certain Lady Kingsmill would be so gracious as to include her. I suspect that until Lord Millsham leaves the area, Lady Millsham will confine herself to the house. I know I would.'

'I believe I shall go for a walk.' Venetia paused by the door, turning back with a speculative expression on her face. 'Do you have any idea who else might receive invitations?'

'I suppose all the nobility, the gentry in town. Lady Kingsmill is of the first consequence in Society, you know. Everyone who is anyone shall be invited.'

Venetia beamed a catlike grin. 'Lovely.' She ran up the stairs to her room, shortly returning with her smart leghorn bonnet draped with black silk riband plopped on her head.

'Going out so early in the day?' Clare wondered aloud.

'Oh, I should like to get to the draper's for a length of pretty silk before the selection is all picked over. I intend to find a nice lavender silk. Just because my Aunt Peasely died does not mean I intend to forgo the ball. Besides, my three weeks of mourning shall be nearly over by then. Bath is so excruciatingly dull.'

'Dull?' Clare echoed softly. She had found the city anything but dull. She drifted over to the window to watch Venetia hurry along Brock Street. Would she actually call in at the draper's shop? Or would she be off on a mysterious meeting?

Yet even with her suspicions, Clare hesitated to suggest Venetia move elsewhere. With the death of her aunt, it seemed poor Venetia had no place to go. A priority would be to find a place for her to reside. Perhaps Sarah would know of someone who might have need of a companion?

Or did her suspicions exceed reality? How unseemly to judge Venetia guilty, without a jot of proof. Most unfair. And if there was anything Clare prided herself on, it was her fairness and tolerance.

When Miss Oliver called in at the residence at the Royal Crescent later on that day, it was to find Venetia in a flurry of activity, busy with planning her gown. Having succeeded in finding precisely the deep shade of lavender desired, a particularly lovely black lace, and ells of satin edging, Venetia consulted one and all as to the best way to complete the gown.

'Dear Miss Oliver, how wonderful you are to have a ball,' Venetia burst forth enthusiastically. 'Though it is a wonder that you will marry Lord Adrian, him being a younger son and all. Clare would have it that true love can overcome all difficulties. But then, what can she know of problems?' Venetia smiled, her mouth tilted up in what Clare considered a rather malicious grin.

'There are a few that I grant you are exceedingly tiresome,' Clare replied, looking straight at Venetia.

The reproof was lost on Venetia, for she shrugged, then drifted out the door with the fabric and trimmings.

'How does it go?' Susan inquired, with a faint tilt of her head toward the door.

'Oh, well enough.' Clare dismissed Venetia in favor of discussing the fascinating details of the ball, not to mention the forthcoming wedding. 'I am pleased for you. From all I have seen and heard, it appears you have found a true love match.'

Susan blushed. 'Indeed. We shall have a comfortable life. Do not share this with another, but Lord Adrian is to receive a new peerage. The Letters Patent is being prepared, and once the title is gazetted, I shall let you know. Then I shall be a lady in truth for my new baron,' she said, giggling a little at Clare's admonishing face.

'You are a lady now, as far as I am concerned. Lady Grove, is it to be? I think it delightful, and I am terribly happy for you.'

They fell to discussing the gowns each planned to wear, until Susan declared it time she returned to Lady Kingsmill's. The house on the Royal Crescent seemed oddly quiet once she left. Upon investigation, Clare discovered that Venetia had gone to find a mantua maker.

In the ensuing days, Clare spent quite a bit of time with Lady Millsham. They found much in common and shared innumerable cups of tea while chatting about favorite books and people. Little William had cooed his way into Clare's heart, and she did not like to think of the day when he might leave.

'I think it a shame you cannot come with us to Miss Oliver's ball at the assembly rooms. Yet Lord Talbot assures me you are correct in your assessment. It is best for you to remain here with the baby. Rest assured that Lord Talbot and I have seen to it that extra men keep an eye on the house at all times. I am determined that the true earl shall be restored to his rightful place at Millsham Hall with you at his side to guide him.' Clare smiled fondly at Lady Millsham before scowling at the next thought to claim her. 'It is utterly appalling that that odious man should usurp the title after such a horrible deed. Alas, I fear we have no proof . . . as of yet.'

'Does Lord Talbot intend to find such? I believe it to be a difficult matter,' Lady Millsham replied earnestly. 'He must be careful. The present earl is not one to trifle with.'

Knowing just how true that statement was, Clare agreed. By mutual agreement, Clare and Lord Talbot had not told Lady Millsham about the shots fired at Clare or her ruined bonnets.

Across the Avon, Lord Talbot chatted with Lady Kingsmill. 'You sent him an invitation?'

'But of course. He is of the nobility, even if in a havey-cavey manner, and I prattled to everyone within my hearing that I intended to invite everyone of the *ton*.'

'Has he accepted yet?'

'Do you know,' Lady Kingsmill dropped her voice to a raspy whisper, 'he did so at once! I vow that surprised me. Perhaps he seeks to establish his credibility? We shall have to keep a close eye on him during the ball. I cannot trust the man.'

'True,' Lord Talbot replied, his eyes twinkling at Lady

Kingsmill's notion of conspiracy. 'He must wish to be convincing in every way.'

'So,' the old lady leaned back on her sofa, well satisfied with the progress of events, 'I am pleased that the ball for my dear niece will accomplish two goals.'

'We can but hope that it will. I am persuaded the man is a loose screw. Yet I suppose that others have succeeded with this sort of mad scheme.'

'Yes, only think of the story of the little princes!'

They reflected on past history a moment, before Lord Talbot rose to take his leave. Lord Welby came up the stairs just as Lord Talbot left the drawing room.

'A word, sir,' Lord Welby said, his voice low and confiding as he searched the area for possible listeners.

Lord Talbot gave him an encouraging nod.

'I happened to see an odd couple in secluded conversation while on my way over here. What do you think? Miss Godwin together with Lord Millsham!'

'Egad! What a curious turn. Upon reflection, I cannot say it astounds me, however. She is a particularly annoying female, and you know they can be depended upon to do all manner of peculiar things.'

'Quite so.' Lord Welby exchanged a significant look, then took himself off to enjoy a comfortable coze with his favorite lady while Richard Talbot continued out of the house, then across Pulteney Bridge into the center of town.

By the evening of Miss Oliver's ball, Clare found her nerves at a fever pitch. Lord Talbot had sought to reassure her. He had strolled along with her while she went to the millinery shop to hunt for a suitable evening hat.

Trying on a confection of white satin trimmed with tiny pearls and an elegant plume of white feathers, she blushed when she caught sight of Lord Talbot's approving look.

'It will go well with my gown, which is also white satin,' she explained, trying to justify this extravagance.

He nodded. 'I can scarce wait.' A slow grin crept across his handsome face to disconcert her.

She darted a glance at him to see if he was teasing her. His eyes held an intense, serious gleam in them that set her heart to fluttering again, as it seemed to do so often when in his company. Abruptly thrusting the hat at the milliner, Clare told her in a slightly strangled voice that she would purchase the thing. She quickly paid for it, and allowed Lord Talbot to carry the hatbox for her when they left the shop.

'Really, it is too bad of you to put me to the blush so often,' Clare scolded.

'But, your blushes are so very delightful, my dear Clare,' countered Lord Talbot.

'You ought not tease so, you odious man,' she stated in firm tones, then sent him a look intended to be reprimanding. Somehow it got lost, becoming a searching study of green eyes that possessed strange depths to them.

'I shall continue, however,' he replied, bestowing a lazy grin before escorting her across Milsom Street. 'It is by far my favorite pastime.'

Clare ignored this provocative remark. She caught sight of two of the tabbies who had cut her so severely when she'd first come to Bath. While it offered small comfort, she noted they both now bowed most correctly and even assumed polite smiles.

'I believe things are improved for you,' Richard said, taking close note of the gossips. He appeared to have achieved his aim, removing the stigma from Clare's name. That he had managed to do far more than that, as far as he was concerned, was another matter.

'Yes,' she replied. Memories of the moments in the coach, in his arms while on the boat ride, all the many hours spent together in excellent conversation, tumbled about in her mind. 'I must thank you for helping me. You have given so generously of your time, and you reap danger in exchange. I fear it has cost you a goodly sum,' she said, her face earnest. Her heartfelt smile dazzled him.

He cleared his throat. 'Once this business with Lady Millsham and her baby is cleaned up and she can be restored to Millsham Hall, we have things to discuss, my sweet.'

Fearing, yet hoping, Clare gave him a tremulous look, then took a fortifying breath. 'Yes, well, we shall see.' Which was an obscure statement at best.

Instead of leaving her at the door of the house on Royal Crescent, Richard entered, handed his hat to Bennison, then strolled up the stairs with Clare. At the landing, Clare handed the hatbox, her light pelisse, and gloves to Priddy, then took off her bonnet as they walked into the drawing room. She examined it while terribly aware of his presence.

'I spoke with Lady Kingsmill this morning,' he said. 'She informed me that Lord Millsham has accepted her invitation to the ball. It seems that we shall have the pleasure of seeing the man again.'

'Oh, dear. I suspect my feelings toward him will be difficult to hide. I am not an actress.' She tossed her bonnet aside, then raised her face to give Talbot a rueful look.

'Thank heavens for that.' Talbot's eyes glittered with amusement at the very thought of Miss Fairchild on the boards. 'Lord Welby was forthcoming with another piece of information. He observed Lord Millsham in close conversation with Miss Godwin. In the center of Bath hard by the abbey, if you please.'

'Good grief! It wanted only that.' Clare sank down on the nearest chair, obviously disturbed.

Bennison entered at that moment with a tray holding all that was necessary for tea, with a glass of fine sherry for Lord Talbot.

Clare glanced at the butler, then back to where Lord Talbot sat savoring the wine. It seemed that Richard Talbot had become quite a favorite with Bennison.

'I shall collect you well in time for the ball.'

'Would you care to dine with us beforehand, sir?' Clare knew what she suggested was totally improper. Never mind that Venetia and Lady Millsham would also be present. Unless she could think of several others to ask. 'Perhaps Sir Henry would care to join us?'

'While Miss Godwin is having secret assignations with Lord Millsham? Best leave her be. I shall enjoy dinner, however. Remember our breakfast at the inn following the accident? You were scandalized that I should eat so much, I fancy.' He chuckled at her indignant expression.

'You, sir, are a complete hand. Your arm is completely healed, is it not? I shudder every time I consider what might have happened had he been a better shot.'

'I still say it is dashed odd that he kept firing at your bonnets. And, no, I do not believe some milliner in Bath is setting out to snabble new business in such a queer manner,' he chided.

'I once considered that he perhaps knew how stubborn I am, and decided that was the best way to prompt me to find Lady Millsham.'

'Ah, but your determination stems from the purest motives. You are a prudent woman even while tenacious.'

Clare blushed at these kind words from the man she admired so greatly.

'Clare?' Lady Millsham bustled into the room, then paused when she saw Lord Talbot perched on a chair, glass of sherry in hand. 'Oh, dear. I did not mean to interrupt.'

'Nonsense. Bennison must have anticipated you would join us, for there is an extra cup.' Clare poured out the tea, then offered a ratafia biscuit.

They chatted a few moments, then Lord Talbot rose to take his leave. Clare followed him to the top of the stairs, watching him march down the steps with a reflective gaze.

'I trust you do not think me a totally improper female, Lady Millsham, but I asked Lord Talbot to dine with us before Miss Oliver's ball.' She gazed at Lady Millsham in apprehension.

'Not in the least. I perceive he is a very unusual gentleman,' she replied complacently.

'That he is,' Clare replied absently, her mind slipping back to the reminiscences shared with Lord Talbot. She had worried so about him when he had been shot. One look at that fiery red arm had sent her into a near panic. Shaking off her doldrums, she smiled at Lady Millsham, then continued their chat, concentrating on the clever things William had learned to do.

Venetia was not pleased to learn Lord Talbot would be joining them for dinner. She said so, long and loud.

'Venetia,' Clare remonstrated, her patience fast sliding away, 'he is coming, and that is that. I had thought to invite Sir Henry Berney, but you have hardly mentioned him, so I hesitated, lest I offend you.'

'Well, to invite a gentleman to dine while alone . . . it scarce bears thinking.'

'There will be three ladies to one man. I hardly believe anything will come amiss. You can glare at him.' With that Clare flounced down the stairs to consult with the cook.

'Well!' Venetia stomped her foot before stalking to her room in miffed silence.

The white satin ball gown and dainty new evening hat were spread out on Clare's bed, waiting for her to put on. Once Cook informed Clare that everything was well in hand, she returned to her room, intent on making herself as lovely as possible.

She must have at least partially succeeded, for when Lord Talbot entered the drawing room shortly before dinner, he inhaled sharply, then strode to Clare's side, bowing low over her hand and lingering far more than was seemly.

'Fair enchantress,' he murmured as he straightened and searched her eyes for a clue to her feelings. He had seen Clare Fairchild in quite a variety of garments. This one far surpassed all others for beauty and style. White satin overlaid with patent net, with clever little puffed sleeves and a minuscule bodice served to lure a man's eyes across an expanse of creamy skin. Her single strand of pearls echoed the tiny pearls in the hat he had watched her select.

Clearly a London gown, it skimmed over her slender figure, revealing just enough to whet his appetite. He knew the form beneath, for he had been made most aware of it when she tumbled on him in the carriage, and he had discovered all manner of alluring aspects while they floated along in the canal. Now he wished for nothing more than the right to hold her in his arms forever. Yet she remained so reserved, in spite of all he did. He almost began to despair.

When assembled, they repaired to the dining room, Lord Talbot leading Lady Millsham as was proper.

'I declare,' Venetia began once seated, 'the prices are quite shocking.' Ignoring Lord Talbot as a fly on the wall, she continued, 'A chip bonnet costing one guinea! And silk gloves at four and sixpence! Well, what is the world coming to, I should like to know. Good English muslin is now five shillings a yard, and the mantua maker charges another two and sixpence to make it up. Well! I shall find myself in the suds before long.'

Knowing this to be precisely the case, Clare did her best to soothe Venetia and entertain Lord Talbot. Why Venetia had to select this moment to digress on the cost of clothing was beyond Clare.

'La, Clare,' Venetia said after being successfully diverted from the subject of prices, 'that is an exceedingly low neck on your gown. I should not care to be seen in such. I daresay I should tuck in a fichu of blond lace were it mine. It is all very well for young girls to display themselves for the marriage mart, but I believe you quite past that sort of thing.'

Having endured quite enough of Miss Godwin's snipes at Clare, Richard gave her a steady look, then said, 'But then you have more need to cover, I believe, and have no fear of being on the marriage mart.'

Venetia gave a horrified gasp, flying from the table in a show of outraged sensibilities.

'Good grief,' Clare murmured, sharing a look of commiseration with Lady Millsham, then gave Talbot a glance of rebuke. Dinner ended on a rather unhappy note.

Clare paused before leaving for the ball to speak with Lady Millsham. 'Now, mind you hide yourself. I shan't have a moment's peace if I think you are in danger.'

Clare accompanied Lord Talbot, using a chair while he elected to walk along close by. Venetia had disappeared, and Clare worried she would get into trouble.

'You refine too much upon her. She needed a setting down,

you know. It is unthinkable that a guest should so abuse her hostess.' Richard felt that the sooner Venetia Godwin left the house on Royal Crescent, the better.

They entered the Assembly Rooms with the assurance of those who are welcome by their hostess. Clare was amused to have a young woman she barely knew flutter up to her and exclaim, 'What a marvelous idea to hire the rooms for a ball. Summer can be so dreadfully dull.'

'Odd,' Clare replied, after a darting glance at Lord Talbot, 'I find Bath most stimulating!'

The ballroom glittered with candlelight from the magnificent chandeliers. Lady Kingsmill held court just inside the entrance, with Susan Oliver modestly gowned and at her side.

'Venetia would approve that dress,' Clare observed to Lord Talbot in a soft aside.

'I far prefer yours.' The warm approbation in his voice could not fail to please.

What did he intend, pray tell? She well knew she had responded to him in a near abandoned manner. Could he be planning to seduce her? She lifted her chin, giving him a reserved smile. 'Thank you, sir.'

Richard watched with frustrated eyes as she drifted off to speak with Susan Oliver. Drat and blast it all anyway. Just when he thought he was making headway, he appeared to hit a blank wall with the object of his affections. He wondered if little Miss Goodwin poisoned Clare's mind when he was not around to nullify it.

On the far side of the room, he espied Lord Millsham. The man stood surrounded by several hopeful mamas and their dutiful, simpering daughters. How a woman could thrust her child at a man like Millsham, Richard didn't know. Yet he supposed that if she did not know his darker side, he might seem quite eligible.

Venetia Godwin entered by herself, curtsying to Lady Kingsmill, then blending in with the increasing throng of people who came to enjoy Lady Kingsmill's largess.

An evil imp prompted Richard to seek her out. 'Miss

Godwin, there is someone I should like you to meet.' He firmly escorted her to Lord Millsham's side, then made the introductions. As he had expected, they pretended to be total strangers.

Just as Venetia began to murmur polite nothings about becoming acquainted with the elegant Lord Millsham, the orchestra hired for the occasion struck up.

Turning to see where Clare might be, Richard found her not far away, allowing her card to be signed by Sir Henry. Richard swiftly made his way to her side. While Susan opened the dance with Lord Adrian, Richard boldly signed for three dances, then gave Clare a defiant 'I dare you to object' look.

She shook her head at him, a reluctant grin slipping out. 'You are a perfectly wicked man, sir. You know I cannot dance three times with you. What would the quidnuncs say then!'

'And they would be quite right, too,' murmured Richard in her ear as he led her forth into the minuet Lady Kingsmill had decreed to open the ball.

Clare advanced, then retreated, twirling about on her toes in the most graceful fashion. It seemed to her that her feet had wings, that nothing she did could be awkward or ill-advised. The touch of his hand was magic, she decided.

'I introduced Miss Godwin to Lord Millsham.'

'Did you indeed! And what happened?'

'They pretended not to know each other. I believe Miss Godwin is due to move on.'

'But Richard, she has nowhere to go,' Clare cried softly in distress. 'Now her aunt has died, she is alone. No other relative will have her, I suspect.'

'She needn't cotton onto you. If you are too gentle-hearted to do the necessary, I shall.' With that ominous note, he changed the subject.

Later Clare stood by herself in a moment of peace, listening to the chatter between dances. Richard had gone for a glass of lemonade. Mysteriously, he had become Richard once again. She couldn't explain that, it had merely happened in a moment of emotion.

'Miss Fairchild, may I have this dance?'

'Lord Millsham!' Clare tried to think of a way out and could not. She extended her hand in courtesy, then went through the motions of a country-dance while wondering why this man had sought her side.

'You find sufficient to occupy your days while in Bath?' he asked while they moved through a pattern together.

'Indeed. Bath is anything but dull. I cannot imagine why so many believe it to be so.'

'But then they do not have your penchant for poking about where you do not belong. Have a care, Miss Fairchild. One of these days you might lose more than your bonnet.'

CHAPTER FOURTEEN

He threatened her! Clare finished the country-dance in a daze. Oh, he was subtle, but he spoke about her poking about where she did not belong, and he knew about her ruined bonnets. Since she had not dwelt on these with anyone, save a word or two to Venetia, he had to have been the one who ordered the pursuit, not to mention the shots. Even Lady Millsham had not been informed as to the extent of the threat against Clare. It surely would have put the poor dear in a pelter.

'What has happened?' The low voice came from over her shoulder.

'Richard!' Clare whispered, trying to conceal her distress as she whirled to face him.

'What did Millsham say to give you such trembles?' Lord Talbot guided Clare toward the scarlet-covered settee where Lady Kingsmill reigned over the assembly. Outwardly one would assume that nothing more than polite words were being exchanged between these two.

'He as much as admitted he ordered that man to pursue us! He accused me of interfering where I did not belong, and Richard,' she cast a shaken look into the malachite eyes, 'he knew about the bonnets. His eyes frightened me, they had such a fierce expression in them. I believe he is quite, quite mad. He must be, to order murder.'

'Do you wish to go to the ladies' withdrawing room so you

may compose yourself?' His tender regard nearly undid her self-possession.

'Thank you, no.' Clare reflected that she felt far safer at Richard Talbot's side than in any withdrawing room. He might be tantalizing, teasing, and certainly tormenting, but he offered security at a moment when she badly needed such.

'Allow me to fetch you a glass of ratafia. You'd best remain with Lady Kingsmill while I am gone.' He paused, glancing down at her with an expression of such great concern that Clare found her heart rising with hope. He threaded his way through the throng of people, his broad, blue-sheathed back easily visible. Watching him walk toward the tearoom where refreshments were to be found, Clare realized that she knew more than mere regard for the man. She had tumbled disastrously into love with that exasperating and excessively compassionate gentleman.

His kindness had been marked toward her. At times he had been almost paternal. Of course, there were the other times when he made her feel deliciously wanton. Those kisses . . . She sighed, then applied herself to answering Lady Kingsmill's questions.

'I saw you dancing with him.' She cast a significant glance to where Lord Millsham parried the attentions of a determined young girl who was of an age to make her come out when next in London. 'I trust he said sometthing utterly disgraceful to put you in the quakes.'

'I hope it was not so evident to everyone that he so discomposed me, ma'am. Actually, he merely told me that I had a penchant for poking my nose where it did not belong. Oh, and he knew about the ruination of my poor bonnets.' Clare sank down on the end of the settee next to Lady Kingsmill, her legs quite refusing to support her with any reliability.

'Gracious!' Lady Kingsmill replied behind her fan, watching with narrowed eyes as the man in question led that determined miss through a sedate minuet. 'I fancy I need not tell you what that means. He must be considered ruthless. You have made a dangerous enemy, my dear. You must realize that for him, the stakes are enormously high. Promise me that you will depend upon Lord Talbot to see you through this ordeal. He is one you can trust with your life.'

'I daresay Lord Talbot has had quite enough of rescuing me from the brier patches I find myself in. Witness the injury he sustained to his arm.' Clare turned to see Richard wending his way to her side. Was that concern or pity for her in his eyes? Most likely he thought her past praying for, yet quite well enough for amusement. Or was she being unfair to him?

Yet she could never forget his expression when faced with what propriety dictated regarding their involvement. What bleak despair had shone from his eyes as they climbed up the footpath from the canal; the green had turned almost black. Her pride insisted she attain more regard than this if entering a marriage. She desired an abiding love.

She behaved like a silly schoolgirl plucking petals from a daisy. Did he love her, did he not? For all her years, she felt vulnerable, unsure of herself.

'Sorry. There is a crush near the refreshment table. Here, drink this. I fancy you still have need of it.'

Talbot handed her a glass of ratafia, observing closely until she had consumed most of it before speaking again. 'The thing we must decide now is what we do next.'

'I say that you deliberately lure the man on,' inserted Lady Kingsmill in a confiding tone.

'It seems we have done that, ma'am, and look what happened. Lord Talbot nearly was killed.' A shiver darted down Clare's spine at the very thought.

Nothing could be decided during the ball. To preserve an outward appearance of normality, both Clare and Lord Talbot felt required to dance.

When Sir Henry Berney sought Clare, she couldn't help but glance in Richard's direction. Her eyes gleaming, she went off to the dance floor in better spirits. He seemed most annoyed; she could only hope it was because she danced the waltz with Sir Henry.

The third dance he had so audaciously demanded, Clare insisted they sit out. 'I will not offer any more food for the tabbies to devour. It seems to me they have had quite enough on their plates as it is.'

He had agreed with a swiftness that she found disconcerting. He might have protested just a little, she thought with total irrationality. She led him to Lady Kingsmill's side, preventing any private conversation for the moment.

The hour was late before Richard brought her to the house in the Royal Crescent. He dismissed Bennison with but a lift of a brow.

'It is too late to think now, Lord Talbot. If we are to plan, I fear you had best appear in the morning when my brain is better able to function.' Clare gave him a rueful smile while she edged her way to the stairs. 'I shall look forward to deciding our best strategy then.' She pretended to yawn, fearing, yet desiring to be alone with him. What if he assumed that horrid expression again? The very thought proved more than she could bear. She turned away, preparing to make her way up the steps to her room.

'Not yet. You cannot look like an angel, then elude me.' He reached out to touch her arm, stopping her in her flight.

She spun about, a half smile quivering on her lips. 'You dare say that after demanding three dances with me? The gossips shall have a wonderful time debating the meaning of that, I am bound, even if we managed to sit one of them out by Lady Kingsmill. Outrageous man!'

He slowly drew her into his arms, cradling her gently close to him. 'Let them talk. We shall show them soon enough.' He tilted her face up to his, covered her lips with his own, and drew the sweetness from her to strengthen his resolve. He must have her, and have her he would. A taste was not nearly enough to satisfy his craving.

Yielding, forgetting all about the particular dreadful expression that so depressed her when she considered it, Clare returned his kiss with fervent ardor. Her passion kindled, she quite succumbed to his charm and expertise, melting against him in spite of all her resolve to the contrary.

'Well, I daresay you have sunk quite below what is acceptable, dear Clare! That I should see such licentious behavior in the very house where I reside. I never!' Venetia stood just inside the door, her body fairly quivering with indignation.

Focusing on her houseguest, Clare blinked, then hastily withdrew from Richard's arms. 'Good evening, Venetia. I see you managed to get yourself home in safety. Please go up and I shall join you directly.' The polite words were spoken firmly, with a thread of steel through them.

Venetia sputtered, tossing a dark look at Lord Talbot, then glaring at Clare. When neither of them added anything to the sternly worded request, she flounced up the stairs in high dudgeon.

Richard swiftly reached out to touch Clare's face, stroking it lightly with a gentle finger. 'Do not allow her to vex you, my dear. If my suspicions are correct, this will all be over before long.'

Clare glanced up the stairs where she knew Venetia waited, then back to his precious face again. 'Over? I daresay you are right. Nothing lasts forever, or so I've been told.' She shivered, then backed away from him, turning and running up the stairs as quickly as possible.

Richard stood a moment, watching her fluid, graceful movements. She was quicksilver, and just as elusive. What had flashed into her mind before she left him? Nothing good. Blast that Godwin woman. He had a score to settle with her. He could not permit her to cut up Clare's peace as she did. Clare was too kind, too tolerant and caring to do what had to be done. But he would see to it. He shut the door behind him, approving that Bennison had silently appeared to lock up for the night.

Upstairs, Clare entered the drawing room with a dangerous light in her eyes. Unfortunately, Venetia failed to take note of that militant gleam.

'I believe you were invited here to be my guest and companion. Is that not true?' Clare said in the most dulcet of tones.

Venetia fiddled with the tassel of her fan. 'Yes.' Raising her face, she bestowed a defiant look at Clare. 'However, you need someone to point out the pitfalls of the path you choose.'

'At no time was anything said about your being my chaperon? Or the guardian of my morals?' At Venetia's reluctant nod, Clare continued, 'I shall warn you only once. If there is a repeat of tonight's manners, I shall request you to leave. Is that clear?'

Not bothering to wait for an answer, Clare spun about and marched to her room, shutting her door firmly behind her with a decisive snap.

What had Richard meant by his behavior tonight? she wondered as she dropped her fan and reticule on the dresser. Her hopes had grown with each touch, each kiss, until she knew she was dangerously close to commitment.

Priddy entered, yawning hugely as she crossed to assist her mistress. Thankful her maid was in a silent mood, Clare allowed her to help her from her gown and put things away, then brush her hair before she said, 'Get to bed, Priddy. I shall see you in the morning, I trust.'

Once the door was closed again, Clare slipped on her dressing gown and wandered to the window to stare out into the night. Linkboys could be seen here and there escorting people home from the ball and other entertainments. The lights bobbed up and down, reminding her of demented glow-worms.

'It will all be over soon, he said. Does he refer to the plot against Baby William and Lady Millsham? Or does he mean the attraction between us? I vow he must be the most aggravating man alive.' With this off her chest, she found her way to her bed and slid beneath the covers positive that she would not sleep a wink.

Not so. The next thing she knew, Priddy entered with her morning chocolate. A glimmer of sun filtered through clouds to cheer the day.

'Good! You slept late. The ball must have been prodigiously wonderful. Baskets of flowers came for you this morning. Lord Talbot and Sir Henry for two. Another with a sealed note.' Priddy sniffed her disapproval at any gentleman who would spoil her pleasure.

Clare drank her chocolate, wondering why she felt gloomy in spite of the reasonably pleasant day outside. Then she recalled what had happened before going to bed.

'Is Miss Godwin up yet?'

'That one? I should say so. She went out for a morning walk. At the moment, I believe she is in the dining room attacking her breakfast. Nothing wrong with her appetite.'

'I must speak with her.' Precisely what she might say, Clare had not decided. Her own guilt at her conduct had been partly responsible for her angry words of last night. She had lashed out at Venetia with good cause, and yet had she not been blameworthy as well? Scandalous behavior, indeed, for one who had always been held up as an example for proper manners.

Arrayed in a favorite gown of jonquil muslin with a fetching ruff at her neck, Clare skimmed down the steps positive she looked more serene than she felt.

At the door to the dining room, she paused. Venetia sat before a plate showing the remains of an excellent breakfast. Did that perhaps mean that the scene of last night had not affected her as deeply as Clare?

'About last night . . .' Clare gathered the words for an apology. She feared she had been too harsh on Venetia. There could be no mistake about Clare's guilt, nor her own feelings of blame in all that happened. Chagrined, she had lost sight of that last night, in Richard's arms while being soundly kissed. Before she could commence her apology, Venetia stood up, advancing upon Clare with an air of righteous pique.

'I have considered it at great length, dear Clare. I feel it my duty to keep you from a highly improper liaison with Lord Talbot. What do you know of him, pray tell? He is a practiced seducer, that is plain. Something tells me that I do not know the whole of it. But consider this, my dear, you made that call on Millsham Hall together. You visited his mother – and did he propose anything honorable? No. You traipsed off with him to Marlborough, then remained at the inn overnight when collecting Lady Millsham. All in all, my dear, you are hardly the proper lady I thought you to be.' She waggled her finger beneath Clare's nose, while not bothering to veil her distaste for such sordid behavior.

The list of social wrongs had Clare gasping with outrage. How well it was that Venetia knew nothing of the canal trip in the narrowboat. She would have had a spasm!

While the basic facts were true, surely Clare had a right to expect that her houseguest would have more faith in her virtue. Small thanks she won for risking life and limb to restore a young peer to his rightful place! She was about to counter with a few home truths, when a deep voice from behind her cut through the air.

'I believe you have said more than enough, Miss Godwin.' Richard Talbot stepped into the dining room, drawing close to Clare as though to protect her from further insults. 'It is past time that you take yourself off from here. Today!' he barked in a voice accustomed to giving orders to those who jumped to obey him.

Venetia looked to Clare, quite as though she expected her hostess to rise to her defense. When Clare stood in silent anger, Venetia flounced from the room, tossing her napkin in a crumpled heap on the floor. 'Well! If that is the thanks I get for trying to salvage dear Clare's reputation from the likes of you, I have no desire to remain in this benighted house.'

But something happened on her way to the stairs. She paused, her shoulders slumping a shade. It occurred to her that her family had forbidden her to darken their doors again, that her Aunt Peasely had been so thoughtless as to die, and she was now quite alone. Turning to face Clare again, she said in a shaken voice, 'But I have no place to go. Besides, you cannot live here alone. It would be vastly improper.'

Fearing that she would forgive the harpy, Richard stepped in front of Clare to shield her from that look of entreaty. His stern face offered no change of heart to Venetia. 'I should have thought that might have manifested itself before you launched into your tirade against a woman who is as good, kind, and gentle as you are spiteful. Pack your things. Something tells me that a shelter will turn up that you had not considered. Remember that Lady Millsham resides here now, and as a widow with spotless reputation, she will do well enough for a chaperon even though young. Besides, it is entirely possible that Miss Fairchild will have little need for such a one before long.'

Absorbing that cold, nasty smile, Venetia whirled about and marched up the stairs with her dignity barely intact.

Listening to the orders flung to one of the maids from her now departing guest, Clare turned upon Richard. 'I fear that was ill done of you, sir. I cannot think as to where she will go, for she has scarcely a feather to fly with. I wonder if there is anyone in her family who will relent and take her back.'

'I've no doubt but what she alienated the lot of them.' Richard studied the closed expression on Clare's face, wondering if he had angered her. Yet he had found it impossible to contain his ire when he heard that ... that shrew speak as she did. For her to say such drivel to a fine lady like Clare Fairchild was beyond belief.

'I felt sorry for her.' Clare wandered across the hall to the study, her appetite totally gone for even a bite of breakfast.

'You will not change your mind.'

'That sounds remarkably like an order, sir. You have no right to give such in my house.' She tore her eyes from him, strolling to the window overlooking the green while wondering what he had meant about the business of her not requiring a chaperon much longer. She turned at a rustle by the door.

'Good morning, Miss Fairchild, Lord Talbot. I have decided that I cannot tolerate being cooped up in the house another minute. What with the unheaval in Miss Godwin's room, I suspect the baby will never nap. I intend to take him for a breath of air.' There was a hesitancy in Lady Millsham's statement not missed by Clare or Richard.

'Let me have Priddy bring down my pelisse, and I shall join you.' Clare walked over to pull the rope for her maid.

'I believe I should enjoy a bit of fresh air as well,' announced Richard with a smooth and very swift insertion. He did not wish for Clare to go out for a walk in the park with Lady Millsham, but he also realized she was in no mood to be ordered about by him at the moment.

Clare spoke briefly to Priddy, requesting her green pelisse and parasol, with her prettiest straw bonnet. She also gave orders regarding the removal of Miss Godwin.

'Well enough, Miss Clare,' approved Priddy with a sniff. 'She has exalted notions, that one.' With a nod of her head, Priddy stalked up the stairs, returning moments later with the requested pelisse, bonnet, and parasol.

Bennison had sent for a hackney to convey the party to the Sidney Gardens. By the time Clare was ready, the hackney awaited beyond the front door. Clare paused, directing a look at the butler. 'Miss Godwin shall be departing once she has packed. Be certain you call her a hackney, and do try to find out *where* she goes, if you please?'

Bennison exchanged looks with Lord Talbot, then nodded. 'Miss Godwin is rushing off. I hope that my presence and the baby, especially, have not alienated you.' Lady Millsham bestowed a timid look on Clare.

'Nonsense. She decided to go.'

'*After* giving Miss Fairchild the benefit of a most unde-served set-down. That any woman as fine and noble as Miss Fairchild should be accused of the implications Miss Godwin asserted is beyond belief. She has a very petty mind,' Lord Talbot assured Lady Millsham. He sat across from the two women, admiring the way Clare offered to hold the baby while Lady Millsham adjusted her skirts.

'Let me carry him a bit. You are near worn-out with all you have had to do this past week.' Clare cuddled William in her arms, chuckling at his bubble blowing and arm waving act.

'I vow it is a treat to get to the park,' Lady Millsham said as she peeked through the window at the sight of the trees and lovely gardens.

'I feel certain that this nightmare of yours will soon be over,' Lord Talbot vouched. 'The pretender tipped his hand last night. I suspect we shall not have long to wait until he moves again.'

Lady Millsham shuddered, then exited the hackney, hold-ing Lord Talbot's hand with trembling fingers. 'Thank you, kind sir, for all you have done and continue to do for my son and me. Believe that I shall acquaint him with his great debt to you.'

Clare strolled along the walk, cooing to the baby. Lord Talbot walked at one side, while Lady Millsham clung to the other. Richard took care to search the area on either side of their path, occasionally glancing back to see if Timms followed behind them. Good thing that the man had come along.

The trio had reached the pretty bridge that arched over the Kennet and Avon Canal when it happened. Lady Millsham leaned over to point out one of the pretty painted narrow-boats when a sharp discharge halted their steps.

'The baby,' cried Lady Millsham in horror.

Red stained the long white shawl that was drapped about the infant. Clare clenched her teeth, then said in a strained voice, 'I believe you had better take him. He is fine, but my arm is not, and I'd rather not drop him, if you don't mind?'

Lady Millsham hurriedly grabbed the baby. Clare leaned weakly against the bridge, the pretty boat ignored as she sought the figures speeding off along the path behind them.

Richard dashed in the direction of the shot with Timms closing in on the man at the same time from the opposite direction. Fortunately, Timms had espied the suspicious character hanging about. Lamentably, he had not been able to prevent the shot fired at Miss Fairchild.

The man fell to the ground as Richard jumped on him from behind, a particularly satisfying thud, to Richard's ears.

'Let me go, oi did nuffink.' The poorly clad fellow wiggled like an eel in an effort to get free.

'Really?' drawled Richard as he plucked the pistol from the man's pocket. 'You neglected to toss this away, I fear. It's off to the magistrate for you. Attempted murder is a felony that will see you hanged.'

The gunman blubbered all the way to the hackney Timms had reserved. Once hands were firmly tied, ankles confined, the fellow was in no shape to escape.

'Who hired you?' demanded Richard. 'I might make it easier on you if I could know.'

' 'Twas a gentry cove what done it.' The description that

followed fitted the sham earl to the tee.

Timms accepted the instructions regarding the pathetic fellow, then set off toward the nearest magistrate.

When Richard hurried to Clare's side, he apologized for leaving her for even a moment. 'I wanted to know if my suspicions were correct. The sham earl hired the man, but why he was to shoot you and not Lady Millsham, I do not know. But then, it was you who carried the baby!'

Clare glanced at Lady Millsham, swallowing with an effort to seem calm. 'Perhaps we had best cut short our visit to the park. I fear it was a foolish idea, at least until Lord Millsham is put to flight.'

Horrified that her longing for a breath of freedom had brought injury to the dearest lady who had sheltered and helped her, Lady Millsham agreed, urging Clare along the walk to the park entrance.

'How fortunate that no one else was about,' murmured Clare, leaning on Lord Talbot's arm. She had pulled a handkerchief from her reticule to press against the wound, but the faint red grew deeper as they neared the hackney stand. As soon as Richard noticed it, he muttered imprecations against stubborn women and acted at once.

Ignoring any thought of impropriety, he swung Clare up in his arms, striding to the first hackney in line, tersely ordering the man to take their party to the Royal Cresent at once and as fast as possible.

She found herself enfolded in his arms, held tightly against his chest during the ride. Lady Millsham sat quietly, wide-eyed and fearful for Clare. Even little William remained silent.

'I really am able to sit . . . I believe,' Clare said in an oddly remote voice. Could it really be hers?

'He shall pay for this,' Richard muttered as he cradled her even closer, if possible.

Bennison gasped when he opened the door. Lady Millsham slipped in and up the stairs to alert Priddy, then made her way to her room as quietly as possible. She intended to return once William was restored to Jenny.

Upon reaching the landing, Richard found his way blocked

by none other than the departing Venetia.

'Well, I daresay this is more of her just desserts. If you ask me – not that anyone ever does – she attracts danger.'

'Be gone, woman, before I throttle you myself.' Richard glared down at her with his most fierce look.

Venetia took one look at the savage expression on his face, and hurried on her way down the stairs.

'You are rather good at ridding the house of unwanted guests, sir. Tell me, do you hire out for that sort of thing?' murmured Clare, leaning against his chest while she might.

'Silence.' He marched down the hall and into her room, where a worried Priddy had efficiently opened the bed and laid out a night rail of sheer white lawn.

He inspected the preparations, then nodded as he set Clare on the bed. 'I want to see your wound, my dear. I ordered Timms to fetch my case with the remains of Mrs Dow's most effective preparation.' He shook his head in dismay once Priddy pulled off the pelisse, then bared Clare's arm.

'I believe we are to have matching scars, Lord Talbot,' Clare offered in a faint but determined voice.

His bark of laughter faded as he tended her graze. 'Fortunately, this is not as bad as mine, dear girl. We shall have you up and about in no time at all.' He turned as Timms entered with a small black case in hand.

Priddy, seeing that perhaps the nightclothes would not be required after all, slipped from the room, returning with an array of flowers to cheer the wounded.

Her arm neatly bandaged, Clare leaned against the pillow, studying the flowers while trying to decide which ones Richard had sent her.

'Spicy carnations, if you need ask,' he supplied in answer to her unspoken question, that wicked brow tilting to tease her. 'They remind me of you.' This sally was ignored.

'Sir Henry sent the others. But who is the third?' She pointed to the folded and sealed note, indicating Richard open it for her. 'What a peculiar expression,' she said in puzzlement. 'Pray, who placed it there?'

'The Earl of Millsham, my dear. We now have an answer to

at least one of our questions. He writes that you exemplify the type of woman who has spurned him one too many times. You are privileged, wealthy, and far too aristocratic, it seems. He also demands you return Lady Millsham and her son to the Hall at once. I gather he has plans for them.' Richard took care she not see the written tirade against deceitful women in general. How thankful he was that he might spare her the sight of it.

'We must ensnare him now that we know for certain . . . but how?'

CHAPTER FIFTEEN

'I recall seeing him in London before he acquired his title,' Clare mused. She slid from her bed and smoothed down her sleeve. Inclined to make light of her injury, she crossed to the door, then moved into the drawing room on the far side of the landing.

Richard followed her, pausing in the hallway to speak to Bennison.

Sinking down on the sofa, Clare studied Richard Talbot. For one thing, it took her mind off her aching arm. For another, she wondered what went on in his mind. For all that he seemed to be easygoing, there was an uncompromising streak in his character. He had been quite decisive when he spoke to Venetia. Clare knew she would not wish to severely cross him, for that glacial stare promised dire threats she had no desire to test.

She thought back to the revelation that had popped into her mind last night. Could it have been but hours ago? It seemed whenever they were together, the time raced past and life proved anything but dull. She slanted a look of mischief at him. 'At least I still have my bonnet. I am particularly fond of that one.'

'This is nothing to mock,' he scolded, giving her the notion he would dearly like to shake her.

'Have you any idea what we must do next?' She sobered at his expression, leaning back against the sofa feeling more pinched than she wished to admit.

Richard grimaced, then rubbed his chin with a hand that for the first time in his memory seemed to be a bit shaky. 'I thought he might reveal himself if we offered him a quarry, but I truly never dreamed he would attempt to kill you in the very heart of Bath. Clare, we cannot go on. I'll not have you endangered again. I feel certain Lady Millsham would not wish you ill, and if you think about it, her boy is in greater danger than ever, especially if we venture from the house with him. We dare not take chances again. I shall engage a twenty-four-hour guard on the house.'

'Oh, pooh.' Clare gave a dismissive wave of her good arm. 'We cannot stop now. I'll not permit that madman to harm anyone else. But we have not a shred of proof, you know. There is nothing but the admission of that hired assassin with the gun, and no judge would accept his word against the word of a peer. Most likely any trial would last a few minutes at the most.'

Bennison entered the room bearing a tray with the requisite tea plus an assortment of cakes and biscuits. Clare poured out the tea, trying not to wince when she moved her arm.

'You are nothing if not tenacious, dear Clare. I insist you put up your feet.' He suited his words by raising her feet, then placing several cushions at her back.

'I wish you would not call me "dear Clare." I believe I have heard quite enough of that for some time to come. Besides, you have no right to be so familiar, sir.' She leaned against the cushions, glad for their support yet unwilling to admit she had need of them.

'That can be remedied.'

Frustration seethed within her as Lady Millsham timidly entered the room. The interesting turn in the conversation was cut abruptly short.

Lady Milisham's soft voice cut through Clare's annoyance. 'I hope you are feeling more the thing. Priddy assures me that given your hardy constitution, you will be as good as new in a trice.'

There was a note of questioning in her voice that Clare felt impelled to assure.

'Oh, I am never downpin for long. I daresay she is right, that I shall resume my disgustingly good state of health in no time at all.' Then seeking to divert the conversation from herself, she went on, 'We have been discussing the sham earl. Frankly, my dear, I do not know why we simply do not go to the proper person to assert William's claim to the title. With your marriage lines in hand and little William in your arms, it ought to be an easy matter.'

'It would not keep him safe,' Lady Millsham reminded them.

'Well,' Clare said consideringly, 'I shan't stoop to murdering the man, no matter how much he deserves it.'

'I believe I shall go have another chat with the person we apprehended in the park. Perhaps a short time in custody will have loosened his tongue.' Talbot rose, then came to stand over Clare. 'I trust I do not need to say anything so obvious as that you need to remain quiet, or perhaps take a nap?'

'Hardly. Although I admit, my curiosity is as high as ever. Return after your "chat" and tell us what you learn.'

He left the room with a fierce look on his face that told Clare he was not pleased with her reply. Did he perhaps sense that she would not be dictated to by anyone? Or maybe he resented her demand that he return to them?

'I hope he took my request in good grace,' she murmured to Lady Millsham. 'Only, this all seems such a muddle. I'm of a mind to confront the earl. Do you know, I cannot recall what his name was? We always call him the earl, never anything else.'

'Basil Kibbler.'

'Good grief, that family? They are perennially under the hatches. I seem to recollect his pockets were always to let. My brother knew him, you know. Some of the things Tom said about him are coming back to me. But I cannot say I did more than dance with the man once or twice. In his former position, he was quite beneath my touch.' Clare recalled the words of the note that had come with the flowers, or what Richard had read to her. She wondered precisely how the exact wording had been. 'That bothered him, it seemed, being beneath my touch, for I am well to grass. Yet once he became the earl,' she threw Lady Millsham a glance of apology, 'his station in life changed. He ought to have been acceptable to anyone, particularly since there is a considerable fortune involved.'

'He refused to pay off the family debts, or so I heard,' Lady Millsham offered hesitantly. 'The housekeeper wrote to Mrs Dow about the scandalous lack of family feeling.'

Knowing it was unusual for servants to write to one another, Clare raised her brows.

Lady Millsham answered, 'He franked her letter. I rather suspect he hoped to see if the housekeeper would find anyone who knew of my whereabouts. Naturally, Mrs Dow never mentioned me.'

Priddy entered with a glass of milky liquid. Clare grimaced, knowing full well what she held.

'A distillation of willow bark, Miss Clare. It will help your aches and pains.'

'I do not have such,' Clare replied in a gentle tone, only to give lie to her words, wincing at her sudden movement when she warded off the glass.

'Aha,' Priddy exclaimed, pouncing on her mistress with glass in hand.

Knowing it futile to put it off, Clare drank the nasty stuff, then grimaced at Lady Millsham. 'They ought to make it into tablets or pastilles. I shouldn't mind it half so much then. Not that I am required to take it that often.'

They chatted about aches and remedies, although each wore an abstracted expression, indicating her mind strayed elsewhere.

Footsteps bounding up the stairs brought both heads around in amazement.

'Lord Talbot!' Lady Millsham exclaimed in dismay.

'Yes, Richard, whatever is the matter? You look positively wild,' Clare added, half rising from the sofa.

He swiftly crossed to touch her shoulder, pressing her ever so gently downward. Plumping himself on a chair without being asked, a behavior quite unlike his normal good manners, he shook his head.

200

'When I arrived at the jail, I found the fellow dead!'

The women gasped, Clare demanding to know, 'But how?'

He shrugged. 'No one seemed to have the faintest idea. 'Tis not so unusual, for a man to die in jail, for the place is an unspeakable horror. But it seems dashed odd for this particular man to go aloft when he is the only witness we know about.'

'I wonder where Venetia went?'

This non sequitur caught the attention of Lady Millsham. 'Poor woman. Life can be very hard for a woman alone.'

'For you, perhaps,' Lord Talbot said. 'I venture to say that Miss Godwin shall find her feet. Mark my words. There is more to that woman than you know.'

'Lord Talbot, you cannot tantalize us like that, and not reveal the whole,' Clare chided.

'In due time' was his only reply.

'Did you know,' retorted Clare, seeking to redirect the subject, 'that the present earl is none other than Basil Kibbler? I thought his face looked familiar, although he was not in my circle, you understand. I cannot recall seeing much of him this past year, even at a distance.'

Lord Talbot nodded. 'I knew his name. But for all I knew, his finances had improved in the years I was gone. I gather they had not?'

'Precisely,' Clare murmured.

'That family lived in Queer Street if my memory serves me right. Not worth a bean,' he added in reflection.

'He was ever hanging out for an heiress. My brother forbade me to have anything to do with him. Which I suspect did not endear me in the least.'

'Others are dished up, and they don't commit murder.'

'They do not call arsenic "inheritance powder" for no reason, Richard,' Clare reminded him. 'I would like to challenge the man, force him to leave the country. Something. Lady Millsham cannot continue to live in terror for her life. And how is little William to grow up with the threat of death hanging over his head? Everyone will be suspect; the child cannot have a normal life.'

'We have no proof, especially with our only witness dead.'

'Hm. What if another witness appeared?'

He straightened up, staring at her with questioning eyes.

It was not easy to tear her gaze from the depths of malachite, but she managed. 'Oh, we do not have one,' she confessed. 'But *he* does not know that. I suggest we tell Mrs Robottom, and permit her to direct the information in the proper channel.'

'What then?'

'Then we confront him.

'My dear girl, you have to have a better plan than that!'

'Give me time. I shall think of something.'

Clare thought she heard him mutter words to the effect that he feared just such. They were lost with the arrival of Bennison closely followed by Miss Oliver and Lord Adrian Grove. He announced them, then at Clare's nod took the tea tray to replenish it.

'What's this? Are you not well, Miss Fairchild?' Miss Oliver cried in alarm.

'A small matter of a grazed arm,' Clare replied, bestowing a warning glance at Richard and Lady Millsham. 'My dear friends fuss over me far too much, not to mention Priddy. She is a dragon of the highest order.' Clare smiled with affection for her maid.

'I seem to recall similar circumstances when you were not quite so sanguine about a grazed arm,' Richard murmured as he adjusted one of her cushions.

'Odious man,' she whispered. 'There is scant resemblance. My wound is nothing so deep or painful.'

'I suspect you are being exceptionally brave. If I see one indication you are less than you ought to be, I shall cart you off to bed at once.'

Clare's cheeks flamed at the very image that popped into her mind from his words. 'Wicked man,' she shot back in return, then realized he was chuckling at her. She had been better to hold her tongue. His actual words carried no impropriety in them; it was her own naughty thoughts that led her unbidden to seductive fantasy.

Miss Oliver turned from chatting with Lady Millsham to

direct her gaze to Clare. 'I do not suppose you will explain about this latest episode in your life. I suspect there is more involved than a simple graze.'

Clare firmed her lips. 'Do you know I was ever considered the epitome of propriety for most of my life? At least until I came to Bath.'

A provocative grin crept over Richard Talbot's face. 'I cannot imagine where they acquired such an odd notion. Not that you are not, ah, interesting, dear girl.'

Susan Oliver glanced at Lord Talbot, then transferred her gaze to Clare Fairchild, taking note of pinkened cheeks, sparkling eyes.

'I expect you spoke to the odious earl last night. May we be of help?'

'Actually, you could,' Clare reflected, hoping the fire in her cheeks would quickly subside. 'Let it be known, in an underhand sort of way, that we have a witness to the murder of the sixth earl. I want to see what happens.'

'You are too curious for your own good, Miss Fairchild,' Lord Talbot protested, his disapproval ringing in his words.

'Oh, pooh,' Clare said, a hint of laughter in her voice. 'We must make an attempt. I refuse to lose another bonnet to the cause.'

Her unguarded words brought a horrified exclamation from Lady Millsham, which must needs be explained. While the ladies chattered, Clare fervently trying to pass off the events as mere trifles, the gentlemen wandered over to the window looking out on the green.

Lord Adrian tugged at his chin, then half turned to Lord Talbot. 'It would seem you have had quite a series of adventures with Miss Fairchild.'

'True.' The tone did not invite further questioning.

'You appear to run tame in her house.' The glimmer of questioning continued, subtle, yet unmistakable.

'It might seem that way,' Richard agreed tightly.

'Don't cut up stiff with me,' Lord Adrian admonished. 'It may have been remarked that you seem to be in each other's pockets these past days, but that does not mean you must heed the tabbies as far as I am concerned. Dash it all, man, no point in getting leg-shackled unless there is good reason. If your heart is truly caught, or you need the blunt – which I daresay you don't, that might do.'

A grim look flickered on Richard's face before he turned to the man at his side. 'Gossiping, are they?'

'Lady Kingsmill suggested I put a flea in your ear as to what is drifting about town. When an oh-so-proper lady is seen frequenting the side of an eligible bachelor, tongues are bound to wag.'

'I was afraid the quidnuncs would have at us. In due time we shall put it all to rest.'

'Indeed.'

Lord Adrian appeared on the verge of inquiring if he might wish Lord Talbot happy, then seemed to think better of it.

When Miss Oliver and Lord Adrian left, Lord Talbot went along with them, frustrating Clare in her desire to plan what they were to do next. That man would answer for his high-handedness. She'd see to that.

It was not until the next day that he returned, entering the study where Clare was curled up in the most comfortable chair with a book. Thin smoke spiraled up from the small fire in the grate. A neighbor's cat had been enticed to pay a call and sat in Clare's lap, cosseted with tidbits.

'Lord Talbot.'

'I thought I had been elevated to Richard?' He sauntered across the room, leaving the door open behind him so Bennison might know his mistress was being treated in a proper manner.

'That was before you left the house without telling me when we are to see the bogus earl. Playing tricks?'

'Never.' He shook his head, then dropped down on a chair near where she reposed. He reached out to stroke the cat. Clare watched his hands, strong yet gentle, as they caressed the animal, and she envied the cat not a little.

'So? I can be ready in a trice.'

'You are not going along.' He braced himself for a furious

reaction, and he was not disappointed. Clare jumped to her feet, dumping the visiting cat in his lap.

She bared her arm, blazing a flaming look at Richard. 'My wound is well to being healed. There is no reason, other than that you are old-womanish about my going with you, for me not to be there. You will not leave this house without me at your side.'

'You are the most exasperating female it has ever been my misfortune to work with.' He set the animal aside, then rose to face her. His hands came up to grasp her shoulders. 'How anyone in his right mind could think you a *proper* miss is beyond me! When I am near you, *my* thoughts certainly are most *im*proper.'

She struggled to free herself, then caught a sparkle of green mischief in his eyes. Suddenly quiescent in his hands, she tilted her head., studying his face with knowing eyes. He was finding all this quite as irresistible as she!

'I say we ought to . . .' she lowered her lashes, giving him a most deliberately provocative smile. At least she hoped it was such. She hadn't much experience at this sort of flirting. It was dashed difficult when one had spent most of one's life doing the virtuous.

'Yes?' His hands tightened, drawing her closer.

'I say we ought to go see the earl. The sooner we close this matter, the better.' Clare fluttered her lashes a trifle, just enough without appearing blatant. Then, deciding to test his intentions, she added, 'My sister writes she desires my company.'

He gave her a shake, 'Visiting, indeed.'

It was impossible to know what was going on in his head. Clare wished she knew. However, it was a heady experience to flirt with him like this, and she might as well enjoy herself. 'Can it make any difference to you if I leave to stay with Sarah?'

'None,' he admitted cheerfully.

Her mouth dropped open a trifle, and her eyes grew wide with dismay. 'None?' All of her assumed wiles dropped away at his desertion.

'No. I fully intend to be there with you, you see.'

'Indeed?' Turning reluctantly from this intriguing thought, she said, 'When do we see the earl? For I suddenly perceive you are merely attempting to draw me from the topic by enticing me in another direction entirely.'

He inched her closer. 'And could I? Entice you, that is?'

He was not to have the answer to that important question, for at that very moment the soft patter of steps on the stairs came quite distinctly through the open door.

'Drat and blast,' he muttered, dropping a hasty kiss on that slightly open mouth while promising himself to do a more thorough job of it later on. 'I see Bennison is protecting you by informing Lady Millsham that you have company who is likely to cause you a blush.'

'Really? How fascinating.' Her eyes abruptly narrowed as she observed his uncomfortable expression. 'Why that expression? Have you heard something I ought to know?'

'Good day, Lord Talbot,' Lady Millsham hesitantly said, her timid voice barely reaching him in his preoccupation. 'How charming to see a cat in here. I am quite lost without my Muffin.' She glided silently to scoop up the tabby cat, stroking it until it smiled with bliss.

'I have never seen a cat smile before,' Clare observed before rounding on Richard again.

He braced himself for her onslaught. He was utterly wrong.

'Lord Talbot has graciously agreed to escort me to see the earl, Jane.' Clare sidled up to him, entwining her arm in his in a manner totally unlike her usual forthright way. Then she pinched him. 'Is that not correct, Richard?'

He knew when to yield. 'Of course. I would not dream of pursuing this without her at my side.'

'Good,' Lady Millsham replied softly. 'The tattlers have it that you are a pair, one way or another. You may as well stir things up a bit.'

Clare dropped her hold on his arms, stepping from his side as though he were too hot a fire. 'I see.' Now she knew why he had not wanted to be seen with her. It would exert pressure on him, forcing him to ask for her hand, whether he wished it or not.

'I doubt it,' he countered. 'We shall have to sort this out later. Excuse us if we make our way to Queens Square. We have urgent business.' He added for Lady Milisham's benefit, 'My man, Timms, will be close at hand, dear lady.'

'Good,' she repeated. 'I trust you to see to everything. You remind me a little of my Peter.' Her eyes misted over, and Richard nudged Clare from the room.

'All right, little termagant. Fetch your pelisse and we shall be on our way.'

'Are you certain?' Clare could not have been more torn. She wanted to confront the earl. Yet if anyone saw her with Richard, it would tighten the screws on his freedom. How frustrating to desire him, yet feel constrained to allow him breathing space.

'I had not thought you a coward, Miss Fairchild,' he taunted.

'Oh, what an insufferable man you are, to be sure.' She flounced about and ran up the stairs, wondering if she had taken leave of her senses to go with him, knowing what it could mean.

In short order she returned, her most proper bonnet in place, hands demurely gloved, and a composed expression on her face. They went out of the door, catching sight of the waiting Timms standing respectfully not far away.

'It is not far to Queens Square. If we walk, it shan't take us long. I should rather not use a chair.' Although it would offer distance, she might as well listen to what he had to say. He wouldn't speak with the chairmen all ears.

Surprisingly, he uttered no more than commonplace remarks. The weather, the serious condition of the economy with returned soldiers hunting for work, grain in dire supply, and other equally dismal subjects. Clare absorbed his comments, thinking him to be a man of uncommon sense. At least in matters of this nature.

When they turned down Gay Street to locate the earl's house, her stomach performed peculiar flip-flops, and she discovered her hands to be clammy inside her demure gloves.

Her fingers tightened perceptibly on his arm.

'Getting cold feet, Miss Fairchild?' His voice had an oily righteousness she utterly loathed. Her brother sounded like that when he knew he was right.

'Nonsense,' she countered stoutly.

The Millsham butler took a dim view of the pair who presented themselves at the door. Upon receiving their cards, he unbent to allow them into the house, even going so far as to announce them to his master, who was upstairs.

Clare glanced about the small drawing room with curious eyes. It seemed the usual sort one found in a place to let. Deep red draperies hung at the windows, with the same red covering a backless sofa and several chairs in the new Regency style. The arrangement was definitely uninspired. How fortunate she was to have the house on the Royal Crescent. They heard steps in the hall, and she turned to face Richard. Her composure being severely tested in this hostile environment, she stiffened her spine, tossing him a challenging look.

The door opened and the earl entered, a cold expression on his face that seemed scarcely encouraging to two who hoped to intimidate him.

'Talbot? Miss Fairchild? I confess I am surprised to see you here.' He drew near, but did not invite them to sit down.

Clare thought his manners had suffered greatly since the trip to Millsham Hall.

'Miss Fairchild has been a trifle indisposed for the past day or two. Someone took a shot at her in Sidney Park. Fortunately, he missed. I caught the man and spoke with him before he mysteriously died.'

'Really,' interrupted the earl in a bored voice. 'I fail to see what this has to do with me.'

'Have patience, my lord, and you shall,' Clare said after finding her voice. She had stared at the earl, wondering what possessed a man with his looks and charm to go so far as to murder. Then perhaps, never having been without money, it would be impossible for her to fully understand his motives. As well, she had been so blessed as to circulate in the highest of the *ton*. She clasped her hands together and tried to concentrate on what was being said. Richard had been leading the earl along, teasing him with the knowledge that the hired assailant had talked.

'Aye,' Richard said. 'The man insisted you employed him to shoot Miss Fairchild. Your peculiar note substantiates that, did you know? It provides a motive, however repugnant.'

'You cannot prove a thing one way or the other if the man is now dead, Talbot.'

'There is another witness, and he to a murder.'

Although his expression remained unchanged, there appeared a definite uneasiness about Basil Kibbler's eyes.

'Mr Kibbler, it would seem to me that the climate in France ought to be highly beneficial this time of year,' Clare inserted, finding the going too slow for her liking.

'I have not traveled to France.'

Hearing the implacable note in his voice, she shrugged, then said, 'Italy, perhaps? I am told the food is marvelous.' He ignored her.

'How can you prove there is a witness to this so-called crime you accuse me of committing? You see,' the man's voice grew dangerously quiet, 'I did not do a thing.'

'One of the stable lads has talked.'

Kibbler's face grew ashen. 'To whom?'

Seeing that he had convinced Kibbler he told the truth, Richard advanced a few steps, his attitude menacing. 'To the proper authority. He was most believable. I daresay it will not be long before you stand accused of murder, Mr Kibbler.'

Clare found it fascinating that the man did not dispute the name in the least.

Richard paused in his speech, then continued, 'It is imperative for one so accused to either give proof of his innocence or flee, I believe.'

Basil Kibbler drew himself up, raking Richard and Clare with a frosty glare. 'Since I am innocent, I shall prepare myself for that event, sir. I must bid you good day.'

CHAPTER SIXTEEN

'A piece of gross impertinence if I ever heard one! To speak so to us!' she exclaimed as they marched along Queens Square. 'Did you notice his eyes? He is guilty.'

'He did strike me as uneasy when I claimed we have a witness to the murder.'

'Shall you have Timms follow him?' She glanced back to see Timms lingering in the area, unobtrusively melting into the scenery.

'Perhaps. I suspect we shall find out Kibbler's intentions before long.'

They crossed Gay Street, Clare intent on discovering what Richard Talbot intended to do next. Absently she observed several ladies on the opposite side of the street, but paid little heed to them.

'I have seen nothing of Miss Godwin,' she reflected aloud. 'Although she is the most aggravating woman alive, I still worry about her. It cannot be easy to have your family turn their backs on you, find yourself all dished up, and no place to put your head.'

Her subtle appeal for any information about Venetia was totally ignored.

'Lady Kingsmill sent a message that she would like to see you. I suspect she wishes to confirm your continued good health. Miss Oliver must have unduly alarmed her.'

'Oh, pooh. We had best go there now, I expect. You do think that Lady Millsham will be all right, even though Timms is away from the house?'

'As we were leaving, I noticed Mrs Robottom coming toward the house. I fancy she will keep Lady Millsham company. She said she was quite taken with the young widow.'

'How lovely.' Clare gave a choke of laughter, not daring to look at Richard lest she compound the problem.

They changed direction after he checked to see if she wished to walk. At her nod, he continued with his comments, then asked, 'Are you pleased now that you went to see Mr Kibbler?'

Clare turned to face Richard, aware of a subtle alteration in his voice. 'I own that I was a bit afraid of him,' she said quietly. 'I truly believe that man is not right in his head. That can only be frightening.'

'Yet knowing that, you insisted upon coming with me?'

'What could he have done? You were there to protect me, after all.'

'Woman, your logic nearly unmans me!'

'With Timms watching Kibbler's house, we no longer have a watchdog of our own,' she pointed out in a carefully polite voice as they crossed a busy Milsom Street.

'True. That bothers you? I would have thought an intrepid girl like you would be beyond such things.'

'I am not a girl, Lord Talbot.'

He sighed. 'I thought we had put that particular nonsense behind us.' He guided her into New Bond Street, ignoring the lure of fashionable shops.

'My age?' she queried, clearly befuddled.

'My name.'

She stopped at the corner of Broad Street to give him a narrow look. 'I only call you Richard when I forget myself.'

'Come, we are attracting attention.' He firmly took hold of her arm, guiding her over the cobbles in an expert fashion. 'I do not understand you in the least.'

211

'That makes us quite even, then.'

'I believe I should like a chair for the rest of the way,' she snapped, vastly annoyed that things were not going as she wished.

'No. It is but a short walk from here across the bridge to Laura Place. An intrepid girl like you should . . .' He winced at the jab from her elbow.

She did not pretend ignorance. 'I fail to see why you insist on that odious term. Intrepid, indeed.'

'It has a certain appeal.'

She disregarded his presence at her side by the simple means of looking in the windows of the tiny, attractive shops on the bridge. Her silence continued up Argyle Street until they came to Laura Place.

Lady Kingsmill required a complete retelling of the episode in the Sidney Gardens. By the time Clare finished, she felt as exhausted as after the incident.

'Well,' prodded Lady Kingsmill, 'have you no other news for me?'

'We shall tell you more when Timms gives us news of Mr Kibbler. For you must know we cannot call him the earl anymore,' Clare insisted.

'That was not what I had in mind,' muttered Lady Kingsmill. 'Talbot, I'm disappointed in you,' she began, and was ruthlessly cut off by Lord Talbot, who rose to his feet saying they absolutely must depart.

'That was excessively rude of you,' Clare scolded when they were once again outside before the house on Laura Place.

'It was, wasn't it?' he agreed placidly.

'I believe I should like a chair, *now*.' Clare looked about, noting one lone chair across the diamond-shaped area.

Richard hailed the chairmen, then tucked Clare inside, waving her off with a sigh of relief. Once she had reached the Pulteney Bridge, he strode off in the same direction, taking a different turn when he reached the far side. Within minutes he had reached Queens Square to confer with Timms.

*

'He has fled? Just like that?'

'You sound disappointed, my love.' Richard took her hand, leading her to the sofa in the drawing room where he pulled her down beside him.

'No, not in the least.' But she suffered a vague feeling of being let down somehow, as irrational as that might seem. She knew comfort from Richard's hand until she recalled it was highly improper for her to be sitting alone with him and holding hands like a pair of besotted lovers.

'I thought you might be glad to know he hightailed it for the coast sometime after we left his house yesterday. His baggage looked suspiciously heavy for its size. I fear Lady Millsham will find he dipped badly into the coffers of the estate.'

'But he is gone?' She searched his face to assure herself he told the utter truth.

'I believe it is safe to assume he will not return to Millsham Hall.'

'I see.' This meant no more ruined bonnets, no mad drives across the countryside with Richard, no more stealthy trips on the canal. How deadly dull!

Richard leaned back, keeping a firm hold on that dainty hand, thus forcing Clare to join him, although she didn't seem aware of his maneuverings.

'He had a passenger with him who might interest you,' he added casually.

'Who?' She studied the clasped hands, wondering if she ought to quibble with him about his presumptions. If it hadn't felt so good and so right, she might have been so inclined. However, since their adventure was concluded, there was every chance she might not see him again, what with her being nearly on the shelf and he continuing in his preposterous ways.

'Miss Godwin entered his coach, and a great number of trunks belonging to the lady were placed in the boot and on top along with his.'

Clare sat up in amazement. 'You jest, sir!'

'At least that's better than Lord Talbot. I think.'

'*Will* you be serious?'

'I have been trying, but you are singularly uncooperative, my love.'

She ignored his disgressions. 'But Venetia! Going with Mr Kibbler? Impossible!'

'I saw it myself. Joined Timms over in Queens Square when he sent word of activity.'

'But she continually plagued me with the need to be proper! She thought it grossly indiscreet for me to drive with you, even with Priddy along! Well, I never.'

'I can only hope so, my heart's delight.'

'Richard, you confuse me.'

'Ah, we make progress.'

Steps in the hall brought Clare to her feet. Lady Millsham entered the drawing room, the sound of her greeting covering the muttered imprecations from Lord Talbot.

Clare led Lady Millsham to a chair, urging her to sit down, while ignoring the disgruntled form of Lord Talbot. 'We believe Mr Kibbler has decamped for the coast, it is to be hoped for France or wherever he intends to live now. He left the house on Queens Square.'

'So suddenly? How can you be certain?' She turned to face Richard, knowing the information would come from him.

'I watched them pack up the baggage and depart. My man will follow them until he discovers their intent.'

Lady Millsham proved quicker than Clare. 'They? You mean Mr Kibbler and his servants? Or did someone join him?'

'Actually, Miss Godwin went with him.' Clare peered anxiously at Lady Millsham, wondering how she would react to this bit of scandalous news.

The young widow gave Clare and Richard an irrepressible grin. 'Oh, how delicious. I know it is quite shocking, and I am wicked to laugh, but she was always one for being proper, and now she . . .' Lady Millsham looked at Clare, then Richard.

They all burst into quiet laughter. Lady Millsham leaned forward to where the others sat close by on the sofa.

'I vow it will be wonderful to return to Millsham Hall.'

Placing one hand on Clare's arm, the other on Lord Talbot's capable hand, she added, 'I do not know how I can ever sufficiently thank you both for all you have done for my son and me. Rest assured the new seventh earl shall know of his great debt to you.'

'Please, do not refine upon it,' Clare urged, near tears what with feeling the end of her association with Richard in sight and the conclusion of the drama with Lady Millsham upon her. Clare had grown fond of the brave young widow. Her feelings regarding Richard, she buried under a pile of good intentions.

Lady Millsham stayed them both with her hands, looking embarrassed but determined. 'Once we get word that it is quite safe for us to return to the Hall, I should like you to go with me. As much as I long to be there, I dread facing that place alone. I do not know if I can trust anyone at the Hall again. Dare I ask that of you after all you have done so far?'

'Of course,' Clare replied instantly, knowing the trip would prolong her contact with Richard.

'We would not think of permitting you to make the journey alone,' added Richard, smiling for reasons of his own. 'With Jenny and Priddy, not to mention Mrs Dow – for I feel sure you will wish her with you for a time – we shall be a comfortable party, and you shan't have to fear a thing.'

Placing her hands to her face, Lady Millsham wiped away a few stray tears of joy, then gave them a watery smile. 'You are very good, sir. I can only pray you get your heart's desire.'

Richard's face slowly lit up with a grin, his eyes quite unfathomable pools of deep green. 'I quite agree.'

The air simmered with tension, Clare thought, as the carriage bound for Millsham Hall made its way out of West Overton. Some distance ahead, her coach with Jenny, Priddy, Mrs Dow, Lady Millsham, and Baby William could be seen, a trail of dust in its wake. She rode with Richard in his new curricle.

'Nice to see the scene of the crime, so to speak, again.'

'There was no crime committed against you in West Overton, sir.'

'I recollect a particular young woman giving me a dose of laudanum enough to make me sleep for a long time. My wound was not sufficiently bad for that. Why did you do it?'

'You had a fever and were restless. Truly, your arm did not look good.' Clare fidgeted with the cords of her reticule in her lap. Taking a surreptitious glance at the man next to her, she wondered what went on in his mind. Why bring up ancient history now?

'You make a very tender nurse,' he mused. 'And you are good with children, too.'

At that moment a dray turned onto the road a short distance ahead, requiring Richard to maneuver his horses and carriage around them. Clare knew better than to chatter while this was in progress, though she longed to ask him what point he wished to make.

Then Marlborough came into view and the Castle Inn in particular. Clare's coach stood in front, and the party wandered about, Jenny and Mrs Dow debating on what to do to stop the baby's crying.

Priddy met the curricle, taking note of Clare's flushed cheeks and Lord Talbot's glum expression.

'Fine day,' she observed to no one in particular.

Clare ignored her, rushing to see if there was anything she might do to help. Taking William from the two arguing nurse-maids, she patted his back while strolling around the inn yard, crooning a tuneless lullaby.

Within a brief time, William had sobbed himself to sleep. Richard had ushered the others in for restoring tea, and now he came back for Clare.

'You look fetching like that, although I daresay your bonnet will never be the same again. At least it will need new ribands.' He stretched out a hand to touch her bonnet, and succeeded in gently caressing her cheek.

Clare grimaced, suspecting the baby had mangled her pretty ribands in his distress. 'I shall require my very own milliner if this keeps on.' She moved away from Richard's highly disturbing touch.

'Can you not put him down in the coach so you may enjoy a cup of tea and a biscuit? Or shall I take the lad?'

One look at Richard's dubious expression and Clare smiled. 'Hardly, sir,' she reproved. Seeing Jenny scurry across the yard, Clare carefully handed the sleeping infant to her, admonishing with her eyes that the girl take care not to wake him.

'However,' Clare continued as she watched Jenny return to the coach with her precious burden, 'I believe the best thing to do is to separate Mrs Dow and Jenny. I suggest Mrs Dow drive with you, and I shall go in my coach. You may again thank Mrs Dow for her most efficacious medicine.'

Richard gritted his teeth as Clare gave him a saucy look before waltzing off to enter the inn, then return to the coach. He didn't know what she had said to Mrs Dow, but the lady came out beaming and marched straight up to the curricle. She accepted his reluctant hand up, then spent the remainder of the journey telling dear Lord Talbot about every treatment in her vast store, offering to send him whatever he needed by way of repayment for helping her dear little girl.

Never had anyone been so glad to see the gates of Millsham Hall.

The atmosphere at Millsham Hall was not welcoming. The butler permitted the group to enter, giving a frosty nod of recognition to Lady Millsham. Not one footman stood in the entry; no one else was in sight. The house might have been empty, but for the knowledge that only a staff could have kept it in such excellent condition. Yet it was oddly silent.

First, Lady Millsham directed Jenny, Mrs Dow, and Priddy to see to various needs, William's in particular. Then she turned to order a light repast.

She bravely led the way up a flight of stairs to the drawing room. Once Clare, Lady Millsham, and Richard were safely inside with the doors firmly shut, they drew together.

'This is a fine kettle of fish,' murmured Richard, taking note of the pale cheeks and worried eyes of both women. 'What can they be thinking of, to give you a snub like that?'

'I cannot help but wonder if Mr Kibbler actually crossed the

Channel as Timms reported. Perhaps he only appeared to go, then means to return here to do away with us all!' Lady Millsham whispered. She placed a trembling hand against her mouth, her fear a palpable thing in the quiet room.

'I vow I did not dream you would receive such a reception. Although word was sent ahead, not a soul came to greet you, not even the housekeeper!' Clare whispered back, darting a frightened look at Richard. 'I am very glad we decided to come with you. Where do you suppose everyone is? And why are they behaving so oddly?'

A click of the door brought the trio about to stare as the butler entered bearing a massive tray. It contained the light repast Lady Millsham had ordered. He placed it on a side table, then lit a spirit lamp beneath the kettle. Since the water had been hot, it boiled within minutes. He poured the water over the tea leaves, then replaced teapot lid and kettle. 'Will that be all, my lady?'

Lady Millsham glanced timidly at Clare, then nodded, unable to speak.

'Do you suppose we dare eat the food?' wondered Lady Millsham as she hungrily surveyed the dishes on the tray. 'I did not eat on the journey, lest I upset my stomach. Now I am starved.'

'Lord Talbot shall taste it first,' Clare said with a defiant look at him. 'And I shall as well,' she amended at the dangerous sparkle she glimpsed in his eyes.

Feeling no ill effects, they loaded their plates with an assortment of salads, cold meats, and dark bread. Clare poured out the tea as Lady Millsham looked as though she might faint if asked to do so.

'I simply do not know what to do.' Lady Millsham nibbled at her salad, glancing at Clare and Lord Talbot as she did.

'I think the sooner we get to the bottom of this mystery, the better,' Richard said. 'If you like, I will approach the butler on your behalf. He may tell me something, whereas he is reluctant to speak to you.'

'Again I must trespass on your good nature, Lord Talbot. What a good husband you will make some lady.'

As there was absolutely no guile in her face, nor any flirtation in her voice, the others accepted it as a compliment.

'I trust so, dear lady,' he quietly replied, sending Clare into a flurry of speculation.

Once they were reasonably satisfied, Clare replaced the plates on the tray, then drew a chair close to where the others sat. In a soft voice, she said, 'We must have a plan.'

Richard murmured, 'I believe I have heard that before.'

'Hush,' she reproved. 'I shall search out the housekeeper while Richard speaks to the butler. Who were you closest to while here?' she inquired of Lady Millsham.

'The upstairs maid, I suppose. I did not live here all that long, nor were the servants ever forthcoming in the least while I did,' she apologized. 'I shall see if *she* is about.' She timidly left the room in her quest.

Clare untangled the mess of riband on her bonnet, surveying the ruin with resigned eyes. Placing the bonnet on the table, she glanced up to meet Richard's amused gaze.

'You were correct, I fear. I shall require another trip to a milliner.'

'A man would have to be deep in the pockets to keep you in bonnets,' he observed.

'I have a competence of my own sufficient for that, I daresay. My husband, should I ever marry, will have more important things to secure.' Then she blushed as she realized the interpretation he might place on her words.

'You do have a way with words, my love.'

She would have scolded him but for Lady Millsham's return.

'She has gone. In fact, I do not see any familiar faces about.'

'I shall see what the butler says. Evenson is his name?'

Lady Millsham trailed after Clare, reluctant to be alone, while Richard sought Evenson. When Clare at last located the housekeeper, she turned to Lady Millsham, saying, 'Jane, dear, what was it we wished to know? Oh, yes, where is the little upstairs maid who was here before?'

'Gone, my lady,' said the dour woman in response.

'Why did you not come to greet her ladyship and the new

219

earl when we arrived?' Clare demanded. 'And where are the others who worked here when Lady Millsham was here?'

Clare spoke in a pleasant tone, but one she had used over the years in dealing with fractious children, thieving servants, and social enemies.

The housekeeper delved into a capacious apron pocket to pull out a handkerchief with which to dab her eyes. 'They were all fired, my lady. Only Evenson and I were retained, so as to know the running of the place. We feared, that is, the new staff thought you would fire them as well. As soon as your letter came, they all sought other positions. Like as not, they forged letters of recommendation,' she concluded bitterly.

'That is why the house is so silent, then?' Lady Millsham said at last.

'Aye, milady. 'Tis unnatural, but there you are. I fear there is no one to prepare a thing for you, other than what Evenson and I can manage.'

Clare took stock of the woman dressed in black bombazine and white apron. She was thin and on the shady side of forty, with her graying hair tucked neatly beneath her cap. Not formidable, more like capable.

'Do you suppose it is possible to find the previous staff, the ones Lady Millsham remembers? Otherwise, I fancy you will wish Evenson to hire new people,' she added to Lady Millsham.

Grateful for this suggestion, Lady Millsham nodded. 'Oh, yes. We must have a cook and maids and footmen, not to mention the others. Enough to keep the house tidy and in good repair without being extravagant.' To Clare she added as they walked away from the interview, 'I do not mean to beggar my son's inheritance.'

'I see you found out the truth of the matter,' said Richard as he joined them. 'I believe Evenson will confer with the house-keeper, then ask those he can find to return. What a jumble.'

'The staff might have waited,' Lady Millsham mused.

'Yet you would have felt uneasy at keeping on those who had worked for Mr Kibbler. Could you have trusted them?'

Lady Millsham nodded at these words of wisdom from Clare.

The following hours were a trial for all. Priddy bustled about in importance, settling in the two ladies and establishing herself in the upper region.

Mrs Dow and Jenny reached a truce between them regarding the baby. No one was informed as to what it was, but as long as the two were satisfied, it was doubtful anyone cared.

Clare was everywhere, helping with this, assisting with that, her years of experience at aiding her family standing her well.

By evening Richard had had quite enough. He sought out Clare in the kitchen where she endeavored to assist the housekeeper with arranging for something to eat.

'There is something I wish to see,' he said with an air of mystery that Clare found intriguing.

She went along with him, tossing an apologetic glance at the housekeeper as she left the room. He drew her along to a side door that led to a grand terrace that stretched across the back of the house. They quietly made their way down an impressive flight of steps to an expanse of grass that had not been scythed in some time.

'What is it?'

'I have had quite enough of this.'

'What?' she said, wrinkling her nose at the harsh tone in his voice. 'Millsham Hall? I daresay it will be a week or more before we can leave, what with all that needs doing. That poor, darling girl.'

'You had best take notice of this poor, darling man, my dear, or I shall be forced to take matters into my own hands.'

'Really?' she mocked him, feeling immeasurably better for some odd reason.

'It's a good thing you've no bonnet on, or I fancy it would end up crushed.' With which he proceeded to indeed take matters into his highly capable hands. He scooped her up in his arms, then carried her off to a pretty garden he had scouted out shortly before.

'Lord Talbot, er, Richard, this is most improper!' she cried, though not very loudly.

He found the stone bench he sought, then sat, placing her carefully on his lap.

'Well?' She tried to keep a saucy note from her voice and suspected she failed.

'For some time now I have held my tongue, though goodness knew it took the patience of a saint, but this is the final straw. I refuse to wait another moment.'

'For what?' she prompted.

'You.' As a reply it lacked in originality, but this was more than compensated for by his direct approach to the subject. She nestled in his arms, thinking she had never been so content in her entire life. As kisses went, and she had known a few, his was by far the best.

'Um,' she murmured as he at last released her a second time. 'I fear I have compromised you well and truly, sir.'

'Have you, by Jove? And here I have been doing my best to achieve that goal since the day we met.'

'You might have merely asked me, you know,' she reproved.

'Every time I got near the sticking point, some woman would interfere. Be warned, I intend to keep you here until you agree to marry me. I'll not take a no for an answer, either.' He searched her eyes for a clue to her feelings.

'Yes,' she promptly replied, for which she was rewarded with another highly satisfactory kiss.

'And,' he continued when they both needed to breathe once again, 'we shall not wait. I have waited quite long enough.'

'We must. The banns, the gowns, the wedding breakfast,' she said, twinkling up at him. 'So much to do.'

'I wrote to Doctor's Commons for a special license soon after I met you. I am well prepared. As for the rest, I wouldn't worrry about gowns,' and he gave her a look that sent tremors down to her toes, 'and anyone who is so rash as to appear at our front door can jolly well feed himself. At least for some time to come.'

'Just so you keep me in bonnets, my dear.'

'As long as that's all you desire.'

Her giggle was lost in his embrace, and neither one heard the calls from the house.

It seemed that Miss Fairchild no longer need fear being left on the shelf.

Also by Emily Hendrickson
and soon to be published:
ALTHEA'S GRAND TOUR

Althea Ingram longed for a gentleman to look up to – but found none among the London dandies who found her dowry more to their taste than her regally tall and lovely person. It was only when Althea fled to Europe that she found what was sorely missing in her life. John Maitland, the Earl of Montmorcy, with his towering physique and dazzling good looks, his strengh and mountain-climbing nerve, was all she dreamed of in a man.

Unfortunately, she was more than he wanted in a wife. Althea's delicate, beatiful companion, Cecily de Lisle, far better fitted the arrogant Earl's ideas about the weaker sex than the fiercely independent young lady whom he mocked as an Amazon. But Amazon or not, Althea had no armour on her heart when she was in the Earl's arms and on the top of an alpine peak – as she tried not to fall in love with a man pressing her over the precipice of dangerous desire. . . .